NICK & CO
IN A FIX

NICK & CO
ON HOLIDAY

BOB CROSON

Copyright © 1985, 1987 Bob Croson
This omnibus edition copyright © 1997 Lion Publishing

Published by
Lion Publishing plc
Sandy Lane West, Oxford, England
ISBN 0 7459 3755 1
Albatross Books Pty Ltd
PO Box 320, Sutherland, NSW 2232, Australia
ISBN 0 7324 1625 6

First edition of *Nick & Co. in a Fix* in 1985
First edition of *Nick & Co. on Holiday* in 1987
This omnibus edition first published 1997
10 9 8 7 6 5 4 3 2 1 0

A catalogue record for this book is available
from the British Library

Printed and bound in Great Britain
by Cox & Wyman, Reading

NICK & CO. in a fix

NICK & CO
IN A FIX

Bob Croson

CONTENTS

CONTENTS

1

TROUBLE

'Give me the ball,' I screamed.

Sparky passed it to me just as he was forced against a wall by the heavy body of Franco Granelli, called 'Lump' by friend and enemy alike.

I took the ball and with clever flicks raced along the pavement carefully avoiding the potholes, lost in the dream of a Wembley Cup Final with one goal each and two minutes left: *'Nick Baker hurtles down the wing on a breakaway, the referee looks at his watch, we're almost out of time.' 'What do you think about it, Mr Clough, will he be sick as a parrot or over the moon?' 'He turns in, rounds the defender, and shoots.'*

I kicked the ball as hard as I could in the direction of Norman, our very unwilling goalkeeper. It soared high over his head and disappeared over the back of the garage gates which formed the goal.

'Now you've done it,' he said.

Adrian Blake, another of the gang, raced up. 'Hey man, why d'you do that? We'll never get it back now,' he said.

I slumped against the wall, fed up. The difference between where I thought the ball should go and where it actually went was still a bit too much for the England manager, or even Scruffy Jones, the PE master who selected the school team . . . But one day . . . All it needed was practice. I could still play for

England . . . if only I could get the stupid ball back.

'Well, who's going to face old Crabfeatures then?' asked Adrian. 'And it's not going to be me! I can still feel the clip round the ear I got last time.'

Old Crabfeatures was the owner of the garage. His more usual name was Mr Booth, and he had been very nasty to all the gang since he had bought the business a year ago.

I sat silently, with my head in my hands, desperately trying to think of a way to save face and solve the crisis. Then I had an idea. 'Let's see where it is before we do anything else. Come over here, Lump, and stand against this gate.'

Franco Granelli wandered over reluctantly. He always got roped in for this sort of thing, and he didn't like it. Just because his Dad owned the chip shop at the end of the street, 'forcing' him to 'have to' eat lots of chips, he couldn't help being a little on the large side. It was his Dad's fault.

Lump stood, facing forward and leaning with both hands against the garage gates. As nobody else volunteered to climb up I had to do it myself. Putting my hands on Lump's shoulders I leaped up. My knees dug into his back and he collapsed in a heap, with me falling heavily on top of him. He let out a great yell.

'You great wally,' I howled, rubbing my side.

'You shouldn't have put your knees in my back. How would you like it?' groaned Lump, lying like a stranded whale on the pavement.

'I suppose I had better try,' interrupted Adrian, 'before anybody else gets hurt.'

Adrian lived in Church Street, like the rest of us. He was in the same class as me and Sparky, my best

10

mate. He was very athletic and loved to run everywhere, so we all called him Whizzer. Like Norman's family, his grandparents had come over from the West Indies and settled here. Now his father had died, leaving his Mum to bring up five children, and he was the youngest. He told Lump to cup his hands and stand with his back to the gates. Then he put one foot in Lump's hands and launched himself up, grabbing for the beam above the gates. The rest of us stood back and watched in admiration. I opened my mouth to say, 'Well done, Whizzer!' when the gates opened, and there stood Mr Booth.

Lump fell backwards at Mr Booth's feet because he had been leaning against the garage gates and Whizzer was left hanging from the beam. He couldn't keep his grip, and as everybody watched him in stunned silence, his hands lost their grip. It was like slow motion in films. He fell to the ground right on top of Lump, who gasped and groaned as the wind was knocked out of him again.

'I'm sick of this. I'm not a bloomin' trampoline you know,' he complained noisily. He looked up and saw the angry face of Mr Booth looking down.

I knew what was coming next.

Sure enough, off he went!

'You lot again,' shouted Mr Booth. 'What do you think you are doing? This is private property.'

Good grief, what a bore! Always on at us.

I wanted to stand up to him, but chickened out. So I said, 'Can we have our ball back, please?'

'Now look, I'm fed up with you lot. This is the third time this week, you're nothing but a nuisance,' Mr Booth growled.

I was starting to get angry with this silly man now.

11

'But we only want our ball back,' I repeated through gritted teeth.

Mr Booth was a big brute of a man, with a bald head and a red face. He wore baggy trousers and a large brightly-coloured anorak which had seen better days. He always seemed to be angry. Well — that was the way we always saw him. Now he looked round, saw the ball lying by a pile of old tyres, and walked over to it.

'This ball you mean?' he asked. 'I'll show you what I'm going to do with this.' He picked up a sharp metal spike that was lying on the ground and fiercely pierced the ball. It burst with a loud bang. Then he threw the ball on to the heap of tyres with the spike still stuck through it.

'Now clear off,' he growled, and slammed the gates shut.

I was dumbstruck. That swine had burst our ball! I was steaming. I turned and walked quickly and angrily down the road. What else could I do? The others turned and followed me. No one said a word.

We made our way to the youth club which was by the church. It was separated from Mr Booth's garage by a plot of long grass where all the children in our street played.

When we went in, Doug Jones, the church curate, was tidying up the games cupboard helped by Sparky's sister. Her real name was Samantha, but we always called her Sam. We all liked Doug, though I did think he was a bit too religious, always going on about Jesus and God. I was also a bit miffed because Sparky spent so much time with him. Sparky went along to Doug's youth meetings at church, which were good, but I wasn't too keen to get involved like Sparky had.

12

But then, he's not that bad — Doug, I mean. After all, he persuaded the old lady who owned the hut and the patch of grass to let him use it for a youth club. Then he got the church and the local council to help set it up and spent a lot of his free time running it.

My pain-in-the-neck little sister, Mo, was helping too. Strictly speaking, she was too young for the club, being only seven, but she always follows me around and Doug had given up trying to keep her away.

Lots of children used the club, but me and my mates — Sparky, Whizzer, Lump, and Chip (Norman's nickname), — together with Sam and Little Mo, were the regulars. It was my gang — with me as the boss.

Anyway, we all stormed in and threw ourselves down in the old chairs. I was really mad, steaming. 'It ain't fair,' I said.

'Oh?' replied Doug from inside the cupboard.

'No, it ain't,' agreed Sparky.

Doug got up from the floor, carefully and calmly put down the table tennis bats he was holding and turned to face us. 'Would someone mind telling me what isn't fair this time?' he asked.

'Old Crabfeatures has done it again,' moaned Lump, still rubbing his bruised but ample stomach.

'Ah!' said Doug. 'Now let me see if I have the picture right.' 'You were playing football on the street outside Mr Booth's garage. Right?'

'Mm,' I grunted.

'And someone. . . ' Doug looked around at the gang's faces. I scowled. 'And someone,' he said, looking at me, 'got carried away and belted it over the fence into his yard. Right?'

13

How come he always knew? He must have second sight!

'Now he won't let you have your ball back,' continued Doug.

I was boiling inside. Why is it that adults never see the real point? 'The old faggot face did more than that,' I blurted out. 'He deliberately burst it.'

'I see,' said Doug. I don't think he did.

'Well, that wasn't fair, was it?' said Whizzer.

'No,' replied Doug. 'But he did tell you to stop playing outside his garage. You did get a warning.'

That was the end. Being patient and understanding isn't my strong point and this was too much. 'Are you on his side?' I demanded. 'It's not his road — it belongs to all of us. My Dad pays his rates as well, you know.' Then I really got going. 'Sometimes I don't understand you. You're always saying how you want to help us, you're forever reading bits of the Bible to us and trying to persuade us to go to church, but when it comes to something important, you back off.'

'Oh, come on, Nick,' Doug responded.

I was angry and upset, and couldn't think what else to do, so I decided to make a big fuss of going. 'I'm going. You don't understand,' I said. I stormed out and banged the door so hard that the wall of the hut shook. I didn't look back, but I knew the gang would follow. They'd better! And they did.

I had to do something. I didn't want my mates to see me beaten. That rat Booth was standing at the entrance to his garage. I stormed up to him. Sparky tried to stop me but I wouldn't listen.

'You toad,' I said. 'Bet your cars are all nicked old bangers.'

He turned angrily. 'What do you mean?' he

14

hissed. Then he stopped himself, sneered, and said, 'Go away, little boy, before I twist your scraggy little neck.'

He looked very nasty, and suddenly I felt scared. At times like this you have to resort to tried and trusted practices. I blew an enormous raspberry, and ran like fury. The rest followed at speed.

'You've not heard the last of this, you little monster,' he shouted after me.

He couldn't possibly catch me. I was beginning to feel better. But that was only the start!

2

BAD NEWS

As usual, the club was very busy. It was early evening, we had all done our homework, and were now letting off steam. Sparky and me were on the snooker table — I was winning as usual — and loads of kids were watching us and drinking cans of Coke.

Whizzer was playing non-stop table tennis with three other kids. He was so quick and never still for a moment, forcing them to go faster and faster. They were yelling and whooping with delight. Chip was by the electronic games, thumping the buttons and taking his score higher and higher. Lump just sat in a corner, watching, and eating through his usual vast quantity of crisps and chocolate before going for a bag of chips from his Dad.

Lots of kids were playing darts and dominoes, cards and other games. Some were just relaxing, listening to music. Standing by the coffee bar were Sam and Little Mo, helping Doug to sell soft drinks and crisps.

After I had done my Steve Davis on Sparky and finally potted the black, I wandered over for a refill of Coke. Sam was talking to Doug. 'You're a bit quiet tonight, Doug,' she said. 'Has the Vicar been having a go at you again? Are you in his bad books? What you done? Been riding your bike over the graves again?'

'You musn't talk about him like that. He's a very

kind man,' replied Doug.

'Well, he don't like us. He's always wincing when he comes in here, and wrinkles his nose like we smell or something,' said Sam.

'It's just that he finds the music a bit loud, and it's a long time since he was a kid,' said Doug, with a smile.

I couldn't picture the vicar ever being a child. As far as I was concerned he'd always been about three hundred and five years old. 'Anyway,' I butted in. 'You've still not told us why you're so grumpy.'

'I'm not grumpy. I've just had some bad news, that's all,' replied Doug solemnly.

These Christians, I thought, always pretending nothing is really wrong. Why can't they be more honest?

Doug carried on serving customers with Coke and crisps. Sam looked at me, shrugged her shoulders and tried again. 'Well, are you going to tell us then, or is it a secret?' she asked, turning to him.

'I was choosing the moment.'

'What do you mean? Is it something to do with us?' I asked, curious now.

'Yes, I'm afraid it is,' said Doug quietly. 'I had a phone call earlier today from a firm of solicitors. The old lady who owns this building has died, and it's going to be sold, together with the land between Mr Booth's garage and the church.'

'*What*?' I groaned. 'What's going to happen to us then? There's nowhere else to go.'

'I don't know,' replied Doug. 'It's a tricky one. But I do believe God will help us if we ask him.'

Some good that'll do, I thought. But as I couldn't think of anything better I kept my mouth shut and sat in a chair sulking, trying to make it look like I

17

was coming up with a master plan of my own.

As we made our way home that evening, we were all very gloomy. Hands were in pockets, heads were down. Whizzer kicked an empty can along the gutter. I felt awful.

Just as we passed the gates of Mr Booth's garage, he appeared and began to open them. He stopped, folded his arms, and looked at us. 'You must have heard the news then,' he said.

'What's it got to do with you?' I snarled.

'Oh, you'd be surprised,' smirked Mr Booth.

That man really was a toad! 'Whaddya mean?' I grunted back at him.

'Well, there's going to be an auction, isn't there?' he said.

'So what?'

'I'm going to bid for that land,' he continued. 'There aren't many people interested, so it won't fetch much. I shall buy it and tear down that rat-hole of a hut you use. Then you'll be out of my hair and I can get on with my business in peace.'

'Why, you mean thing!' said Sam, in disbelief.

'Mean, is it?' replied Mr Booth quickly. 'Well, there's nothing you can do about it!' He turned and went into his garage.

We just stood there feeling helpless. I was fuming inside, all bottled up with anger. I had to do something. I picked up Whizzer's can and hurled it through one of the garage windows. Then, realizing what I had done, rushed off, with the others close behind. Over my shoulder I could see Mr Booth coming out of his garage, shaking his fist after us.

We rounded the corner and skidded to a stop by the first lamp post. Not only was it just far enough away from Mr Booth to be safe, but I was also

18

puffed out, and needed the support of a friendly lump of concrete.

Sparky wasn't very happy. 'Why did you do that? What good did it do? Can you see Mr Booth doing anything to help us now?' he asked, looking straight at me.

I knew underneath that Sparky was right, but I was annoyed. Annoyed with Mr Booth, with myself — and now with him. Ever since he had got too involved with Doug and become a Christian, things had not been as good between us. We had been best mates all our lives, and our Dads before us. When it came time for us to show we were the tops in the district, he was at my side. Every fight I had ever been in, there was Sparky alongside sorting somebody out.

Now he was different. I mean, I don't swear a lot, but he had stopped altogether. I even had to use Whizzer to help me with a few punch-ups because he wouldn't. There was no point in arguing with him, though, because, to cap it all, he'd even stopped shouting back at me! At first I thought it wouldn't last—I knew Sparky and I knew he couldn't keep it up, but he had! It really gets me angry now when he doesn't lose his temper.

'I suppose you're going to suggest we pray about it as well,' I said scathingly.

'Why not?' he said. 'It takes more guts than chucking cans through windows and running!'

Before I could think of a nasty answer, Sam butted in. She didn't like seeing us at each other, so she changed the subject. 'Look—we can't do anything about that at the moment, but we do have to do something about the city youth club five-a-side competition. Don't forget, Nick, you entered a team, and you also bet that stupid dope Ram that we could beat his team.'

'Mm,' I replied. This was another of those situations that my mouth had got me into. If only I could keep my big mouth shut! I don't know how Sparky manages it.

'Now, let's see,' I thought aloud. 'A team.'

'Don't forget, we need six including the sub,' said Whizzer.

'Right,' I replied. 'Now, there's me, Sparky, and you Whizzer, 'cos we're good. That's three. We need three more. Chip, you're not bad, if you concentrate.'

'Oh, it's so boring, football,' said Chip. 'Do I have to?'

'Yes,' I replied. Actually, he was not much good but there was no alternative. I could see Sam bursting to say something, and I knew what it was, so I quickly carried on speaking. 'You will be goalie, Lump. You're the right size — you fill a third of the goal just standing there,' I quipped.

Everybody laughed, except Lump. He wasn't too pleased with either the teasing or having to play, but I wasn't giving him any choice.

I still had the problem of a sixth person, and I had run out of players. I also knew what was in Sam's mind. 'We shall have to play without a sub. There isn't anybody left,' I said firmly.

Then Sam said exactly what I expected, and dreaded. 'What about me? I'm better than Lump and Chip put together,' she asked.

Now, for a girl, Sam wasn't too bad, and it was true that when she played with us, when I let her, she was better than Lump and Chip. But how could I possibly let her play in the team? I'd never hear the last of it, particularly from that rat Ram. 'There's a simple answer to that — *No*. You're a girl, and girls don't play in the five-a-side competition,' I said to her.

I think I touched a nerve. Sam went berserk!

'Just because I'm a girl, what difference does it make? We have to beat Ram and his mob, it's important. You men are all the same, and it's about time you changed. I'm playing, and that's that!'

Nobody spoke. Well, what can you say?

Sam continued, 'And besides, if six don't start then you aren't allowed to carry on, it's in the rules.'

I had no answer, so against my better judgement, I gave in. 'All right,' I said. 'But I don't know how I'm gonna face Ram and his mates at school.'

'Great,' yelled Sam. 'Let's get practising.'

So we did, and I must admit — she isn't bad!

Over the next week we spent a lot of time talking and arguing about our club. For years there had been nothing in the area. My dad, who's the local policeman, had tried all sorts of things. He couldn't get anybody interested, even the council wouldn't do anything to help. Then Doug came along and set something up at the church, which was better than nothing, but still pretty hopeless. People like me feel a bit out of place in a church. After that, Doug managed to get the hut set up and we'd had our own club. Doug's good at that sort of thing. I don't understand how these things work out — he says it's through prayer and stuff like that, but I don't believe it.

Then the dreaded day came — the day of the auction. We sat with Doug on the old club chairs in the hut. Across a narrow aisle sat Mr Booth and one of his men from the garage. We called him the Hulk because of his size. There were a few people sitting behind us. At the front, by the coffee bar and behind a desk, sat a man in a smart pinstripe suit with a secretary alongside him.

The auctioneer rose to his feet. 'In accordance with the wishes of the solicitors,' he said, 'I hereby auction the property as stated in the brochure. The method of auction will be by presentation of sealed bids. I have a number of these already. Are there any more to be handed in before I close the bidding?'

'Yes,' said Doug. He got up and handed the envelope to the auctioneer's secretary.

'Any more?' he asked.

Silently Mr Booth got to his feet, looked across at Doug and the rest of us with an expression between a snarl and a sneer, and handed over an envelope to the secretary. There was a long silence as the auctioneer opened all the envelopes. After what seemed an age, he got to his feet, banged his gavel on the table, and called the meeting to order. 'As there are no more bids,' he announced, 'I hereby declare that the land and hut is sold to Mr Booth of 43 Church Street.'

There was a gasp from behind. Mr Booth got to his feet, smirked, and walked over to the auctioneer to sign the necessary papers. The gang sat in stunned silence.

Mr Booth returned down the aisle. He stopped alongside Doug, and said, very bluntly, 'I want all this lot out in one month or I will throw it out on the street.' With a nod of his head he called over the Hulk, and they walked out with an arrogant swagger.

The auctioneer picked up his things, and together

with his secretary, made his way out. As he passed us he spoke to Doug. 'Sorry about that. It was an extremely generous bid by Mr Booth, no one else came anywhere near.' He moved on and out, quietly closing the door behind him.

'What do we do now?' asked Chip.

'I don't know,' replied Doug. 'I shall have to think about it.'

I sat numb and blank, the conversations echoing in my head but seeming a long way off. It was a disaster. I had to take it out on someone, and Doug was the nearest. 'Some use the church was,' I said. 'Jesus was supposed to help those who asked,' I grumbled on.

'Did you ask him then?' replied Doug.

'That's beside the point,' I grunted back. 'You did.'

'Maybe it's not the end of the story yet,' Doug responded.

'That sounds like a cop-out to me,' I said angrily. Then I thought better. It wasn't really Doug's fault. 'I'm sorry, Doug. It's not really your fault. You've done a lot for us. We just don't want to lose the club,' I said.

There was a miserable silence, broken only by the banging of Whizzer's foot on the chair. He couldn't sit still, even now. Eventually Doug spoke. 'Come on. All is not over yet. We've still got a month left. Look, you have been a right nuisance to Mr Booth. Why don't you go and see him? Apologize for all that has happened in the past and try to persuade him to let us keep the hut. He can't be wanting it for anything, he hardly uses the buildings he's got already,' he said.

Nobody answered. They were all waiting for me.

I hated the idea but couldn't think of a better one just at that moment.

'Well, all right,' I said reluctantly. 'I don't really see why I should apologize for anything. I've done nothing wrong, much. But if it means keeping the club, I'll do it.'

'Right,' said Doug. 'I'll ring him and make an appointment.'

3

◆

THE CAMPAIGN BEGINS

We stood around in the club hut feeling uncomfortable and edgy. Sparky was aimlessly bouncing a ball against the cushion of the pool table; Whizzer was batting a table tennis ball up in the air over and over again. Lump was stuffing himself with chocolate.

Then the door opened and Doug walked in. He had his crash helmet under his arm. 'Sorry I'm late,' he said, as he put his helmet down on the coffee-bar. 'Right. Let's get going.'

'I'm not at all sure about this,' I muttered. The more I thought about it, the more stupid the idea seemed.

'Do you want a club or not?' asked Doug. 'Because if you do, you should be willing to swallow your pride and try anything.'

He had a point. I owed it to everybody to try. 'Oh all right, let's get it over with,' I said, with a sigh.

It had been agreed that me and Sparky, together with Sam, would go along with Doug to see Mr Booth. Reluctantly, we followed Doug along the road to the garage. We passed the main gates and made our way to the small office alongside the open stretch of concrete where second-hand cars stood ready for sale. I felt funny inside, scared and angry all mixed up together.

Doug knocked politely on the glass door. I could see Mr Booth sitting behind his desk, but he had his back to us and was looking into a filing cabinet. He turned in his chair in response to the knock, a smile on his face. He must have been expecting a customer. The smile quickly changed to a scowl when he saw Doug, me, Sparky and Sam. 'Oh, it's you. You'd better come in,' he said.

Boy, what a toad, I thought.

We went in, Doug leading the way.

'Well, you asked to see me, and time is money, so get on with it,' said Mr Booth gruffly, leaning back in his chair.

There was a long silence.

Mr Booth looked at us. Sam and Sparky looked at the floor. I pursed my lips and stared hard at the wall behind his head thinking, 'What on earth am I doing here?' and, 'Here's another fine mess you got me into,' and other equally useless and irrelevant thoughts. Doug was looking at each of us in turn, desperately willing one of us to say something.

The silence was getting embarrassing. I knew it was up to me really, so I sucked in a big breath of air and began. 'We have come to apologize for any trouble we may have caused you and your garage, and promise we won't do it again,' I said quickly and breathlessly.

'Huh, I should think so, and about time too,' answered Mr Booth.

'And,' I went on, 'And to ask you if you would let us keep the hut in the corner of the land by the church. We promise that we won't interfere with anything to do with the garage, play outside, or

26

cause any sort of bother.' I sucked in a great breath of air, relieved to have finished.

'I see,' replied Mr Booth slowly. 'If I allow you to keep the hut, you won't cause any bother.'

'Yes, that's right,' butted in Sam hopefully.

Mr Booth got to his feet, put both hands on his desk, and glowered at us. 'I don't respond to blackmail,' he barked. 'What you're saying is that if I don't let you keep the hut, you will cause a lot of trouble around the garage!'

'No, no, we . . .' began Sparky.

'Let me tell you,' continued Mr Booth, 'that if there is the slightest bit of trouble anywhere *near* the garage, I will use any method I like to stop it, and I don't need your protection. It strikes me that some of you lot need a rattling good hiding.' He looked straight at me, then he turned his anger on Doug. 'And as for you, Vicar, or curate, or whatever you call yourself, I didn't think blackmail was part of the church's business.'

'I think you're missing the point,' put in Doug.

'On the contrary, I think I'm only too well aware of the point,' replied Mr Booth quickly. 'There is no way that hut will remain. You have three weeks and two days to remove all of your equipment. I want no more bother from you or any of these young ruffians.' He waved his arm in our direction.

'I think you're being rather unfair,' said Doug.

'That's enough,' grunted Mr Booth. 'I have bought the property, you get out. Now go away, I have got work to do and you are stopping me from doing it.' He thumped the table.

Sam turned abruptly and rushed out crying. Sparky followed her silently. Doug pushed me out, but he wasn't quick enough. I had something to say to Booth, and nothing was going to stop me. I was going to give him something in return for what he had got to say. 'You're a rotten, mean, nasty swine,' I said, desperately struggling for words. 'And I'll get my own back on you for this.'

Doug forced me through the doorway, and shut the door. Mr Booth stood at his desk, hands on hips, and looked through the glass door with a surly smirk.

Doug managed to drag me away. I felt like kicking and screaming.

Back in the hut, the rest were waiting.

'What happened?' asked Whizzer.

We just slumped in the chairs and didn't say a word. Nobody moved for a long while, apart from the odd swinging foot or tapping finger. I was boiling up inside. In my head many thoughts were bubbling and brewing, all nasty. Why are adults so unreasonable? Old Booth could have let us stay. I bet there's something fishy going on in his garage that he doesn't want anybody to know about. We didn't do anything to him — well, not much. I'll get my own back on him. I'll make him wish he'd never done and said those things. What we need is to get organized for some action, our way! It's time for me to take a grip on the situation.

'I'm not finished yet,' I said, the thoughts whirling through my mind. 'I'm not going down without a fight. Look, if you're with me then meet me on the street tonight at six o'clock.'

I turned towards Doug. 'I'm sorry Doug,' I said. 'It's not your fault, but we're going to do it my way. When someone gets nasty, you have to get nasty back, or they walk all over you.' I got up and walked to the door. 'Anyone coming?' I asked, but

28

was really telling.

'What about helping Doug with all the moving that has to be done?' asked Sam. I wasn't in the mood for co-operation.

Sparky turned to me. I could see that he was upset. 'I'm not going to leave Doug in the lurch,' he said, 'just because you've lost your temper. This is no way to treat a friend who's done a lot for you.'

I was confused, mad, and upset, and didn't know how to answer that one. There was a sort of empty pause.

Then Doug said, 'I have persuaded the church to let us start a more limited club in the church hall and meeting rooms. We have to agree to stop some of the more noisy activities, and we can only meet two nights each week, and we have to clear everything away afterwards, but it's better than nothing.'

He shouldn't have said that. I had been beginning to wilt, but that finished me off. I remembered all the trouble we had before. I turned to the others. 'You can do what you like,' I said. 'But I'm off. I'll see you tonight if you really want to do something to sort this out.' I didn't know what I was going to do, but I'd think of something.

That evening at six o'clock I met the others on the street and began to plan a campaign. I knew Sparky wasn't keen, but at least he came.

'I've been thinking,' I began. 'What we need is some publicity. I've seen it on telly. First we organize a petition, get as many names as we can, then we take the names in a march to the City Hall.'

'Sounds a bit far-fetched to me,' grumbled Lump.

'Oh shut up, Lump,' put in Sam. 'If anyone mentions work you have a heart failure. I think it's a great idea.'

29

'What's your dad going to say?' retorted Lump. He really is a wet blanket on anything, except for food that is.

'I know what my dad will say,' added Chip. 'He'll go crackers.'

'Well, I think it's great, man,' said Whizzer. 'Lots of fun and a good rumble.' He turned to Chip. 'Your dad's just scared because he thinks he might lose his job if he gets involved in anything risky,' he said.

Lump asked me again, 'But what will your dad say?'

I didn't really want to think about that one, but the best form of defence is attack, so I attacked Lump.

I put my face a short distance from his. 'I'm not going to be put off,' I said. 'I'm not going to let Booth or anybody walk all over us. He plays mean, so will I. Anyway, what can go wrong? Dad's always telling me about democracy and freedom in this country — that's why he's a copper. Well, I just want a piece of it for us. He can't argue with that.'

'I just don't think he'll see it that way,' replied Lump.

What a softie! What did it matter what my dad thought? 'I'm fed up with this,' I said. 'Are we doing it or not?'

In their own way they all eventually agreed, although some were not too happy about it, and Sparky insisted on telling Doug.

We set about organizing the petition first, taking sheets of paper and getting lots more local kids as well to help. Then we canvassed the whole area, getting people to sign. We stood outside the local shops and knocked on lots of doors.

My dad didn't really mind this. He had heard all about Mr Booth, and wasn't too keen on the man himself. We weren't doing any harm, and he had a word with the other local policemen to keep an eye on us. It was a good job he didn't know about the march, though. That would have been a different story. Before long, we had everything ready. It was too late to go back now. Anyway, nothing could possibly go wrong. Could it?

4

THE MARCH

Getting the petition together had been hard work. But we had enjoyed it. Now we had two huge boxes full of assorted bits of paper with the signatures of all the local people who could be persuaded to sign. In an empty shed at the bottom of Whizzer's extremely overgrown garden, we had made placards and banners out of old sheets and canes, taken with some stealth from under the noses of curious mums.

It was the final meeting before the march. I got there first and unlocked the door. I could hear Lump coming from a long way off with a crackle of crisp paper and thud of heavy feet crashing through the assorted rubbish at the bottom of the garden. I opened the door just as Lump arrived.

'Can't you be quieter?' I demanded.

'I was being,' replied Lump innocently.

There was no point in going on about it, that was Lump! Quietly, Sparky and Sam slipped in behind Lump through the door. 'Come on, you two, we haven't got time to waste,' said Sam as she and Sparky unfurled the banner they were working on. It was fortunate for her that I was busy or that remark would have earned her a thick ear, girl or no girl!

It was not long before Chip arrived, and Little Mo as well. He set to work on a placard, while Little Mo

32

wandered around getting in everybody's way. Sisters!

Eventually Whizzer arrived, wearing a pair of headphones, and clicking his fingers to the Reggae music which only he could hear. One thing Whizzer could never do was arrive on time, and he got a mouthful from me every time he let us down, but it made no difference.

'Where have you been?' I demanded.

Whizzer swayed with the music and smiled.

I reached over and switched the small cassette off.

'Hi, man,' he beamed.

'You're late,' I grunted. 'This isn't a game you know.'

'OK, man, OK, keep cool, don't panic,' replied Whizzer. 'Whaddya want me to do?'

'Shut up and listen for a start,' was my curt reply. Nobody was taking it as seriously as me. Didn't they realize how important this was? But the gang sensed the edge in my voice and everyone stopped and listened to my instructions for the march.

'Right. In the morning I want everybody outside the doors of the club by ten o'clock. Whizzer, Lump, Chip, you bring along the banners. Sparky, you and Sam bring the boxes of signatures. Remember, we only want club regulars along on the march. Get as many as you can, but only club members! Nothing can go wrong if we do it properly. My dad says everybody has a right to demonstrate peacefully, and the trouble with marches is that they are badly organized. Well, we won't be. So, he'll be happy then.'

'Are you going to tell your dad?' asked Chip.

Trust him to ask that! 'I might,' I replied. 'He's told me lots of times about people's freedoms and

33

rights. Well, I'm taking him at his word.'

'My dad's going to be hopping mad,' said Chip ruefully.

'You're not backing out, are you?' I asked sharply.

'No,' replied Chip weakly. 'Just anticipating a sore backside!'

He's not the only one, I thought to myself. Then I said out loud, 'Let's get everything finished and go home. And remember, don't tell *anyone*, except club members!'

They all finished off their tasks and left, except for Sam, Sparky, and me. We tidied up then left, locking the door and leaving through the broken back fence of Whizzer's house.

Something was troubling Sparky, I could feel it. We walked along as far as the gates of our houses not saying anything. Sam knew something was wrong and walked off quickly, saying, 'See you tomorrow.'

I stood with Sparky. He needed to say something. I didn't know what, but I figured I had better let him get it over with. I didn't have long to wait!

'You're doing this all wrong,' he said.

'You got a better way?' I asked. Before he had a chance to start I said, 'And don't go on about turning the other cheek and all that stuff. I'm not a Christian, and I don't want to be. Every time I turn the other cheek someone slaps that one as well!'

I was defensive because inside I was beginning to have my doubts about the whole thing. But I couldn't back down now — a man's got his pride! Everybody would think I was chicken, and I wouldn't be able to lift my head on the street.

'Look, we're only going to upset more and more

people doing it this way,' said Sparky, 'and I bet Ram gets involved and causes trouble, too'.

'That's a risk we'll have to take. I'm not backing down now,' I replied. 'And don't you dare say anything to anybody or I'll never speak to you again.'

Sparky stood silently. 'All right,' he said eventually. 'So long as you don't do anything daft.' He turned and walked in.

Boy, friends are really funny sometimes. They always want it their own way!

The next morning was grey, damp, and very unwelcoming. Usually on a Saturday my mum has a terrible time trying to get me out of bed, but I was up and dressed and ready to go before she had even focused.

She knew I was up to something, but none of the usual tactics worked to find out what was going on. Little Mo was the usual informer, but not today. All she said to Mum was, 'You'll have to wait and see.'

We left the house to head for the club. In my mind I had the picture of a great march to the City Hall, meeting the Mayor, handing over the petition, being promised the club would be saved at all cost, and returning shoulder-high in triumph.

I turned the corner of the road in this glowing anticipation, and was pulled back to reality by Little Mo tugging at my sleeve. I looked ahead and gasped. Ahead of me the road was full of kids. There must have been at least two hundred. Brightly-coloured banners broke through the grey of the day as people jostled about, laughing and talking, making too much noise. I pushed my way through to the steps of the club where the rest of the gang were.

'What happened?' I demanded. 'I said only club members.'

'I guess there were more club members than we thought,' replied Chip helplessly.

'Hey, man, what does it matter?' said Whizzer. 'We'll sure make an impact with this lot.'

I felt uneasy about the whole thing, but there was no way back now. Things had gone too far. Sparky looked sick.

I shouted out, 'Quiet!' and then louder, 'QUIET!'

'Now, everyone get in fours, no more than four in a row, follow the people in front, and don't do anything daft,' I shouted.

Slowly, everyone milled round until there was some sort of order. Then I gave the order to move off.

All went well as we passed through our district. When we reached the park on the edge of the main shopping area of the city I decided to walk back along the column to see how things were. I was horrified. As we had marched, other local kids had joined in, so there was now a huge crowd. Worse still, in the middle of the column, was my hated enemy Ram, together with some of his mates. I knew they were out to cause trouble. He smirked at me.

'Don't cause any trouble, Ram. This isn't the place to sort out our differences, it's too important,' I said firmly.

'What, me?' replied Ram sarcastically. 'I've only come to help.'

His mates jeered and chanted. I realized there was nothing I could do, and went back to the front of the march. I told Sparky and the others what was happening further back. Little Mo suggested that we might try what Doug would do in such a situation — pray — but I shut her up with a gruff, 'Don't be stupid.' Inside however, I was thinking of a quick prayer, just in case.

As we reached the shopping area the chanting grew louder. The orderly procession of four in a row broke up as Ram and his mates jostled the marchers. They started shouting and swearing. It wasn't long before a police car turned up to investigate, followed by more cars as the word was spread by police radio.

Where the road narrowed near the front of the big department stores, a posse of police were waiting. It was a big relief to me that my dad wasn't one of them. They stopped us and wanted to know what we were doing, so I told them. The sergeant in charge wasn't very pleased that they hadn't been given advance warning, but accepted my explanation.

'I want twenty only to carry on to the City Hall,' he said. 'And the rest to go back to the park and wait.'

This seemed a good idea to me, so I passed on the message. Ram had other ideas. Suddenly, from among the mass of kids, a brick was hurled through the nearest shop window. It broke with an awful crash. As if they were at a football match, Ram and his pals used the tactic of surging the children round like a stampede of cattle, all in different directions. More windows were smashed and people were knocked to the ground. The noise, shouting, and screaming was terrible.

I just looked on in absolute horror. I mean, I'm no angel, but I had never been involved in anything like this before. Before long, lots more police arrived and we were all herded back to the park.

All of the gang, including Sam and Little Mo, ended up at the police station. We were asked lots of questions and then told to sit and wait on a long wooden bench in the entrance. I was terrified that Dad would walk in any moment and I wasn't looking forward to it. I was also very angry and frustrated. Even some of the kids themselves didn't care about losing the club. Why were so many people uncaring and selfish?

A door opened, and my father appeared. He didn't look too pleased. 'In here, you lot,' he ordered. We shuffled past him into the room and turned to face him.

'What on earth do you think you are doing?' he demanded. 'Don't tell me,' he turned to me, 'I don't need to guess very hard to find out who's behind it.' My dad always looks large and frightening in his policeman's uniform. I could tell that some of the others were scared stiff and near to tears. But not me!

'We did what was right,' I blurted out. 'We didn't do anything wrong. We can't help it if trouble-makers do things like that. Somebody's got to care and somebody's got to do something.'

'Shut up Nick. I'll talk to you later,' cut in Dad. I was angry but did as I was told. 'I'm not wasting time on you all now,' he added. 'Fortunately, the sergeant spoke up for you and said that you had nothing to do with the broken windows and other damage. You will all go straight home now and I shall see each of your parents to tell them what has happened and let them deal with you all.' He paused. 'Now go home,' he said.

38

We all turned and shuffled out slowly. I didn't dare think about what he'd do to me later. I knew it wouldn't be pleasant!

5

NICK'S MASTER PLAN

We walked home very slowly. It's funny how distances seem greater when you're feeling depressed, and it was an awful long time before we came to our street. I was miserable and walked along the gutter kicking a stone. Nobody spoke. We were all thinking about what our parents would say.

Suddenly from behind me there was a fierce 'PARP!!' A huge low-loader lorry passed by and I jumped on to the pavement for safety. 'Idiot,' I yelled, and shook my fist. It was carrying a very big, yellow earthmover, and I wondered what on earth that was doing down our road.

It wasn't long before I found out. It drew to a halt alongside the land between the club and Mr Booth's garage, behind some other vans and cars. A group of men stood around talking and the driver joined them.

'What's going on?' I said to the others. Immediately we all broke into a run in the direction of the activity and noise. As we got nearer we could see what was happening. The grassy area was already churned up and machines were scraping the ground flat.

I butted into the group of men talking by the parked vehicles. 'What are you doing?' I demanded.

A large, red-faced man turned his head. 'Shove off, kid,' he said.

'Look, mate,' I replied, 'there's no need to be like that, tell us what's going on.'

The man turned right round now and looked at us all aggressively. 'Mr Booth warned us there might be some trouble from local kids, and you fit the description of the ringleaders. Now get lost!'

He turned away and then turned back again. 'You might as well know that we have orders to pull down that hut over there tomorrow,' he grunted, jerking his thumb. Then he turned again to carry on his chat with the others.

We stood, stunned that the crunch had finally come and the club was finished. I couldn't bear to watch, and turned away in the direction of home. First, the disaster of the march — and now this!

Running through my head were thoughts of home and what was going to happen, the disasters of the day, and images of the club building being ripped down. I could have cried, but I knew I couldn't. Everyone would think I was a softy. To stop myself from blubbering I tried to think of ways to get back at Mr Booth. I knew it was hopeless but I couldn't bear the thought of that horrible man winning.

Then it came to me — a last defiant act of heroism in the face of defeat. Custer's last stand. It was my Master Plan. We would have to sit-in! I turned to the others and told them my idea.

'Let's organize a sit-in!' I said, trying to make it sound really exciting.

The groans were loud and long. 'You must be joking,' replied Chip.

'What a load of softies,' I cut in, stung by their defeated attitude. 'Come on, we're not going to give in without a fight, are we?'

'Yes,' said Lump bluntly.

41

'Give me one good reason why we shouldn't?' I demanded, ignoring Lump.

'I'll give you two,' put in Sparky. 'One, it's stupid, and two, it's wrong.'

'Well, I think we should,' added Sam, loyally. 'Why should we let him win that easily?'

At last, someone on my side. If this goes on much longer, I thought, I shall have to revise my opinion of girls. But I mustn't allow a crisis to colour my judgements too much!

I could see the others squirming a bit in embarrassment. 'Well, look at that,' I said. 'The only one with any guts is Sam. I know what you lot are afraid of — you're scared of getting a good hiding. Well, you're going to get one anyway, so why the fuss? It'll be tomorrow before my dad tells your parents, and by that time we'll have started the sit-in. They won't punish you twice, so what are you afraid of?' I could see the heads beginning to nod. 'I'm the only one who's going to be punished tonight,' I continued, 'and I'm not scared.' I was, I was terrified, but I wouldn't let on.

There was a silence, ended by Sparky. 'But it's still wrong! It's stupid really,' he added. 'We can't win and it'll only mean more trouble.'

I was really mad with Sparky. For a best pal he was being very difficult. He might have been right, but that wasn't the point, was it? I hated myself for saying it, but I just lost my temper. 'If you're not with me, you can get lost!' I said.

He turned, then looked back to say something, but stopped himself, and walked off slowly down the street.

'You tell anybody and I'll thump you,' I shouted after him. To the others I said, 'I want to see you all at midnight round the back of the club hut, and not a word.'

Everyone nodded, some more willingly than others, then turned for their homes. Sam walked alongside me. 'We'll show 'em, you and me, won't we, Nick?' she said.

'Mm,' I replied. I hoped she wasn't getting the wrong idea. Thank goodness Little Mo was there to protect me!

When Little Mo and I got home the inevitable happened. Mo was sent straight to bed with a smacked bottom and no supper. I was sent to my room to wait for Dad to come home. It wasn't long before I heard the bang of the front door, and after hearing heated discussions downstairs, the call came for me.

'Nick, down here, now!' They must have heard Dad's voice three streets away! I came downstairs, trying to look as apologetic as I possibly could. Experience told me not to argue but to keep my mouth shut and take the punishment.

Dad blasted me out. I don't know what he said because I sort of switch off and just watch the mouth movements in a kind of hypnotic stare. Then the inevitable happens. The wooden spoon is ritually taken from the kitchen drawer and I am forced to bend over with his heavy hand on my neck. It's funny, you don't really feel it after the first one, but it's best to make some sort of noise or he claims it as a miss and adds one on at the end.

I always cry. It's expected. Anyway, it hurts as the numbness wears off. Then I'm sent to bed with the usual line of 'it hurts me more than it hurts you'. Who believes that? What gets me is that Grandma reckons no one was as bad as my dad when he was a child, but he never mentions that. As far as he is concerned, nobody has ever been as bad as me. It doesn't seem right somehow!

At midnight I was woken by my alarm clock. I had wrapped it in a scarf. Now for my Master Plan — the sit-in. I had insisted to Little Mo that she shouldn't come because the route out of the house was dangerous. Carefully I climbed out of my bedroom window, over the kitchen roof, along the top of the garden wall, and dropped to the ground in the back alley. Then I quietly plodded down the street, hopped over the fence and round to the back of the club hut.

Sam and Whizzer were already there. Chip followed me in, and eventually Lump arrived, muttering about the cold, and how stupid all this was, and why on earth he had let himself be talked into this, until I shut him up with a threat.

I broke the lock on the back door with a brick, and we eased it open. We had brought a couple of torches, and using them for light, I gave everybody orders and we set to work. The few old bits of furniture left were heaped against the two doors. Fortunately the side windows were boarded up anyway because they kept getting broken. Then I called everybody together again.

'Chip, you take the first watch while we all get some sleep. After half an hour wake up Whizzer to take over, then Sam, Lump, and me,' I said. 'We'll keep that up till the first workmen arrive. When they do, we stand behind the two front windows and chant. Try and think of something good to chant.'

Sam, Whizzer, Lump and I sat against the wall of the hut and tried to sleep, but it was impossible, so after a while we all kept watch together. The street

44

outside was eerie and empty, very much quieter than usual, with pools of orange light around each lamp stand. We were all cold, tired and miserable. Somehow, I wished Sparky was with us. He always cheered me up. Maybe he had been right. It didn't seem such a good idea now, but I tried to keep everybody going with occasional comments about Mr Booth, and stories of some of the great things that had happened at the club. I was convinced Mr Booth was up to no good, and the more I thought about him in those boring hours, the more I became sure he was some sort of criminal. But what sort? And how could I prove it?

After what seemed ages, the dawn began to break and the lamps switched themselves off. Lump and Chip wanted to give up but I bullied them to continue. As for Whizzer — well, he always treats everything as a lot of fun, however serious it is. Only Sam was taking the thing really seriously. People were beginning to appear on the street — the early risers off to work, the milkman, and the newspaper delivery boy. I wondered what would happen at home when they found out I'd disappeared. Boy, would I get in trouble this time! My bottom was still sore from the last onslaught, so I guessed a few more smacks with the wooden spoon wouldn't make much difference. I could feel the others getting tense and anxious.

'Let's warm up with a good song,' I said, hoping to raise their spirits. I broke into, 'We shall not, we shall not be moved,' and the others followed, rather half-heartedly.

Suddenly a van drew up and we stopped abruptly. As we watched in silence, the men got out and stretched. The big fellow who had spoken to us the day before got out. He must have been the foreman — I could hear him barking out orders. Then he walked over towards the door of the hut and we instinctively ducked down. He turned the key in the lock, twisted the handle, and pushed. 'That's funny,' he said, 'it was all right yesterday.'

He then tried his shoulder against the door. I could see the furniture we had piled up beginning to move, so I decided it was time for action. I jumped up and shouted, 'You can't come in!'

The man leapt back in amazement. 'Who's that?' he shouted.

Stupidly, I replied, 'It's me!'

'Who's me?' he went on.

This was getting silly.

'We are the members of this club and you can't pull it down. This is a sit-in,' I shouted.

There was a pause.

'Come on out!' the man barked. 'Don't be stupid.' Then he started to get angry. 'If you don't come out this moment, I shall call the police.'

'Go away,' I replied. Then we all began to sing:

'We shall not, we shall not be moved,
We shall not, we shall not be moved,
This is our club and we'll not let you knock
*   it down.*
We shall not be moved.'

The man walked away back to the rest of the workmen. He was pointing and talking, but we couldn't hear what he was saying. One man went off down the road. Soon Mr Booth appeared. He came up to the window and glared in.

'Oh, not you again,' he groaned, looking me

46

straight in the eye. 'Now, you just get out of there. I've had enough of all this. I've a good mind to come in and sort you out myself.' He looked very fierce and angry and I knew he meant it.

'You touch me and I'll have the law on you. My dad's a policeman you know,' I replied quickly.

This seemed to calm him down a bit and he stepped back to talk to the others. Then he returned. 'I want you out in five minutes, or I call the police,' he demanded.

Our only reply was another chorus of 'We shall not, we shall not be moved'.

Mr Booth stood back with the rest of the men looking angrily in our direction. I wondered what he was going to do. Then I saw Little Mo and Dad rushing down the street. Dad was half-dressed and obviously angry. I could see him talking to Mr Booth, then he marched up to the door and thumped on it.

'Nick, Nick! Come out here this minute,' he shouted. For my own safety I decided this wasn't a wise move, and anyway, it would be giving in.

'No, Dad!' I shouted back, 'I'm not. We are fighting for our rights here, and we're not coming out.'

He thumped even harder. 'You get out here this minute,' he shouted, 'or I'll write your principles on your backside with a wooden spoon.'

'You're going to do that anyway,' I replied, 'and besides, what about all those principles and rights you're always telling me about?'

He thumped the door again, and then backed away to the pavement.

I hadn't noticed before, but all the other parents had arrived, together with Doug and Sparky. They seemed to be having some kind of argument, but I couldn't hear them. Doug was talking. People were waving their arms about and the voices were very loud. I could see Doug was trying to calm them all down. Eventually he came towards the window and looked in. 'Nick, you there?' he called.

'Yes,' I replied, aggressively.

'OK,' he said. 'Listen, you've made your protest, and I really appreciate it, but things are getting serious.'

'Good!' I grunted.

'Look, Nick,' Doug went on, 'if you carry on, you'll ruin any chance of setting up a smaller club in the church and you'll also do your own cause no good. Don't expect publicity, or sympathy, you won't get it. If you leave now, then your parents have promised not to punish you, and Mr Booth has said he won't take things any further. But if it goes on, the police will have to be called and your parents will punish you as well.'

'Blackmail,' I retorted.

'Think it over,' he said. 'I'll be back in five minutes.'

I turned to the others. One look told me it was a lost cause. I could see they wanted to give up — all except Sam, loyal as ever.

'I think we should take Doug's advice,' said Chip.

'Me too,' added Lump quickly.

Whizzer didn't really mind, but didn't want to upset his mum any more.

I paused. 'OK,' I said eventually, and we pulled the barricade down and opened the door.

We went out silently and joined our parents who took us off home. I looked hard at Sparky, who just looked sad. I couldn't bear to watch as I heard the bulldozer start up and the sound of splintering wood and cracking glass. I fought back tears of bitterness.

It was a sad day for Nick and Co. What was even worse, was that Dad broke his promise. He didn't hit me; he did something far worse. He had promised me a dog on my next birthday but now he said that I couldn't have one if I got into any more bother. That really got to me! No way could I avoid trouble — that's impossible!

6

RAM'S REVENGE

I didn't go along to the new club set up in the church hall for a while. But then I decided I'd better go along. I was getting very bored at home, and the others seemed to be having a good time at the club. Anyway, I didn't want to lose my position as leader of the gang.

We could only meet twice a week in the church hall and everything had to be put away each time. It all seemed a bit wet to me and pretty useless. Things usually turn out that way when grown-ups get their hands on them, I thought.

The church hall was a big room with a high ceiling, and was painted in bright colours. It had a stage at one end which was used by the drama club and for the big meetings the church had every week. That first time back I paced around and made my presence felt, just to let everybody know I was there. The tuck shop had been set up in the kitchen so I went in to buy a drink.

'Hello Nick,' said a voice from the corner of the room. I turned round and saw Aunty Edna. She wasn't my real Aunty, nor the Aunty of any of the other kids, but we all called her that. She was great. Sometimes we visited her in her little old house at the bottom of the street, and she always had some pop or sweets for us. I had no idea how old she was, but she must have been ancient because she was my father's Aunty Edna before me.

'Hello,' I replied, rather grumpily.

'What's the matter with you, as if I didn't know,' she continued. 'You're just like your father before you — pig-headed and stubborn.' If it had been anybody else, I would have been very rude, but not to Aunty Edna! 'When will you learn?' she went on. 'Everybody's on your side, really. You just have to realize you may not know best all the time.'

I let her go on, but I didn't really listen. Old people do go on a bit, either about how much better, or worse, things were when they were young; or they talk at great length about their illnesses. They think they know it all.

'I don't know,' she said, shaking her head.

Just then Sam popped her head round the door and rescued me. 'Hey, have you forgotten the five-a-side competition?' she asked.

'Oh, right,' I replied, in relief. Before she had a chance to say anything, I said to Aunty Edna, 'See you! Got to get a team organized.' I moved out of the room as quickly as I could and didn't look back.

As the team-sheet had already been handed in I couldn't knock Sparky's name off, and anyway we would have really been in a mess without him because he was a good footballer. But I still wasn't feeling that friendly towards him. I just can't understand people being so unwilling to change, and so stubborn.

I got everybody together and told them what we were going to do, then we went out to the park to practise. Lump was hopeless as usual, but at least his vast bulk blocked quite a bit of the goal. The only problem was, he tended to jump out of the way if the ball was kicked too hard. Chip made an effort for once and wasn't too bad. Whizzer and Sparky were both very good, as usual.

Sam? Well, she was skilful and sharp, but I wasn't going to tell her that! When she asked how well she had played I told her that although she had tried hard, it wasn't quite good enough and she would be the reserve. I could see that this made her really mad. She knew that I would do almost anything to avoid her actually playing, so I quickly got involved in the football to avoid confrontation.

The day of the competition was hot and sultry. The team met outside the church. Doug had persuaded our school to lend us some kit for the occasion. It was all red. I felt great when I tried it on in front of the mirror at home, pretending I was playing for Liverpool.

On the way to the park we all talked excitedly about the competition ahead and our chances. I was sure we could win this year if everybody tried hard. The park was very busy. It had been taken over for the competition and several pitches had been marked out. In the middle was a large white tent where the organizers worked it all out.

We were organized into four leagues, the winning teams making up the semi-final placings. Fortunately, we were not drawn against Ram's team. Nobody really liked playing against them because they were dirty and mean. As we waited and talked we didn't notice Ram and his mates making their way across the park to the organizer's marquee. The first we knew was a yelp of pain from Chip as Ram kicked him from behind.

'Oh, so sorry! Didn't notice you there,' he said, with an evil smirk on his face.

There are some kids you just can never get on with, and this creep was the king. 'Why don't you shove off?' I said.

'What's the matter, sonny?' he replied sarcastically. 'Still crying over losing your little doll's house — sorry — club hut?'

That did it. I was really angry now as I remembered what he had done to us on the march. 'You pig,' I said. 'I won't forget the trouble you caused on our march. I'll get you for that. Now, push off, before I put my foot in your face.'

Ram was always tougher with his cronies round him, and today was no exception. 'You better button your lip, worm,' he grunted, 'or I might have to do it for you. You know what your trouble is,' he added, 'you just can't take a joke.' He turned to his pals and smirked. They laughed obediently, the stupid dopes.

I wasn't going to back down, never, and stood up against him. 'You just clear off,' I said. 'I'm not afraid of you.'

'You should be,' he said, with a sneer.

I could sense a fight brewing. I didn't think we'd win with Sparky the way he was, but I would never back down. Just at that moment there was an announcement over the tannoy: 'Would all teams who have not yet reported to the administration tent, please do so immediately?' demanded a voice.

Ram looked me up and down, then said, 'I'll see to you later. Come on, men.' He turned to go.

Why couldn't I learn to keep my mouth shut? Like a fool I had to take it further. 'I'll be waiting,' I said arrogantly.

'You do that,' he replied. Then, as a parting shot, he moved forward and kicked Chip's leg again. 'Oh, so sorry, it was an accident,' he said. 'I'm so clumsy.'

Chip rolled in agony as they strolled away, laughing to each other. I would have gone after Ram but the others stopped me. I didn't have time to think up any plans for revenge. We were due to play the first round then. We played very well through all the qualifying rounds, with Sparky and Whizzer whipping down the wings, and me in the middle spraying the ball about and cutting back to help in defence where Chip was doing a sterling job in spite of his injury. Lump worked hard in goal and made some quite good saves — sometimes with very unusual parts of his anatomy.

We won our group and reached the semi-final. We were playing against a club from the other side of the city. In spite of having the first goal scored against us, we managed to pull one back so that, with five minutes to go, it was one goal each.

Chip was limping so badly I didn't think he would make it to the end of the game. With two minutes to go they nearly scored but Lump's ample bulk got in the way and the ball rebounded to Chip. He took off like I've never seen him do before, completely fogetting his limp and, after passing several players, made a superb shot that whistled into a corner of the goal. When we had got over our astonishment we leaped for joy and smothered Chip. There wasn't even enough time to restart. When he eventually surfaced we could see that Chip wasn't too well. That last great effort had finished him off and he was in real agony from the damaged leg.

A St John's ambulance man came over to have a look and said Chip couldn't play in any more matches and strapped his leg up with heavy bandages. To make matters worse, the team that won in the other semi-final was none other than Ram's lot. Just our luck! I could have coped with Sam playing in some earlier round. I could just about handle having her in the team for the final, in an emergency. But against Ram's team no way! They would make mincemeat of her. But Sam had other ideas. This was her big chance, and she wasn't going to let it slip. What could I do? I seriously thought of scratching from the competition, but neither Sam, nor my pride, would allow it.

It was time for the final. We marched on to the pitch and took up positions. I could hear murmurs from the crowd as they noticed that one of the team was a girl. It made me squirm with embarrassment. Then Ram's team sauntered out. We looked smart in our bright red gear; they looked like an advert for a rag market, just about managing the same colour — a sort of faded, dirty blue.

Ram looked across at us and sneered. The whistle blew and he and I made our way to the middle to meet the referee.

'This isn't right,' he complained. 'He's got a girl in his team. 'It's not a Brownies' tea-party, you know.'

I was somewhere between embarrassment and anger, and didn't quite know what to say. I heaved a sigh of relief when the referee rescued me. 'There's nothing against it in the rules, so I suggest we get on with the game,' he said straightforwardly.

' 'Ere, hang about,' said Ram. 'I hope that there's going to be no favouritism then, when we tackle her and all that.'

'There won't be,' replied the ref. 'Now, let's get on with it.'

Poor Sam, I thought, I shall have to try and protect her. But then there was no time to think about it, the toss had been made and we were quickly under way.

Ram's lot were really rough, and they set about us straight away. I wasn't sure what was kicked the most — the ball, or our shins. I could feel myself getting angry. The referee didn't seem to be doing much about the pushing or kicking. Then he started telling me off for arguing. Why didn't he tell them off for kicking? Yet another stupid grown-up that couldn't grasp the first principles of fairness! I mean, the only kicking that I did was in retaliation.

Up to half-time there was no score, but we'd lost a lot of blood. In the second half they continued in the same way. They were really pushing Sam around and I thought once or twice she might cry, but she didn't. Then came my moment of glory. Lump rolled the ball out to Sparky, who neatly evaded his marker and passed to Whizzer — who whizzed down the wing and crossed the ball to Sam. She then controlled the ball superbly and dropped it in my path. In spite of being obstructed by that brute Ram I thumped the ball first time and it hit the back of the net with a satisfying sizzle. What a goal!

We went wild with delight. I think that was our undoing. Straight from the kick-off, Ram ran with the ball towards our goal. If he wasn't so interested in cheating, he would be a very good footballer, and he was really turning it on now. He glided past everybody until it was just me and Lump left. I knew he would go to my left so I stepped that way forcing him further out. He tapped the ball past me and made a run. There was no way he could get to the ball, but the next thing I knew he was rolling all over the floor in agony. I never touched him! Honest! But, blow me if the ref. didn't whistle and give him a penalty. Ram deserved an Oscar for his performance, I thought bitterly. As he got up, he smirked at me and winked. I could have kicked his teeth in! Trouble was, I tried to do just that. The referee didn't like it, pulled me over, and told me to clear off the pitch.

What injustice! I was so mad I couldn't contain myself. I gave that ref. a piece of my mind but it didn't help, I had to go! Sullenly and with the sympathy of the rest of the team, I sulked off.

From the side I watched as Ram scored from the penalty, and despite some marvellous efforts from the gang, Sam in particular, they ran out the winners 3-1. I was sick.

We got the award ceremony over with as quickly as possible and skulked off with the jeers and taunts of Ram's lot in our ears. I didn't know whether to be mad with myself for getting sent off or with the referee for letting Ram's lot get away with it, or mad at Ram's gang for cheating. So in the end I got mad with everybody and went off home to sulk.

Why is the whole world against me? What have I done to deserve all this? I felt really sorry for myself.

7

THE PIANO INCIDENT

Things couldn't get much worse. First we lost the club, then there was all the trouble over that crook Booth. The disaster of the march and the sit-in fiasco were bad enough. Now, there was the ultimate catastrophe — defeat in the five-a-sides by Ram's team. Life was getting grim!

The club evenings settled in to a pattern of being quite good, but occasionally spoilt by someone from the church wanting to use our room or complaining about the noise and mess. We hardly ever saw the Vicar. I think he must have been hiding somewhere!

Some weeks later, a stranger walked in to the club. We are a mixed bunch, with kids whose parents come from many different countries, but so far no one in the club had parents who came from India, even though there were some in my class at school. This kid wore a turban and was obviously very nervous of us all.

Doug must have met him before because he went straight over and said, 'Hello again, glad you could come.' Then he brought the kid over to us and introduced him. 'Hey everybody, this is Rajinder Singh Chopra, Raj for short, just moved on to the street.'

Sparky went up to him and said, 'Hi, come on over and have a game of darts.'

I thought I'd better make it clear to him where he stood, so I stopped them on their way to the dart-board and said stiffly, 'I'm Nick, the gang leader, hello.'

He looked at me warily and responded with a quiet 'Hello'. On first meeting he didn't seem to offer any competition so I left it at that, making a mental note to take him on at pool, just to put him in his place. As it was I had a good chance the next week to make my point. First I beat Sparky in a little pool competition we had arranged, so then I hammered Raj out of sight. I felt better after that.

I was getting fed up with club. Nothing much seemed to happen over the next week or so and life was very boring really. The church people were forever moaning about the mess and how rude we were. I told them where to put themselves a few times — I wasn't going to be called rude by anyone.

Then came the incident of the church piano. For as long as I can remember, that piano has sat around without being used much, so why there was all the fuss when 'it' happened, I don't know. Some adults really are unpredictable. I know I won't be like that when I'm old.

It was just an ordinary sort of evening, nothing very exciting. Some of the church members were in the kitchen preparing food and stuff for a bazaar. Aunty Edna was one of them and she and a couple of her mates kept slipping us the odd fairy cake. I'm a sucker for fairy cakes!

But to get back to the story. I've got a soft football which we used to play with in the club hut for all sorts of games. I had brought it along to the church hall, and Doug said we could use it, as long as we played 'gentle' games. He very firmly said that our favourite game, passball, was out of the question because something would get damaged. So we had to wait till he was out of the room before we could put in a quick game.

Passball involved splitting into two teams of four, with one person standing on a chair at each end of the room. The ball was passed around the team until it reached your mate standing on the chair, and that was one point. The only rule was that you couldn't move your feet when holding the ball. Quite a harmless game really. In the old hut we had been allowed to use furniture to gain extra height, and that, together with the speed we threw the ball, caused Doug to ban it.

The night of the 'incident' in question I was just dying for a game of passball. Luckily Doug had to help organize something outside for the bazaar so he put us on our honour to behave. I ask you! The moment he was out of the room, I produced the ball which I had hidden behind a chair for just such an occasion and called out, 'Who's for passball, then?'

'Great,' replied Sam, quickly volunteering with Whizzer who was always ready for some action. Lump absolutely refused to stir himself — just sat there eating crisps as usual. Chip was persuaded but wasn't that keen. We were still one short to play against five of the club regulars not in my gang.

I looked around for another player. Then Raj came up to me and said, 'I'd like to play, if I may.' I wasn't sure about this. Ever since Raj turned up he had been trying to get in on the gang and I couldn't sort out why. I am always suspicious of people until I really know them — most can't be trusted, they only want something from you, or at least that's how it seems to me. But this was an urgent need and he was quite good at ball games, so I gave in, just this once. 'OK, Raj,' I said, then added quickly, 'but don't get any ideas, it doesn't make you a member of the gang.'

We began quickly and the game got noisier and noisier. At one stage somebody came out of the kitchen and told us we were making too much noise. It was lucky that no one was climbing on the furniture at that moment and Whizzer quickly hid the ball behind his back. As soon as they had gone we carried on at an even more frantic pace than before.

Now, when I play games I have to take them seriously. I can't bear just to play and not mind who wins. As far as I'm concerned, everything is a competition, and I'm going to win it, or there'll be trouble. (That doesn't count for school-work, of course. That's different — boring!) If I lose at anything I am cross for ages, like with the five-a-sides. Mum says that I'm just like my dad, which is strange because he's always telling me off for taking games too seriously. Last week for example, he clouted me for shouting at Mum when she messed up our family game of cricket on the park. I bet he did it when he was my age.

But, back to the story. The game of passball was getting more and more heated. I couldn't get past Stewart, a tall guy on the other side, so I decided to resort to using the furniture to get higher.

Out of the corner of my eye I saw the upright piano, and its stool. I made a dash for it, put one foot on the keys, making an awful noise, put the other on the top of the piano and hoisted myself up. It was harder than I thought to keep my balance up there because I got a surprise. Half of the top was open, but I made it and called out for the ball. 'Raj, pass the ball, quick,' I yelled.

Just at that moment Mr Marchbank walked in. He was a retired teacher and always looked very correct, wearing a smart blue suit with a white handkerchief in the top pocket. He was rather fussy and a real stick-in-the-mud. It just so happened that this particular evening he had decided to pop down to the church hall to see how the organization of the bazaar was going on. And I bet he wanted to check on us, because he didn't really approve of us messing up his beloved church hall.

Anyway, as I said, just as I was about to receive the ball from Raj, Mr Marchbank arrived at the door.

'Stop,' he ordered loudly. It was the worst thing he could have done.

Raj had thrown the ball hard because he was trying to impress. I turned in the direction of the shout to see what was going on. I began to overbalance and wobble a bit. When the ball arrived at my head, it put the finishing touches to my wobbling act. Everyone was looking at me. There were gasps of horror as they watched me wobble — to the left, then the right, then back again. Eventually, after what seemed like an age, one foot slipped right down into the piano and the other crashed down on the keys. The crunching and cracking was horrific.

A huge silence fell upon the hall and I just stood there — with one leg in the piano and one out. Nobody moved as I extricated myself and sat on the piano-stool rubbing my leg. But the silence didn't last long.

'You blithering idiot! Look what you've done

now,' yelled Mr Marchbank, advancing across the hall towards me.

'Nick, are you all right?' shouted Sam, dashing to my side.

Doug came rushing in after hearing all the commotion. 'What's happening? What have you done now?' he demanded.

Out from the kitchen rushed several old ladies. 'Oh dear, oh dear, whatever is going on?' they clucked.

There I sat but everybody was looking at the piano, except Sam, who was studiously dabbing my leg with her hanky.

'I knew we should never have let you lot in here,' went on Mr Marchbank. 'You're all nothing but trouble. You have no respect for property.'

But then good old Aunty Edna and her pals took up my defence. 'Now just you calm down Mr Marchbank,' said Edna. 'Just remember, these are perfectly normal children who have to let off steam. I'm sure Nick didn't mean to damage the piano.'

'That's not the point,' replied stuffy Mr Marchbank.

The gang and I followed this conversation like spectators at a tennis match, our heads moving from side to side.

'The point is,' replied Aunty Edna, 'that I remember *you* when you had a snotty nose and holes in your trousers, instead of a posh blue suit and white handkerchief. I also remember you getting up to all sorts of mischief. What would have happened if you had been banned from the church hall, I wonder! Do you want these children to learn about Christianity and God's love for sinners, or do you want a tidy church with no people?' She was marvellous. I felt like getting up and clapping.

'That's all well and good, Edna,' Mr Marchbank replied. 'But at this rate we'll have no hall left for anybody. I am going to report this to the church meeting.'

Doug turned to me and quietly said, 'I think you had better go.'

I wanted to join in the battle but decided this wasn't the best time. While everybody was still arguing, I slipped out of the door and was away. I wandered down the street aimlessly and sat on the wall opposite where our old club hut had been. There was nothing left and there was now an ugly corrugated iron fence with barbed wire on the top blocking my view. Old Booth had gone a bit overboard on security. I just sat there all on my own, feeling pretty low. No one seemed to care, understand or appreciate me. All everybody wanted to do was change me. Why couldn't they accept me as *me*!

As I was mooching about and looking at nothing in particular, I noticed the gates of Mr Booth's garage opening and a couple of shifty looking men appeared. They looked up and down the street, not noticing me, then waved to someone inside. From inside the yard a breakdown vehicle appeared with a car on it. One of the men leapt into the passenger seat and it set off at speed in the twilight. The other man quickly banged the gates to and I heard padlocks being snapped together. It seemed a funny carry-on to me! Why such secrecy about taking a car out of the garage? That shark Booth had always seemed a shifty person to me. Now I was even more convinced he was up to no good.

I wandered over to the iron fence and tried to find

a peephole to look through. There wasn't one. Somebody had very carefully made the whole wall completely secure without one tiny crack.

It was then that I decided something had to be done! It was no use telling my dad or Doug, they just wouldn't believe me after all the recent aggravation. I didn't want to get the gang involved in any more trouble. This time I had to do something myself, on my own. I decided the only thing to do was to investigate the garage and see what I could find out. My mind was made up. Next I had to plan how to do it.

I wandered off down the road home. In my mind I could picture finding a hoard of stolen jewelry, getting a reward, rebuilding the club, being interviewed on television as a hero.

Fame and fortune beckoned!

8

MIDNIGHT RAID

I lay on my bed 'planning the job'. I had always known that watching all those old 'cops and robbers' movies on the TV would come in useful some time — much more valuable than silly homework. From my background knowledge I figured out that I needed to 'case the joint' and also get together some tools for the break-in. Most importantly, I needed a torch.

On my wanderings about cupboards and boxes in search of the elusive torch I unfortunately drew the interest of Mo. At first I fobbed her off with, 'Just looking for something', but that didn't work for long. Then, worse luck, she noticed my prize, which I had found in a box of old toys.

'Why do you want a torch in the middle of summer when it's not dark?'

'Mind your own business,' I replied bluntly.

She followed me back into my bedroom. I could see her suspicions had been aroused. Sisters!

'If you don't tell me what you're doing, I'll go straight to Dad,' she whined. Seven is such a difficult age, and if little Mo didn't watch herself she would never make eight.

'I've got something to do, that's all,' I muttered.

She wouldn't let go. 'You tell me what or I'll go and tell Dad,' she said.

There was no way round it. I was going to have to

tell her. 'All right then,' I said, trying to make it sound as serious as possible. 'If you promise not to say a word to Mum or Dad, on pain of getting your arm twisted and being banned from all gang meetings for ever more.'

'I promise, cross my heart and hope to die,' she replied. She was a real tell-tale but I could usually trust her with important things. Anyway, it seemed a good idea that somebody should know where I was in case of accident. They never seem to think about that in films.

I began with great drama. 'I have seen something fishy going on at Booth's garage, I think he's up to no good and I'm going to investigate,' I said, whispering and looking mysterious.

Mo looked horrified. 'You mustn't get into more trouble, Nick. Dad'll kill you,' she said with wide-eyed concern. 'Why don't you tell Dad and let him sort it out?'

'What good would that do?' I replied gruffly. 'Do you seriously think he would believe me, after all the other disasters?'

'You must be crazy to do it,' she said.

I wasn't in a mood to listen to her. Nobody was on my side. I was on my own, now. I wasn't going to give up and be defeated. I turned on her, 'You keep your mouth shut like you promised, and leave me alone.'

She shrugged her shoulders and left me to get on with sorting things out.

Once again on the stroke of midnight I set off on my favourite escape route. Carefully I eased myself out of the bedroom window, over the flat kitchen roof, then down and along the top of the garden wall. Gently I dropped from the wall at its end, into the back alley.

Then I got the shock of my life. A torch flicked on and I gasped in surprise.

'It's only me,' came a voice I immediately recognized.

'Sam,' I whispered gruffly, 'what on earth are you doing here? And keep your voice down.'

'Little Mo told me all about it,' she whispered, 'and I wasn't going to let you go through with this on your own.'

I could have crowned that stupid little sister of mine! And, what's more, I was getting a bit fed up with Sam's constant attention. But by then I was quite glad she was there because I was beginning to feel just a tiny bit scared. Of course, I didn't say so. I decided to let her stay. Mind you, I didn't have much choice.

'OK,' I said, trying to sound annoyed while whispering, 'but switch that blinking torch off before you wake everybody on the street.'

'Oh, sorry,' she said, and we were immediately plunged into blackness as she flicked the switch. 'Now what?'

'Pick up that crate behind you,' I grunted, 'and follow me.' During the day I had placed the crate ready for a direct assault on the wall of Booth's garage.

'What crate?' asked Sam. 'Owww!' she squeaked, as she turned and tumbled straight over it. There was a terrible clatter as the crate knocked into a dustbin which then fell over. In the still night air the sound seemed to echo for ever. I clapped my hand over Sam's mouth as the window of my parent's bedroom opened and a shaft of light streamed out. The outline of Dad's head and shoulders lit by moonlight was framed in the open window.

'I thought I heard a noise,' he said. 'Better go and see what it is.'

In moments of panic, inspiration strikes. 'Meeow,' I whined, doing my best to imitate the local 'Tom'.

There was a pause which seemed to last forever, then Dad said, 'Good grief! It's that blinking cat from down the street again. I shall have some strong words to say to its owner.' From inside the bedroom I heard a muffled, 'Come back to bed, love, and shut the window.' The window banged shut and all went dark again.

Only then did I remove my hand from Sam's mouth. She gasped for air. 'There was no need to do it so hard,' she complained, rubbing her mouth as well as her shin. Women! There was no point in making a big fuss, so I picked up the crate and muttered, 'Are you coming or not?' and walked off.

We set off down the dark alley, then made our way onto the street, and made for the garage, carefully avoiding the direct light from the street lamps. There was a place where the new corrugated iron wall turned at right angles to run alongside the church. Here it was in shadow and we wouldn't be seen. I put the box down and turned to Sam. 'Wait here and stand guard,' I said, 'and whistle when anybody comes along.'

She nodded, said 'Good Luck' and watched as I placed the box against the fence. Armed with a pair of wire-cutters 'borrowed' from my Dad's toolbox, I stepped up to attack the barbed wire on top. I hadn't guessed the height of the fence accurately, and it was all I could do to reach up and cut. How I was going to get over, I had no idea.

When I had cleared as much as possible I made my first attempt. There seemed to be only one way. I had to get my hands on the top of the fence where there was a horizontal piece of wood and then I had to leap up and pull myself up the rest of the way. The trouble was, when I jumped against the fence it made a sound like a big base drum, so I had to stop. I needed more height.

I persuaded Sam to kneel on the box. She wasn't keen, but if she wanted to be number two in my gang, she had to learn to take the rough with the smooth. She knelt down very reluctantly and I carefully climbed up on her back, then eased myself on to the top of the fence. But there was more trouble. In my haste, I hadn't cut away enough wire, and I now found myself stuck by the seat of my trousers to a particularly sharp piece of barbed wire. It was difficult to know what to do. It was hurting anyway but if I moved it would probably hurt even more. I flashed my torch quickly down on the garage side of the ground and found it was clear. I foolishly made an instant decision.

'Decisions made in haste are repented at leisure,' my grandmother always used to say. She was right! I thudded to the ground and felt a searing pain in my right foot to add to the sharp pain in my bottom from the barbed wire. Stifling a groan, I sorted myself out and looked around. From the other side of the fence I heard Sam calling quietly but anxiously, 'Are you all right, Nick?'

Bravely I replied, 'Yes, now get out of sight.' I then turned my mind to the task ahead. My foot was sore but bearable and my trousers had a nasty tear which my mum wouldn't be pleased about. But now I was here, I was determined to go on. Besides, I had suddenly realized the great weakness in my plan — I hadn't worked out a getaway route! I looked around. In the dim light I could see lots of old cars littering the grassy area where we used to play. Over where the club hut used to be, was a new shed like a large garage. I made my way over and crawled around trying to find a way in.

On one side of the shed there was a small window that didn't seem to fit very well. I carefully eased it open. It was easy to climb through and I found myself standing in the pitch dark of the garage interior. I flicked on my torch and played it around. Over the other side was a workbench and I wandered over to see what was on it. There's one unfortunate thing about torches — they only light a narrow area and a clumsy character like me needs all-round vision. My left foot, in the dark, hit against something and there was a dull clunk.

I shone the torch down to see what I had kicked over. Trust me — it was a pot of red paint! Not a large pot, but big enough to spatter all over my shoe. Torn trousers, paint-covered shoe, Mum really would be pleased! I picked up a rag and dabbed at the paint, and managed to get the worst off.

I went on over to the bench. It wasn't loaded with stuff but there were a few blank pieces of metal that number-plates are made of, and lots of loose letters strewn around. At one end were small pots of paint, templates and stickers, used for decorating cars with stripes and such like.

I was just nosing around these, when I heard a low whistle from Sam, then the sound of voices from outside. Quickly, I flashed the torch on to some large boxes and moved to hide behind them. I was just in time!

First of all the lights went on in the yard outside, and I heard someone moving around. Then the door of the shed was opened, the lights were turned on, and, through a gap between two boxes, I could see the huge body of the Hulk framed in the doorway.

He looked around and wandered over to the bench, then back to the door. I breathed a sigh of relief. He hadn't found me! He was just about to switch off the light when he suddenly noticed the spilt tin of paint and a trail of red footprints. I watched in horror as he followed them — first to the bench and then straight for me. 'Ah,' he grunted, as he followed them. He called out over his shoulder, 'Boss! Over here! I think I've found something.'

Now was the time for decisive action. Just as he reached me, I gave an almighty shove and pushed the whole pile of boxes over on to him. He yelped in surprise, and fell over. I made a dash for the door and escaped out into the grassed area, now floodlit, where the old cars were parked.

Running as fast as I could with an injured foot and torn trousers I made for the spot where the barbed wire was cut and leaped at the fence. My fingers caught on the top, but I just hadn't got the strength to pull myself up. I turned and saw the Hulk appearing from the shed, and Mr Booth from the direction of the main garage. It was no good, I was cornered!

They ran over to me and grabbed me. 'Right, I've got you now, you little squirt,' leered Mr Booth.

'You touch me and I'll tell my dad,' I replied, frightened by his manner.

'How's he going to know?' he said menacingly.

Just then, Sam called from over the fence, 'Are you all right, Nick? What's going on?'

'Oh, there are more of you, are there?' said Mr Booth, startled by the voice. He turned to the Hulk and ordered him to go and catch the little blighters, as he put it. There was something in the way he spoke that really frightened me, and I called out to Sam, so she could go and tell my dad. Mr Booth's tone changed abruptly, and just as the Hulk reached the main garage to chase Sam, he yelled at him to ring for the police instead. He then manhandled me in the direction of his office. I knew I was in for big trouble this time, but was really relieved that Sam had gone to fetch my dad.

The police car arrived at the same time as Dad did. He didn't make a lot of fuss, but quickly got me into the police car and took me down to the station. I made a statement there, then Dad and I were taken home. I could see that he was livid, but all he said was, 'Why on earth did you do it?'

He didn't seem to listen when I told him about my suspicions of Mr Booth. He just sent me straight to bed.

I couldn't sleep that night. I was in big trouble this time. I felt sick and alone, everybody against me. Why wasn't anybody on my side?

9

SPARKY TO THE RESCUE

The next few days were awful. Mum and Dad were very upset and kept shouting at each other. Dad was livid with me, and I was kept in my room and not allowed to play out. He also finally said I couldn't have the dog for my birthday. I hated being locked away like that — it was really depressing. Mo came in to keep me company, but that wasn't much fun because she kept giving me bits of news that I didn't really want to hear.

She told me that Sam was in a lot of trouble with her parents, and was very upset, crying a lot. I knew I should never have let her follow me, but what could I do? Mo also was the first to tell me that Mr Booth was definitely going to prosecute. The whole thing was getting too much, and I was really cheesed off.

I lay on my bed flicking mindlessly through a stack of old comics without any real interest, when there was a knock on the door. A head appeared. It was Sparky. 'Can I come in?' he said.

Why on earth was he here? A few days ago I would have said something rude and turfed him out, but at least he was somebody to talk to. 'What do you want?' I grumbled. 'Come to gloat?'

He didn't respond but sat down on the edge of my bed and fiddled with the edge of a comic. 'Your dad's pretty mad with you,' he began.

'Tell me something new,' I grunted.

'And you've really set Mr Booth against you,' he continued.

This conversation I didn't need. 'Look,' I said to him, 'I don't need to be told about all the rotten things that have happened or are going to happen to me. Also, I don't want a sermon from you. If you've come here hoping to "convert" me, you can forget it. I'll fight my way back. Nobody's going to beat me!' I had a lot of pent-up anger to get rid of.

I stopped. For a long time Sparky didn't say anything, just kept fumbling with a comic. Eventually he spoke. 'You know,' he began, 'you've got it all wrong. I know things have changed in the last year. I know I've changed. I made a new start when I became a Christian. I believe in Jesus Christ and that he died for me. And that he's alive today. I believe it's true, and it's changed the way I look at things. But all that doesn't mean we can't still be friends.'

When he started to talk about being a Christian it made me squirm with embarrassment. I don't know why, but it did. How he still wanted to be a friend of mine after the way I had treated him was beyond me, but right now I needed a friend. 'OK,' I replied, 'but I don't want any of your religion bit. *I'm* in charge of my life, not anybody or anything else. Right?'

We shook hands on it, solemnly. Strange thing to do really, but that's what grown-ups do! We had been friends for so many years and I didn't like the awkwardness that had come between us. Now he had come more than halfway towards me so I was quite happy to give it a whirl, just so long as he kept off that Jesus Christ bit. I didn't want to be brainwashed by anybody.

We sat silently for a moment. Suddenly Sparky picked up a pillow and hurled it at me, then jumped on me and started tickling. He caught me by surprise, and I laughed so much I thought I was going to die. With my last bit of strength I threw him off on to the floor.

There's nothing like a good friendly fight to make you feel better. We pushed and pulled, punched and tickled until we were both absolutely exhausted, and lay on our backs on the floor. It was good to be friends again.

'You know,' Sparky said, staring at the ceiling, 'I agree with you about Mr Booth. There is something fishy about his operation.'

'Then why didn't you join in and help?' I complained.

'Remember,' he replied, 'I'm not going to break the law. There must be some honest way of dealing with this without doing something wrong.' I suppose he was right, and anyway I was too fed up to argue.

When he thought I'd had enough, Dad allowed me out again. He wasn't very friendly towards me, but I think he felt that I was too low to get into any more bother. He was right! I didn't want to go back to the club at the church, but Sparky came along and dragged me in. As soon as I got there I could sense that everything was a bit flat and quiet. Nobody was leaping around, not even Whizzer. The gang came over to say hello when they saw me, but it wasn't with the usual enthusiasm. Sam in particular was very quiet and hardly looked at me. They weren't nasty or anything like that, but I felt like a failed David who'd gone to face Goliath with a sling and stones, then had to go back to the troops and say, 'Sorry, I missed!'

Sparky was being a real pal to me, and played me at pool. Whizzer bought me a drink, Chip some sweets and Lump even offered me a crisp! What a sacrifice! Inside I was feeling really guilty about all the trouble I'd got them into, but I didn't show it.

I had to leave the club to get back home early, as my Dad insisted. Sparky came along as well, just to keep me company, he said. As we made our way down the street, we talked about things that had happened with the gang in the past, and had a real laugh at all the memories. We didn't notice a couple of figures standing in a doorway, until we were up to them.

'Well, if it isn't our local neighbourhood thief,' came a voice. 'A very suitable name — Nick — isn't it?'

It was that swine Ram and his mate. I spun on my heels to face him. Talk about the pot calling the kettle black! I hated Ram. He'd never caused me anything but trouble. For years we had fought over who was top man in our area. We each had our own patch but always wanted to gain ground, to take over each other's territory. Now was the time for Ram to make a challenge, just when I was down.

I could have wished for a better moment, with Sparky so unwilling to fight. But I refused to give in — I'd do it all myself if I had to.

'Did you enjoy your defeat at football?' Ram asked, with a sneer. 'Mind you, with a girl in your team what can you expect? Was it just one girl or should the whole team have been wearing skirts, I ask myself.'

'You pig,' I said. 'You cheated and fouled to win.'

'You were the one who was sent off, not me,' he cut in. He came a step closer. 'Besides,' he said, 'I don't have "foreigners" in my team. If you take in immigrants and have to make your gang up with "them", your team's bound to suffer.' I knew how Ram treated the black children at school. It made me mad!

I was just about to say something when Sparky cut in. 'You know perfectly well that they're not immigrants. Anyway, Whizzer and Chip were born in this country. Besides, the colour of their skin doesn't matter, it's what's inside that counts.'

'Well, well, well,' Ram turned on him, 'if it isn't old goody-two-shoes, the latest convert to the God Squad.' He turned again to me, 'You really have got some queer folk in your mob — religious nuts, girls and blacks!'

I could feel my blood beginning to rise. 'You can say what you like, you skunk,' I said, 'but every one of them is worth ten, or even twenty, of your rag-tag bunch of left-overs.'

'Who says?' Ram took a step towards me.

'I do,' I said, stepping closer to him.

'You gonna prove it?' he went on, coming closer still.

'Yea,' I grunted, taking one more step and trying to stand as tall as I could.

We were nose to nose and toe to toe. He pushed me in the chest so I pushed him back. He barged me with his shoulder so I did the same to him. I knew he was setting up to swing a punch at me and I was watching out for it.

Suddenly Sparky stepped between us, the idiot. He held out his arms and said, 'Hang on a minute!

78

This is a stupid way of settling things! I've got a better way.'

What was he playing at?

'Get out the way before you get hurt,' I shouted at him.

'Yea, push off, so I can flatten him for good,' said Ram. 'You'd do better to go off and pray for him — he'll need it.'

But he didn't. He just stood there. 'I've got an idea,' he said. 'What about a replay of the five-a-side to decide who's best?'

What was going on in Sparky's brainbox? We were bound to lose. There was a long silence. I looked at Ram, and he looked at me. He was obviously weighing up the chances of success. It didn't take him long.

'I like it, I like it,' he said. 'This boy talks sense. You don't stand a chance Nick Baker. When we've taken you apart you can finally crawl into a little hole and keep out of my way.'

There was no way out. I'd get Sparky later, but meanwhile a brave response was needed. 'Oh yea? We'll see about that. Next Saturday, two o'clock in the park, and we'll put to rights the way you cheated us out of the cup.'

I knew we didn't stand much chance, and wished Sparky had kept his mouth shut. It was because he wanted to stop me fighting Ram. I reckoned I stood more chance in a punch-up than in a football play-off. But I couldn't refuse the challenge!

Ram looked aggressively at me and jabbed me with his finger, 'Two o'clock Saturday. Be there.' He turned, gestured to his henchman and swaggered off down the street.

I turned on Sparky. 'You've done it again,' I

complained. 'We stand no chance at football. At least in a fight I might have got one over on him.'

'Calm down Nick,' he replied calmly. 'The way you are at the moment, Ram would have beaten you easily in a fight. And besides, that pal of his was standing by to make sure Ram won. You're not using your head.'

'I would have used my head, given half a chance — on his nose!'

'Listen,' Sparky said, 'it is possible to win without all that.' He paused, then continued, 'We've got a secret weapon.'

I was getting confused. Sparky was talking in riddles. 'What on earth are you talking about?' I grumbled.

'The latest addition to the club — and hopefully to the gang,' he said confidently.

I scowled. This sounded like something fishy going on behind my back.

'Raj,' he added.

'Look,' I butted in quickly, 'nobody's joining the gang without my say-so. That kid's been trying to wheedle his way in and I don't like it.'

'It's up to you,' Sparky said. 'I've not told him anything about being able to be a member of the gang, but I think you better realize something.'

'What's that?'

'Well, before Raj moved here, he played for his district team at football. I've watched him play. He's brilliant!'

I was stunned into silence. I didn't know what to say. What was I to do? Raj seemed all right, so why was I making it a problem for him to join the gang? It wasn't because of his colour — that never entered my head. When it boiled down to it I suppose what really bothered me was that it wasn't my idea and I hadn't been around to find these things out for myself. Maybe Sparky was right. It couldn't do any harm to watch Raj play, anyway.

'OK, then,' I said to him. 'We'll have a knock around and see what he's like. No promises, mind you.'

'Great,' Sparky replied.

We finished our journey home. I couldn't begin to explain all the thoughts rushing through my head. I was beginning to get used to the new Sparky, and he was a good friend. I was also realizing what an idiot I had been over the club hut — getting Sam involved and causing a lot of upset to other people. I hadn't been meaning to do all that. Just look at the mess I'd got us all into. I had only been trying to help.

10

◇

IN THE DOCK

I woke up with that awful sinking feeling in the pit of my stomach. It was the day of my visit to the magistrates' court. We went there in Dad's car, in absolute silence. I felt really awful. During the week the solicitor had seen me and talked about what would happen. And Dad hadn't been exactly comforting. I looked out of the window as the streets and houses flashed by in a blur.

All I could do was concentrate on keeping my breakfast down.

We arrived at the courthouse and parked at the front. Then Dad turned to me and said, 'Just remember, keep your mouth shut unless asked to speak and then say as little as possible.' In silence we got out of the car and made our way between huge, blackened, stone arches, through some mahogany-framed glass doors and into a long corridor. We turned off this corridor and into a smaller passage where there was a long bench. Dad told me to sit down and went on to report to a little man behind a desk. Then he came and sat beside me. It was like waiting for the dentist, but worse. Our solicitor came bustling along in a dark suit and was carrying important-looking files and documents under his arm. He was very tall and had a severe look on his face.

'You know what you have to say, don't you?' he said.

I nodded. Then he and Dad walked off down the corridor talking. Dad came back and told me he was going in now and both he and the solicitor left me. It's difficult to know what to do in this situation so I looked at the man behind the desk and smiled. He scowled back at me then carried on with his work.

Then I tapped my feet on the floor and drummed my fingers on the bench. The man coughed loudly and looked at me crossly, so I stopped. If only it was all over! I stared at the floor and started to count the number of tiles under the bench.

Suddenly a door opened and a man in a black gown appeared, like Count Dracula. 'Are you Baker?' he hissed.

'Yes, sir,' I replied meekly.

'Follow me,' he whispered.

I followed him through the door and into a large room. He motioned me to sit down and I had a chance to look round. I had imagined something straight from a TV movie, complete with scowling judge and earnest jury. Instead the room resembled a small cinema with tip-up seats. Dracula showed me where to sit. I was on my own on a row of seats down the side. On my right was a little three-sided box, the witness-box. Facing the front and ahead of me was another row of seats with a table in front..It was empty except for my solicitor at one end and the police sergeant who took my statement at the other. They were facing a raised platform with a large table on it, behind which were three enormous chairs. In front of the platform there was a man at a desk with a funny little typewriter.

I felt strange. It was as if I wasn't really there but

watching it through a TV screen. But when I looked to my left I was jolted back to reality as I saw people I knew. There at the back sat my father. But what really surprised me was seeing Sparky and Doug. Why on earth were they there?

My stomach churned again and I felt quite sick. All of this was to do with me. What was going to happen? What an idiot I had been! I vowed I would never do anything like this again as long as I live. I even asked God for a bit of help, just quietly. I wonder why you always think of God at times like this?

Then a door in the corner of the room opened and the court usher, Count Dracula, came in. 'All stand,' he ordered. You could hear the squeaks and soft thuds of the tip-up seats as everyone got up. The three magistrates, all ladies, came into the room, and stood behind the desk on the raised platform. I felt the blood draining from my legs and my knees start to knock. The magistrates bowed slightly, then sat down and we all did the same.

The clerk turned to me, motioned me to stand and spoke. 'Is your name Nicholas Bartholomew Baker?' he asked.

'Yes,' I replied meekly.

'And do you live at 102 Church Street?'

'Yes sir,' I replied again, my mouth getting drier all the time.

He then carefully explained to me that I had been charged with 'breaking and entering' and asked me if I understood the charge. Then he asked me whether I pleaded guilty or not guilty. I paused, shuffling my feet from side to side, remembered Dad's instructions, and responded. 'Guilty,' I said quietly.

I was allowed to sit down then. I felt really

relieved. But in my state of nerves I had forgotten it was a tip-up seat and there was the inevitable crash as I landed on the floor. Boy! Did my bottom hurt and my face blush! I wished the floor would swallow me up.

Now it was the turn of the police sergeant. He got up and outlined what I had done. He made me sound worse than Al Capone. After he'd finished I was sure that the least I would get was ten years: Then the solicitor got up, said a few words and to my amazement called Doug to the witness stand. Doug came forward and as he passed me, he smiled and gave me a wink.

'I have known this boy for some considerable time,' he began, 'and although he is very impetuous and lively he has never shown any criminal tendencies. I have found him an enthusiastic member of the local youth club, friendly and never malicious. He is sometimes a little boisterous but I am convinced that, given the chance, he would never allow this to happen again, and I am willing to vouch for him to that effect if required.'

I could have kissed him! We were too embarrassed to look at each other when he passed me on his way back to his seat. Good old Doug. The solicitor finished things off, making me sound like a cross between Mother Theresa and the Pope. I couldn't believe my ears.

We all had to stand then, and the magistrates left the court. I slumped in my seat. They were out for about ten minutes but it felt like ten years. During that time I bit my lips, drummed my fingers on the bench, tapped my feet together — anything to take away the tension.

The magistrates returned and we went through all

the bowing and standing routine again. The bossy lady in the middle of the magistrates spoke. She asked me to stand up, then she looked me straight in the eye.

'Nicholas,' she said, 'you have been a very silly boy. The way you behaved was totally without reason and caused the owner of the garage some harrassment.' I lowered my eyes dutifully expecting the worst. Would it be Pentonville or Parkhurst Gaol? 'I understand that you were angry that the youth club had to close, but that was no justification for your behaviour. We have decided, bearing in mind the excellent character reference from Mr Jones, to dismiss your case with a caution. Should you do anything else and be brought back to court — any court — this will be remembered and will affect any future judgement. You would do well to listen to your friends. It seems they have far more common sense than you have.'

Without further comment she and the other magistrates stood and left.

I couldn't move. Relief washed over me and drained the last of my energy. Dad steered me out and sat me on a bench outside. Doug and Sparky came along and slapped me on the back. I didn't know what to say to them, and could only muster an embarrassed, dry-throated, 'Thanks'.

The journey home passed in much the same blur as the drive to the court, but now it was a blur of terrific relief. As soon as I got home I went straight to my room and lay down. I couldn't get Doug and Sparky out of my mind. When the chips were down, they were there — real loyal friends. It made me think. Perhaps I should try and do things differently. Maybe my way of doing things wasn't always right. I dunno, it was all beyond me. I still couldn't stomach that religious churchy bit, but I decided that things were going to be different now. I was going to try and change — like all the best criminals.

I put my new resolution into action straight away. My Mum got the biggest shock when I asked to do the washing-up. It was the same with making my bed and tidying my room. I secretly thought it was a waste of time because it only gets messed up again, but it pleased Mum. When Dad saw the new Nick in action he just looked suspicious and muttered darkly, 'He'll never keep it up.' I must admit that the same thought had occurred to me. All this 'being good' seemed absolutely impossible to maintain — how did Sparky manage it? He even managed to enjoy it! I was quite impressed with Sparky in fact, because when you tried it, you realized just how difficult it was, not a cop-out at all.

The first time back at the club was difficult. I didn't know what to say to Doug. He seemed to sense my difficulty and spoke first. 'Hi, Nick, good to see you,' he said. 'I hope you've got over things. What about a game of pool?' I nodded dumbly, thankful that I didn't have to make a big deal out of it all. The rest of the gang played it down too.

Over the pool table Doug said, 'You know, I think Mr Booth is up to no good, too. But we will have to find an honest and legal way of finding out about it.'

'Mm,' I agreed. I didn't really feel like being involved with Mr Booth again — not ever!

Later that week Doug called us together to tell us that the church had decided to close the club down. I wasn't surprised. The incident with the piano must have been the last straw. Trust me! But Doug told us that it had been a close vote in the church meeting. Many people — Aunty Edna included — thought closing us down was all wrong. When Doug broke the news I think everyone expected me to explode. But I didn't. That's not to say I wasn't angry inside, but I was learning that it's not always the answer. I was beginning to realize that there were Christians and 'Christians', and that not everyone was against us. Perhaps after a while they would have another vote and Aunty Edna and Doug's lot would win.

Doug had persuaded them to allow us to meet as a group for coffee every week, but I didn't really think much of that. I kept quiet, though. Then I got together with the gang and we decided to take over the hut at the bottom of Whizzer's garden as a proper gang base.

I was beginning to wonder how long I could keep up all this being good before I exploded!

◆

11

THE ACCIDENT

Time continued to fly by in this long, hot summer of disasters. It wasn't long before I could feel the enthusiasm of 'trying to be good' fading. Doing the washing-up had to go — it sometimes looked worse after I'd done it! I was telling Sparky about my failings as we walked along the road after a visit to the park for a practice game of football.

'I hear Ram's telling everyone that they're going to beat us easily at football,' Sparky said. 'He's going to get quite a surprise.'

I didn't have Sparky's confidence in spite of having Raj in the team. Ram's lot were very mean and were capable of using all sorts of ways, fair or foul, to beat us. 'Don't get too confident,' I replied. 'You know what Ram's like.'

To tell the truth, I was very worried about the game. I knew my patience wouldn't last and that I would do something stupid when Ram started playing dirty.

'Have we got a referee?' asked Sparky.

'I suggested Doug,' I said. 'And Ram couldn't find anybody else, so he's doing it.' That at least was something in our favour. He would be fair and honest, and you couldn't ask for more than that.

As we walked along, I saw Aunty Edna across the street, going in the opposite direction to us, on her way to the shops. As usual we both gave her a wave, and she waved back, then we carried on with our chat. We were walking down the street discussing the match when a car turned the corner ahead of us and hurtled down the street at a ridiculous speed. It rushed past us and, before we could turn to follow it, we heard a sickening screech of brakes and a dull thud.

We looked back to see the car slewed across the road and a hunched figure lying there. The car door opened and a large man leaped out and ran off in the direction of Church Street. We ran towards the car and saw that the body lying in the road was Aunty Edna. As we reached her she tried to move, but she groaned and passed out. Sparky knelt by her side and started to help her while I rushed after the man running away.

I saw him disappear round the corner into Church Street but when I reached the same spot and looked up and down the road there was no one to be seen. All I could see was the small side gate to Mr Booth's garage swinging open on its hinges, which was very unusual. It was usually locked and bolted, worse than Fort Knox. I ran back to the scene of the accident convinced that the man who ran off must have been the Hulk, Booth's right-hand man. The size of the man, together with the open gate, was enough evidence for me.

I looked down at Aunty Edna. She was not moving and looked terribly white. I couldn't see any blood but she was lying awkwardly, with one of her legs and an arm in a strange position. Sparky was being very good; he had been to some first aid classes. He had told a woman from a nearby house to go and phone for the police and an ambulance, and was now trying to make Aunty Edna as

90

comfortable as possible. Someone had brought a blanket and a pillow, which was carefully placed under her head. Sparky wouldn't allow anyone to move her and covered her with the blanket. Then we waited in an eerie, hushed silence.

Grown-ups are really strange! They all came rushing out of their houses when the accident happened, but most of them were quite useless. They just stood and stared like it was some sort of circus stunt, occasionally whispering to each other. Two of them came over and tried to do useless things, like sweeping the road around Edna. Sparky had to get very sharp with two other women who suggested we ought to try and lift her into a house. Another woman brought a cup of sweet tea — which was a bit daft because Edna was unconscious. Even I knew that you weren't supposed to do that! So we all just stood there, waiting.

One or two old ladies were saying, 'Oh dear, oh dear, oh dear,' and holding handkerchiefs to their mouths. Then, quite suddenly, Aunty Edna opened her eyes.

'It's all right, Aunty Edna. The ambulance will soon be here,' said Sparky soothingly.

She smiled weakly and gripped his hand. Boy, he was fantastic. I just stood around like a spare part. Then she winced with pain and passed out again. Sparky looked up at me. I obviously didn't look too good. 'Why don't you sit down Nick?' he said quietly.

I thought that was quite a good idea. I didn't want to seem soft, but that sort of thing always made me feel queasy. So I sat down before I fell down!

After ages, or so it seemed, we could hear the sound of the police and ambulance sirens coming closer. As they appeared round the corner of the street, the sound increased dramatically. They drew to a stop and everything flowed into a smooth efficient operation. Two burly policemen got out of the car and began to clear people away, setting up signs and plastic bollards. Meanwhile, one ambulanceman rushed to Aunty Edna's side and took over from Sparky, whilst the other opened the back of the vehicle.

After a quick look at Edna, the man with Sparky called for some straps and bandages from the ambulance. He then carefully straightened out her leg and strapped her legs together. He also fastened her arm across her chest with a broad bandage. Then both men got the stretcher out and carefully placed her on it. Quickly, they slid the stretcher into the vehicle, said something to the policeman, and were off in a flash of white and luminous yellow, blue lights flashing and siren blaring.

Meanwhile, another police car had arrived. This time it was a little patrol vehicle instead of the enormous red and white traffic Land Rover that came first. Out from the vehicle, placing his helmet steadily and carefully on his head as he walked, came Dad. Was I pleased to see him!

He looked at me and asked if I was all right. Sparky answered for me. 'A bit shaken I think,' he said.

Dad turned to Sparky and asked what had happened. 'This car knocked Aunty Edna down and the driver ran off,' Sparky replied.

'Did anyone else see it?' Dad asked.

'No, I don't think so.'

'OK. Go and sit in the car,' Dad said quietly to the two of us.

We did as we were told and Dad went to have a word with the two other policemen. Then he returned to us and got in the car.

'I'm taking you down to the station,' he said. 'You need to make a statement, and you look as if you could do with a strong cup of tea.' We didn't argue.

At the police station we sat in an interview room and Dad brought in some huge mugs of tea, then left us for a bit. When he returned, he half smiled, which was a real effort for Dad. 'For once,' he said, 'you appear to have done something right. The police at the scene said that you were marvellous, and did exactly the right thing.' He looked at us. 'Are you feeling OK now?' he asked.

We both nodded, beginning to relax.

'Right then,' he said. 'Tell me what happened.'

I was feeling a lot better and wanted to make sure that Dad clearly understood exactly who had done it. The thought of Aunty Edna lying in hospital made me very angry. She was a smashing old lady who would never hurt anybody.

'I know who did it,' I said bluntly.

'Oh?' asked Dad, startled.

'It was the Hulk, Mr Booth's assistant,' I continued. There was absolutely no doubt in my mind. I could see Dad's brow furrowing, and a hard look came in his eyes.

'How can you be so sure?' he said. 'Let's start at the beginning. Tell me all that happened.'

I began to recount everything; the screech of brakes; the man running away; the open gate.

Dad listened. Then, after a moment's pause, he turned to Sparky. 'What did you see?' he asked.

Sparky hadn't seen anything, because he had been concentrating on helping Aunty Edna.

'Don't you believe me?' I demanded, amazed that Dad hadn't rushed out to get a posse round to Booth's garage.

'Look,' he replied. 'You had a back view for a few seconds, and you saw an open gate. That's not enough evidence.' Sometimes my father is so *slow*. If he'd been on the Titanic he would still be checking for leaks as the ship went down, saying, 'We must be sure before we do anything, we must be s. . . glug, glug, glug!' Are all parents like this, I ask myself? Or just those who happen to be policemen as well?

'So you're going to do nothing about it?' I asked sharply.

'No,' he replied. 'The car was stolen but we don't know who by. Aunty Edna was badly hurt in the hit-and-run accident. It's all very serious and the CID will deal with it. But I'm not going to let you shoot your mouth off, just because you believe Mr Booth is the city's answer to "The Godfather". When you are interviewed in a minute or so, make sure that you stick to the evidence, not opinions! Remember the bother you are already in, and what that magistrate said.'

He left us, and I turned to Sparky. 'What do I do?' I asked despairingly.

'I think you should stick to the facts,' said Sparky. 'If you make a big thing of this you'll only get yourself into bother, and nobody will believe you.'

My mind ticked over with everything I had seen and the things that had been said. I kicked the table in frustration. But when the detective constable came in I stuck strictly to the evidence and not opinions. I hated myself for it. Honesty's a funny thing, I thought.

But I knew that I wasn't going to let the thing rest there. Not me!

12

∧

RETURN MATCH

Sparky and I sat on the kerb outside our houses flickering stones, waiting for Sam. I was still very bothered about Aunty Edna's accident and the way Dad had reacted.

'I know I go over the top sometimes, but I'm absolutely certain that the bloke who ran off was the Hulk,' I said.

'There's nothing you can do about it at the moment,' said Sparky.

'But do you *believe* me?' I demanded.

'I don't believe you'd tell a lie about it,' he replied. 'But you do sometimes get a bit carried away and let your imagination run riot.'

We fell silent while I thought about that. I was convinced that I hadn't imagined it, and the more I thought about it, I was convinced that Booth and the Hulk were involved somehow.

I flicked a few more stones out into the road. 'I'm sure it was him,' I continued. 'And I don't see why he should get away with it.'

'Well, if you're so convinced, you'll just have to be more patient and wait for some more evidence,' Sparky said.

'You mean another old lady knocked down?'

Sparky shrugged his shoulders. But I was like a dog with a bone and wouldn't let go. 'Why does God allow such things to happen anyway?' I demanded.

'Aunty Edna's a regular down at church, one of the best. Yet she's the one that gets knocked down by a crook. I doesn't seem fair or right to me, particularly when no one gets done for it. Where's God in all of this?'

Sparky was stumped at this flow of questions. I think I must have said out loud the same questions he was asking inside. He sat with his head in his hands and his brow furrowed. Then he said, 'I don't know, I just don't know. But I'm sure there must be an answer. After the match we'll go and ask Doug. He'll know the answers. We'll tell him about Booth and the Hulk as well, and see what he says.' This seemed a reasonable idea to me and anyway Sam appeared then and we had to get on with the arrangements for the match against Ram's lot.

We sat in the hut and began to chat about the game. The gang now included Raj. He was a very quiet lad, but very loyal and friendly, so I had let him join. Besides, he was a fantastic footballer!

Once again I was dreading the thought of Sam blowing a fuse. With Raj in the team we didn't really need her. How to break the news, that was the problem. I remembered the last time.

'Right,' I said. 'The team!'

'Chip, you play in goal,' I continued. As usual he wasn't keen — I could tell by the expression on his face — but he didn't argue. He knew it was useless.

'The four others,' I went on quickly, 'will be me, Sparky, Whizzer and Raj.'

There was an ominous silence.

'The reserve,' I concluded, 'will be Lump.' At this, mouths dropped open and everyone glanced at Sam. Tears of anger formed in her eyes, but she didn't say anything.

96

'I don't really want to play,' groaned Lump. 'I'm useless and I hate football. Besides, Sam is much better.'

I wish he had kept his mouth shut. I knew it wasn't a popular decision but I didn't want Ram to have the chance to give me a verbal going-over, and get Sam as well, all over again. 'No,' I said firmly, 'you're the reserve, Lump, and that's the end of it.'

'Why?' demanded Chip.

'Because this game is going to be rough and nasty and I don't think it would be fair on Sam,' I replied, getting annoyed. 'That's not the real reason,' butted in Sam sharply. 'You're just afraid of what Ram will say.'

She was right!

'Go on, let her play,' put in Whizzer.

I tried another tack. 'I'm only trying to protect her,' I said to him. It sounded really lame!

'I don't need protection,' she responded aggressively. 'I've proved it once and I can do it again.'

I could see I wasn't going to win, again, and gave in as graciously as I could. 'All right, then,' I said. 'Sam is reserve instead of Lump.'

Both Lump and Sam whooped in delight, for different reasons.

It was another warm and sunny day at the park. We were there early and kicked a ball around for practice. There were no special posts this time, no kits borrowed from school. I took along four sticks I had found in the shed and we banged those into the ground for posts. Fortunately all the markings from the tournament were still there, just visible.

Ram's lot came swaggering across the park to join

us, and at the same time Doug appeared on his motorbike. After parking and removing his helmet he began to get the game organized. We were all wearing an odd collection of tee-shirts and shorts. Doug looked around and asked, 'How am I going to sort out the teams? Nobody's wearing the same colour as anybody else.'

Ram leered across at Sam and then said to Doug, 'When we play at school one team takes off its shirts.'

Sam blushed. This was just the sort of thing I expected from Ram.

'Seeing as Nick has to play with girls in his team, we'll take off our shirts. Don't want to embarrass anyone, do we?' Ram said.

I could have strangled him, and knew that this was just the start. It could only get worse. I just hoped that Doug was up to it and wouldn't let Ram get away with things. We needed all the help we could get and Ram was extremely clever at cheating without being caught.

The match began and straight from the kick-off Ram and the rest of his mob set about barging, pushing and kicking — not the ball, but us!

After about five minutes what I had been dreading happened. Ram hit a fierce shot at our goal and Chip parried it. Ram then rushed in to get another kick at the ball, knocked Chip over, trod heavily on his fingers and hit the ball between the posts. He claimed a goal of course, but in spite of Ram's angry protests, Doug wouldn't allow it. Poor old Chip lay writhing on the ground, clutching his hand. It was obvious he couldn't go on. It was bad luck for Chip. Every time he played against this lot he got hurt. So, once again Sam had to come on. She was delighted. To my amazement she went straight up to Ram and said, 'Just you watch yourself, I'll get you for what you did to Chip.' Ram was too flabbergasted to reply.

We put Whizzer in goal and Sam took over Whizzer's place and the game went on. It was a pretty even match, with no one particularly on top. Towards half-time Ram must have said something to his team because they began to get very rough. I knew they were trying to get me going, and they nearly succeeded! Just before half-time they gained a goal using exactly the same trick as last time. Ram was coming past me, then dived as if I had pushed him. Doug blew the whistle and awarded a free kick and they scored. I was sick! There was no point in getting angry with Doug, he was doing his best and Ram was a master at this manoeuvre. But I was ready to stick one on Ram!

For some reason the half-time whistle went early, or so I thought. Sparky and Doug seemed to be chatting, then Doug gave Sparky a knowing nod as he blew the whistle. Sparky dragged me to the side.

'They're stringing you up again,' he said.

'I know, but I can't stop myself.'

'Don't be daft,' said Sparky. 'It's just what Ram wants. Think about it. What do you want most — to win the game, or to smack Ram in the mouth and watch us lose from the sidelines?'

There were merits both ways as far as I was concerned, but after some thought I said to Sparky, 'We have to win, I suppose.'

'Then control yourself,' he urged. Then he walked off.

The second half was worse than the first. Ram began to make nasty comments to the coloured lads in the team when he was near them but when Doug couldn't hear. They tried pushing Sam around but, judging by their bruised shins, she gave as good as she got. They were still trying to get me going as well, but with the help of occasional looks and digs in the ribs from Sparky, I managed to stay in control.

Raj was fantastic. He didn't say much, but boy, did he speak with his feet! And it was from one of his dazzling dribbling runs that our equalizer came and not a moment too soon. With two minutes to go he worked his way down the left and crossed the ball. In spite of some pushing and shoving, I forced my head round a defender and nodded the ball in. What a goal!

It was great to feel the satisfaction of having scored against that foul mob and seeing their heads drop. There was hardly time to start up again and so we finished with a one-all draw. Everything was to be decided on penalties. We each came up to try and in turn scored till four had gone from each team.

Now there was just Ram to shoot for them and Sam for us. Ram came up and placed the ball carefully. Doug blew the whistle and he shot. Like a dream Whizzer leapt athletically to his left and tipped the ball around the post. We all leapt on him with delight while Ram stood with head bowed and hands on hips.

It was all up to Sam now. After quietening us down and shutting Ram's lot up who were making remarks and trying to put her off, Doug went to the side of the goal. Sam came up and placed the ball carefully on the spot. She turned and looked at us. We clenched our fists in encouragement. The whistle went and after a short run she thumped the ball! It skidded past the sprawling goal-keeper, just inside the post. We were in ecstasy, rushing up and slapping Sam on the back. We had won! Totally forgetting myself, I gave her a hug and a kiss. Boy did I blush when I realized what I had done!

The game was over and we were triumphant. First, Doug cleared off Ram's lot who were making dark threats. Then we set off for home. As we left the park we were nearly run down by a car which was taking the corner much too fast. I could swear that it was the Hulk driving it. I looked at Doug and Sparky who looked back, thoughtfully. It had gone before we even thought of taking its number. None of us said anything, but I knew what we were all thinking.

That night I lay in bed thinking about the events of the day. I thought again about what a great pal Sparky was, and his brilliant idea for beating Ram. I wouldn't tell him to his face, but I was really impressed, and a bit envious of how he coped with the situation. What made me squirm was remembering the kiss I gave Sam. What had come over me? I blushed even now at the thought of it. As girls go she was pretty fantastic but, good grief, what would the others think? I just hoped she wouldn't get the wrong idea!

13

WHO DID IT?

It was Doug who suggested we should visit Aunty Edna in hospital. I wasn't very keen but Sparky talked me into it, reminding me of how she had stood up for me in the past. Personally, I would have preferred a game of football in the park. I found this 'doing good' thing a bit of a pain. Mind you, I knew it would give me a chance to ask her about the accident.

So there we were, waiting at the bus stop. Mum had made me bring a bunch of flowers which was horrible. I was having a real job hiding them under my jacket and all the front of my tee-shirt was wet. I wouldn't have been surprised if I had caught greenfly or something. I knew I would never live it down if anybody had seen me with them.

When we got on the bus I put them under the seat. Some idiot in the row behind kicked them, so by the time we met Doug outside the hospital they were looking a bit bedraggled. He took one look at them and one look at me, closed his eyes and sighed heavily. They weren't that bad! Grown-ups do tend to over-react. It was easier for Sparky — he had brought fruit.

Doug showed us the way. We pushed through the glass doors and went down a long corridor smelling of antiseptic and daffodils. Aunty Edna was in a little side-ward with three other ladies. She was lying in bed with one leg covered in plaster, strung up on a frame with weights. She also had one arm in plaster. It looked very uncomfortable but, as usual, she was smiling. When she saw us coming, she waved.

'Well, well, well,' she said, as we arrived. 'A visit by three handsome young men. This is my lucky day.'

Yuk, I thought. Why do old people say things like that?

'Hello, Aunty Edna,' Doug said. 'I thought you might like to see these two.'

'Oh yes!' she replied. Then, to our great embarrassment, she began relating to the other three ladies in the ward how we were the two boys she had been telling them about and how grateful she was and how wonderful we were. It was awful, but nice, both at the same time!

I dumped the flowers on her bed and sat down.

'Flowers and fruit, oh how lovely,' she said.

How quick can we get out of here, I thought. But there were one or two things I wanted to ask her before I went. I was determined to prove that the Hulk had done it.

'How are you?' Sparky asked her after a little pause.

'Oh, I'm all right, bless your heart, love,' she replied.

It went quiet again. It's always like this in hospitals — nobody quite knows what to say to each other, so you finish up asking useless things, eating all the grapes and staring at the person in the bed opposite.

'When do you think they'll let you out?' I asked.

'They said it'll be a while yet,' she said and for

once her smile slipped a little.

'Did you see the man in the car, Aunty Edna?' I asked bluntly.

Doug started and said, 'You shouldn't ask things like that, Nick. Not so soon after what Aunty Edna's gone through.'

'Sorry,' I said. But I did really want to know.

'Oh, I don't mind answering,' replied Edna. 'I didn't really see much, my dear. I do remember a very big man standing over me, dressed in black he was, then I passed out.'

That proved it as far as I was concerned. The Hulk always wore a big black jacket and black trousers, whatever the weather. It couldn't be anybody else. I shot a knowing look at Doug and Sparky, trying to make them understand from my face that I now had all the proof I needed.

'I'm sure the police will catch whoever did it before long,' put in Doug. He was trying to stop me asking any more questions. 'The car was stolen, you know.'

'Was it really?' she replied. 'Well, I never. I'm not angry at whoever did it, but the man has to be stopped from doing it to somebody else, so I hope he's caught quickly.'

Doug nodded.

Aunty Edna sat back. 'You know,' she said, 'I do feel very grateful for being here. I could very well have been finished off by that car. But I don't like seeing so many sad people lying in these beds. They don't see that they have anything to be happy about.'

'You're forgetting something, Aunty Edna,' Doug butted in.

'What's that, my dear?'

'Well, they don't think they have anything to hope for, that's why they're so sad.'

'Yes, you're right there,' Aunty Edna went on. 'Perhaps that's why God put me here. I can tell them all about how much he cares about them and wants to help them.'

This was beginning to develop into one of those uncomfortable conversations which I found very embarrassing, so I changed the subject. 'Anyway,' I said, 'Aunty Edna's just proved that it was the Hulk who did it.'

'How so?' asked Sparky.

'It's obvious,' I went on. 'She said that this guy that stood over her was big and dressed in black. There's only one man around here that fits a description like that! The Hulk in his black leather.'

'Come on, Nick,' Doug put in. 'Edna was half-conscious after being knocked down. No way is that anything like evidence.'

Aunty Edna was looking puzzled. I was just about to explain to her when Doug said quickly, 'Well, we must be going now. Come on, lads!' and hustled us out of the room. I think she was surprised to see us leave so quickly. I was annoyed. Maybe Doug was right and it wasn't enough evidence, but I was *sure* the Hulk was guilty.

We waited for the bus in silence. I kicked an old can in the gutter. But on the bus Doug turned to me all of a sudden and said, 'I think you might be on to something!'

This took me completely by surprise. I had just about given up hope. 'How do you mean?' I asked.

'Well,' he continued, 'bearing in mind all that you have said, added to the time that car nearly ran us over after the football game, as well as everything that's gone on in the past, I'm beginning to think it's very suspicious.'

'What are we going to do about it?' asked Sparky.

'Well, I think the only thing we can do is to go to Nick's Dad and tell him all that we know,' he replied.

I thought he must have finally flipped. Dad would never believe us! 'You can give it a try,' I said, 'but I would like to be some distance away when you do.'

'You've got your dad all wrong you know,' went on Doug. 'He's just concerned about you. He's a very good man and a good father. I'll speak to him. I'm sure he'll help.'

We shall see, I thought, but I didn't want to stand in the way of a just cause.

Doug was as good as his word. The next evening there was a knock on our door and there he was, asking to have a word with Dad.

'What's he done now?' asked Dad suspiciously.

'Charming,' I muttered under my breath.

'Nothing wrong,' reassured Doug. I could see Dad breathe a sigh of relief and he invited Doug in.

'You know,' continued Dad, 'Nick really owes you a lot after all that you said in the court, and I shall always be grateful.'

'There's no need to be,' said Doug. 'I only spoke the truth.'

'Ah, quite so,' replied Dad, flustered. 'What can I do for you then?'

'Well, it's about Aunty Edna's accident,' Doug continued.

'Oh?'

'I think Nick may be on to something.'

'Oh no!' said Dad. 'You're not joining in on this vendetta against Booth's garage, are you?'

'Well, I admit that Nick has gone over the top in the past,' Doug said, 'but I think it's more than that this time. Nick is convinced that it was Mr Booth's assistant that he saw running off. I've also seen him driving different cars around the neighbourhood, always far too fast.'

'It is a garage they run,' said Dad. 'What do you expect? They have to test cars after they've repaired them.'

At this point, I interrupted the conversation. I couldn't keep quiet. 'But they don't do car repairs. They can't! There was no equipment for car repairs when I was caught in there,' I said.

'Nick, I don't want to hear about that. It's caused enough trouble already,' said Dad.

There was a pause. 'However,' he continued, 'I hadn't realized that cars weren't repaired there. Look, I will speak to the Detective Sergeant on the case at the station tomorrow and see what he says. But you'd better be right about this.'

I looked at Doug and he looked at me. It was a step forward.

So it was that the next day I found myself at the garage, together with Doug, my Dad, and the Detective Sergeant, who made an appointment to see Mr Booth and the Hulk. (The Hulk did, in fact, have a proper name, but as far as I'm concerned, he was still the Hulk.) We all crammed into Booth's office. I had some bad memories of the last time I had been there, when Booth had been so nasty. He didn't look too pleased now.

'Well, what can I do for you?' asked Mr Booth sharply.

The Detective Sergeant spoke. 'We have been continuing our investigation,' he said, 'into the accident which occurred last week in the next street.'

'What's that got to do with me?' responded Booth testily.

'I want to ask your assistant something,' went on the Sergeant. 'Can you, or he, tell me where you both were on the day in question?'

'Yes,' Booth said shortly. 'But let me say first that I am absolutely fed up with people poking their noses into my business. That little monster over there and now his father and the church seem to be intent on putting me out of business. I'm going to make sure that the matter does not rest here. On the day in question,' he went on, 'we were delivering a car.'

'Can you prove that?' my father asked.

'May I suggest,' went on Booth, arrogantly now, 'that you ask your Chief Inspector how the second-hand car we provided for his son is doing. It was delivered on that day by us, and please thank him for the delicious tea he provided.'

There was a nasty silence. How could it be? It was impossible. My father looked at me and Doug. If looks could kill we would both be extremely dead.

'I see,' replied the Sergeant. 'I will, of course, be checking this up and will get back to you.'

'Do that,' said Mr Booth angrily. 'Now, I suggest you go!'

Without another word, we left! Doug and I looked very foolish and didn't say anything while the Sergeant spoke to Dad over by his police car. I could see that Dad was getting a right ticking-off — the back of his neck went all red!

The car drove off, and Dad turned. 'Thanks,' he said, sarcastically. 'That's just what I needed. It's the last time I listen to the local do-gooder and the terror of the neighbourhood.'

Doug decided on strategic withdrawal, made his apologies and left hastily. I was taken home — back to the bedroom! As I sat on my bed and stared at the wallpaper I thought to myself, 'If I spend any more time in this rotten bedroom, I shall go bananas!!'

Why do my ideas always go wrong?

14

ON THE TRAIL

With a lot of effort we had made the shed at the
bottom of Whizzer's garden quite neat and tidy. His
mum was happy because it had been a real mess
before. We had scrounged some furniture and a bit
of old carpet, and it all looked very cosy. I only
hoped that there wouldn't be any visitors to our
house which might mean Mum would go to get out
the spare glasses from the front room cupboard.
Orange juice didn't taste the same out of paper cups
and the glasses really helped add a touch of class to
our new den.

We were all sitting round enjoying the orange
juice as I told them about the way Doug had
persuaded my dad to get Mr Booth questioned and
how it had all gone disastrously wrong.

'Doug must have been out of his tiny mind,' Lump
chortled. Chip and Whizzer nodded in agreement
and wonder. I think they all expected me to join in
and say how stupid I thought he was. Well, they
were wrong!

Through all the misery of the previous weeks I
had learned a lot about loyalty and had found out
who my real friends were. There was a lot about
Doug that still had me puzzled, but there was also a
lot about him that I had come to admire and wished
I could be like that too.

'Just you shut your mouths,' I said to them

110

sharply. 'When the chips were down, he was the one that came and helped. I noticed you lot all managed to find something else to do! He's a good guy and you just better watch what you say or I'll thump you.'

Everything had gone very quiet. I thought it was because they were staggered at my defence of Doug. They sat there, their mouths open and eyes wide. Suddenly I realized they were looking straight past me. I turned, and there, standing in the open doorway, was Doug. I blushed like mad and felt sick with embarrassment. No one moved.

In the end, Sparky saved the day. He jumped to his feet and quickly changed the subject. 'I still think Mr Booth is up to something,' he said.

'Yes,' I added, finding my voice. 'Yes, it's still not changed my mind about him.'

'What do you think, Doug?' Sparky asked.

Doug stepped into the hut and looked around. 'I think you have made a fantastic job of this hut,' he replied. He sat down and said, 'And I also think that Mr Booth is not the innocent law-abiding citizen he claims to be.'

'What shall we do about it then?' asked Sam.

I kept the conversation going to get away from that very embarrassing moment when Doug had come in so unexpectedly. 'There must be something, but I'm not sure what,' I said. 'If I cause my Dad any more aggravation he'll lock me in my bedroom and throw away the key.'

'I've got an idea,' Sparky suddenly said. 'What about following them? I saw it work in one of those detective movies on TV once. It's called surveillance or something like that. Then, when we catch one of them breaking the law, we call the police.'

111

'That won't work,' grunted Chip. 'We can't follow more than one person unless we all split up, and if we do that, how could we let each other know if we find anyone?'

'I got a CB radio,' Whizzer butted in. He didn't ever say much, but reckoned to save it for something important. 'In fact I got lots of CB, my brothers and me,' he added.

'Great,' I said. 'What we'll do is this. We'll split into twos and wait at different spots covering most of the area around the church. When anyone sees anything suspicious, call the others up through me.'

Everyone was suddenly very excited, Doug included.

'I'll follow what's going on with the CB and come along in my car,' he added. 'I don't want anybody getting too involved in something they can't handle.'

'Just a minute,' cut in Sparky. 'Did you say *car*?'

Doug nodded, and held up a bunch of keys to prove it. We were amazed.

'Can we see it?' I asked, heading for the door.

. We piled out on to the road, only to behold the biggest, ugliest, rustiest heap of old metal I have ever seen with wheels on. I could see that Doug was very proud of it, treating it like a new toy, but honestly it was terrible. It's funny how some grown men have this awful blind spot when it comes to cars. They just don't seem to see the rust or hear the awful engine. I have even heard my father talking to his car! I could hardly keep a straight face.

'Hey man, who paid you to take this heap of junk away?' Whizzer asked.

'Don't be cheeky,' Doug replied, obviously hurt.

We paced round it, prodding gently at the rotten

bodywork. Nobody had the heart to laugh, but there were a few cutting comments like Whizzer's flying about. Doug offered us a ride so we got in, hoping it wouldn't fall apart as Doug roared off on a short trip round the block. He screeched to a stop outside the hut and we fell out, a bit dizzy and travel-sick.

'Fair enough,' I concluded, nodding my head in amazement, then arranged for everybody to meet back at the hut at six o'clock.

That evening, after tea, we gathered at the hut and Whizzer handed out the CB sets. 'Don't break 'em,' he grunted, 'or my brothers will flatten me.'

'Right,' Doug said. 'Split off to where you're supposed to go.'

We broke up into pairs — Sam with Lump, Sparky with Raj, and Chip with me. We set off in our different directions, trying to look as casual and unconcerned as possible, and Doug settled down in his car.

Chip and I made our way down past the church and garage, and walked on down to the bottom end of the street. We ended up sitting in the entrance to an alley giving us a view along three different roads. Chip had brought a couple of his pocket computer games and we passed the time doing these. Every so often I called up the others on the CB.

'Bandit One to Bandit Two. Are you receiving me? Over,' I called.

'Bandit Two receiving loud and clear,' came the reply from Sparky. 'No contact yet, over.'

'Nor here, over and out,' I replied. This was repeated for Bandits Three and Four — Sam and Lump and Doug, that is.

Time really dragged and, apart from giving a

113

couple of girls from school a fright as they walked past, nothing much happened. I sat and thought about the last few weeks and how my attitude to Doug and Sparky had changed. It was good to be friends with them again. Sparky was such a great guy and lots of fun, and Doug talked a lot of sense, and I wished I could be like him. They both seemed to be having a much better time than me, and because they didn't get worked up so much, got a lot more done. The more I thought about it, the more muddled I became. It seemed the more I tried, the less I succeeded.

Then Chip nudged me and brought me back to the job in hand. 'This is boring,' he moaned. 'And I've got to go home soon.'

I must admit that I was ready to give up as well. Yet another good idea to bite the dust!

Suddenly the CB crackled into life. 'Bandit Three to Bandit One, Bandit Three to Bandit One. Are you receiving me? Over,' Sam was calling.

'Bandit One to Bandit Three, loud and clear, over,' I replied.

'We have contact, over,' she said with obvious excitement.

I nearly dropped the CB before I answered, forgetting the correct way of replying. 'Well, get out of sight and wait for me,' I said. 'Come on, Chip,' I called. 'Action.'

We raced off down the street until we reached the corner where Sam had been patrolling. I couldn't see her or Lump, but I saw the large bulk of the Hulk, sidling along trying car door handles. Fortunately he was walking away from us and we dived behind two cars. Sparky and Whizzer arrived a few seconds later and did the same. I saw Sam and Lump further

114

on behind another car and motioned them to stay down and be quiet. As the Hulk walked on we occasionally ran on to another hiding place just like they do on TV when they are stalking criminals.

Suddenly the Hulk stopped, moved quickly to a very new estate car and dug in his pocket for something. I fell into a garden behind a bush and called Doug on the CB. He had a problem starting the car, which didn't surprise me. 'I'm on my way,' he replied to my urgent request.

I looked back at the Hulk who had now got into the car and was trying to get it started. The engine turned over and he set off down the street with a screech of tyres, just as Doug turned the corner behind us in his car, and screeched to a stop.

'Missed him!' I groaned.

'Never mind,' Doug replied. 'Pile in and we'll try and follow him.'

I opened the door and the gang fell into the back. I got in at the front with Doug. He thumped his foot down on the accelerator and we hurtled away.

'Do you think we'll find him?' Sam called from the back over the noise of the engine.

'We'll have a jolly good try,' shouted Doug.

I was a bit dubious about Doug's driving and also whether the thing would hold together under the strain, but he seemed confident. I was also glad not to be in the back, they were getting thrown about like dice in a pot. There was a wild look in Doug's eyes as he gripped the wheel tightly. I wasn't sure what would happen if and when we caught up with the Hulk.

I'd got another of my sinking feelings!

15

CHASE

Doug's old car rattled off down the road in pursuit of the Hulk, with us inside shaking around like peas in a pod. It wasn't too bad for me in the front passenger seat, but the others were suffering as Doug tried to keep up with the chase. The traffic in the city was very busy, but after a few minutes I saw the car about five vehicles ahead.

'They're up ahead, the blue estate car, that's him,' I yelled, shaking Doug's arm.

'OK, OK, but leave go or you'll have us on the pavement,' he yelled in reply.

'Don't let him get away,' Sam called from the back.

'I'm doing my best,' responded Doug.

We lurched in and out of the lines of cars and lorries, trying to keep within sight of the blue car. Poor Doug struggled to concentrate with the accompanying yells of 'There he is!'

'Don't lose him!'

'Left, turn left!'

'Round that lorry, you can do it.'

Doug's knuckles were white as he gripped the steering wheel and pumped on the accelerator and brake in turn. It was very hard to stay calm and at times I couldn't control my excitement, leaning out of the windows and yelling words of encouragement and abuse to people to get out of the way. The car seemed to be shaking itself apart as bits kept flying off, particularly as we took sharp bends. I hoped there was enough left on to keep up the chase to the end.

We managed to get into a reasonable position about two cars back, which was ideal for 'trailing', until we came to the Ring Road lights. The blue estate whipped through just as the lights were beginning to change. Doug tried very hard to get through but the car in front of us was turning right and blocked our way. We screeched to a halt and everyone was thrown forward.

'Ouch!'

'Ooo!'

'Gerroff!'

'My foot!'

'Ow!' came from close behind me. I looked at the heap of bodies trying to sort itself out, then turned to Doug. He was revving the engine and waiting for the lights to change. 'Go on,' I yelled, 'there's no one coming through the lights the other way.'

'I can't,' he replied. 'It's against the law!'

'If you don't, we'll lose him!' I shouted.

Fortunately the lights changed quickly. 'Go on,' I said again.

Suddenly he rammed his right foot down to the floor, pressing the accelerator to the maximum. We leapt forward, the engine screaming, and were past and away.

After changing quickly up through the gears Doug breathed a sigh of relief and looked at me. 'Don't get the idea I'm going to make a habit of this,' he said. What a guy! Straight up, he's really good. I had really got it wrong about him in the past. I wished I hadn't done and said the things about him that I had, but he didn't seem to mind. He'd forgiven and forgotten! Amazing! I wish I could be like that!

We raced on after the stolen car, and before long, with a shout from Sam in the back, we had caught up with it. Doug tried not to get too close so as not to give the game away. Now we were heading out of the city, the traffic was thinner and we had to drop further back. Soon we left the city altogether and were into the countryside. But there had still been no break, no chance to stop and ring the police. We followed the car off the main road and down narrow country lanes with steep banks blocking the view to either side.

It was really difficult for Doug. We had to be far enough back not to be noticed but not so far as to lose him. More than once we had to reverse at speed when we had missed a turning. I was totally lost now. We seemed to have gone miles and miles down narrow lanes at great speed. There was no time to check signposts and I never was any good at reading when my eyes are travelling upwards of seventy miles an hour.

Suddenly, we realized we had lost him. 'Where's he gone now?' yelled Doug. 'Look out for a turning.' We slowed right down and worked our way along between two high hedges looking for a turning.

'There!' pointed out Raj from the back, nearly knocking my nose off in his enthusiasm.

Through a gap in the hedge we could see the car driving down a track to a farm. Doug drove past the turn-in and drew to a halt further along.

'What do we do now?' grumbled Lump from the back in his usual unwilling way. 'Whatever it is, bags I don't have to leave this van.' What a coward!

The others groaned and chorused, 'Oh, shut up,'

in unison. However, Lump did have a point. I turned to Doug. 'What do we do now, Doug?' I asked. 'We're miles from a telephone, and if we leave, how do we know the car will be here when we get back?'

Doug thought a minute then replied. 'You and Sparky stay here under cover and keep watch,' he ordered. 'I'll drive on to find a phone box. If something happens, don't move, just watch and make a note of anything that will help the police.'

'They won't believe us!' I groaned.

'Maybe not,' replied Doug, 'but we haven't anything to lose.' Sparky and I got out.

Doug wound down the window. 'And remember,' he said, 'no heroics.'

Then, just as we turned to find a place to hide, two cars came hurtling out of the farm and screeched to a halt either side of Doug's van. Out poured six men. They wrenched open Doug's door, dragged him out, forced him against the side of the van and ordered the gang out. Nobody seemed to have noticed Sparky and me, but we were so shocked we didn't move. I came round quickly and nudged Sparky, pointing to the ditch behind us. The others were climbing out of the van and being pushed alongside Doug. They all looked very frightened. Sparky and I dropped into the ditch and scrambled through into the field behind.

We thought we had escaped because they hadn't noticed us, but just as we began to track along behind the hedge a voice from inside one of the cars called out. It was Booth!

'There's two getting away, through the hedge, over there,' he called. I would recognize that voice anywhere!

'Run for it,' I yelled to Sparky, and we hurtled at full tilt along the edge of the field, forgetting all thoughts of hiding.

'Split up,' Sparky called.

So I set off along the hedge whilst Sparky made across the field. I ran and ran. Turning, I saw Sparky making his way across the field with two men in pursuit. I hoped he would make it. I made it to the next field and carried on. Behind me I heard someone yell, 'Get him, he mustn't escape.'

'God, if there is one,' I said to myself looking upwards, 'please don't let anyone get hurt. And especially not Sparky.'

Suddenly, I was knocked sideways to the ground, and I felt a very heavy weight on me. I looked up into the ugly face of the Hulk, who had leapt on me from behind a hedge.

'Right, you little monster, I've got you, so you better come quietly or I'll break your nasty little arm off,' he grunted. He wrenched me up, thrust my arm up my back, and marched me in the direction of the farm.

'What're you going to do with us?' I demanded.

'I'm going to keep you here till the weekend,' he replied. 'By which time we will have finished our business here and be away. Until then you can be my guest in the little hotel round the back. Take him away, boys!'

'You'll never get away with it, my dad will be after us when he knows we're missing,' I retorted as I was dragged away.

'Oh yes I will,' Booth returned. 'Nobody knows where you are and out here we hardly ever see anybody.' He laughed and went into the farmhouse.

I was taken to an old barn. The doors were pulled

120

back. They threw me in and I fell in a heap of old straw. Before I had a chance to get up Sam was at my side. 'You all right?' she said.

'Yes,' I replied. 'Where is everybody? Is Sparky all right?'

'We're all OK,' came a voice. It was Doug.

Everybody was there. They were all looking a bit shocked, but nobody was hurt, thank goodness. Even though we were trapped it was good to be back with the rest of the gang.

'What are we going to do?' asked Chip, obviously frightened.

'Don't worry,' Doug said. 'It'll be all right.'

Somehow his calm voice settled everybody. I hoped he was right!

◇

16

AMBUSH

Meanwhile, back at Church Street, the mystery of the missing gang gradually unfolded. I found out later, from Little Mo, what exactly happened on Church Street after our chase and capture.

As the evening went on, Chip's mum, as usual, was the first to get worried. She rang Sparky and Sam's house to see if he was there, but discovered that none of us were about. That set Sparky's mum thinking! She went round to check on my house, and of course, we weren't there either. At this point my Dad got involved and walked round to Lump's fish and chip shop, then on to Raj's home.

Finally, getting angrier and angrier, Dad went to the gang hut in Whizzer's back garden. By now, all our parents were very worried and Dad decided to give Doug a ring, but of course he didn't get any answer.

Just as he finished trying, Little Mo was brought downstairs because she had told Mum what we were up to. I had threatened her not to tell, but thankfully, in the end, she had talked. Mo told me that my dad was really anxious at this point. He decided to ring his friends in the force and see if they had noticed any of us. After drawing another blank, he contacted his station sergeant and told him what had happened.

A search was organized but Dad decided to go on

his own to ask Booth if he'd seen us. Of course, he found the place empty, but unlocked, and decided to have a look around. Inside he found licence plates and false registration documents just lying around — obviously people had left in a great hurry. He immediately rang the station and brought in the CID.

Then, just as he was coming out of the garage, he happened to bump into the vicar who told him that he had seen us all leap into Doug's car and hurtle off down the street at full speed. It was then that a full-scale search operation by the police swung into action. Of course we didn't know all this, but we were hoping for some miracle rescue as we sat it out in that cold, unwelcoming barn.

There was nothing we could do, but sit there, feeling rather cold, and wondering what to do. I got up and tried all around, looking for a way out, but the walls were made of breeze-block and the floor of concrete. There were a few bales of straw lying about which we used for sitting on. Sam suggested we pile these up against the roof and try to escape by knocking a hole through the corrugated iron. Chip pointed out, quite rightly, that this wouldn't work because there weren't enough bales of straw and anyway, when we tried to break through the metal, the noise would wake everyone up in the farmhouse.

'Well, I think we should just sit still and do everything that they tell us,' said Lump.

'You're just a coward,' retorted Sam.

'I know,' he replied quickly. 'I like it that way.'

'Oh come on, you lot,' Doug cut in. 'Arguing amongst ourselves isn't going to do any good at all.'

We all fell silent.

'What are we going to do?' I asked Doug eventually, after a long pause. I hoped he might have a magic answer!

'There's no point in rushing into something,' he said. 'If we do, someone is likely to get hurt. They're not going to hurt us if we stay quiet and be patient.'

I could see the sense in this and nobody else had any great ideas, so we made ourselves comfortable.

It wasn't long before we heard the sound of voices coming and the padlock on the outside being unlocked. Then the door banged open and in came a scruffy little man with a big tray of bread and cheese and a jug of water and some metal mugs. Behind him stood the Hulk, blocking the door. They said nothing, but backed out carefully. Then we heard the padlock and chain being put back in place.

'Great! Food!' Lump said as he made a bee-line for the tray. We all moved in quickly before he scoffed the lot and we disposed of all the simple provisions without any difficulty.

As I sat munching the cheese a germ of an idea began to grow in my mind. The only time that we had any chance of escape was when the food was brought in or the empties taken out. What had to be worked out was how to take advantage of this.

'Hey, everybody! I've got an idea,' I said enthusiastically.

'Oh no!' spluttered Lump through his cheese sandwich.

The rest didn't look particularly worked up either. I explained to them what I had in mind, how we needed to ambush our captors when they came back for the empties and then make a dash for it.

There was a long silence.

'Well. . .' I went on. I had been trying not to get

124

grumpy again, but the old me started to break out again, and I couldn't stop myself. 'Oh, come on,' I said impatiently. 'We've got to do something and no one's thought of anything better.'

'Well,' said Doug. 'It's rushing things a bit. We must be very careful. I have been thinking along similar lines myself. But we need time to plan it out.'

'That's the style, Doug,' I responded, pleased that at least someone was on my side. I knew he was still not sure about it, but I decided to ignore his doubts.

'Right,' I said. 'Let's get organized.'

'I've got an idea,' Sam suddenly said. 'Why don't we pile up the bales of hay to one side of the door and push them on to those thieves when they come in.'

'Great idea,' I replied. I like to see people getting on with things.

'Look,' said Doug, 'we mustn't rush into this. Let me think.' By this time everyone was busy piling up the bales. Doug turned to me, 'For safety's sake, let me take the risk. If you all make a lot of noise and cause as much confusion as possible, I'll make a run for it.'

'OK,' I replied. Doug was probably the fastest of all of us so he stood the best chance. I couldn't argue with that. So we all prepared ourselves, taking up the positions that Doug and I suggested. I knew that Doug was worried for us because he kept telling everybody to be careful and not do anything silly when the time came. Not knowing when anybody was going to come, we just had to wait, some more patiently than others.

I could see Doug quietly closing his eyes. I realized he must be praying. We could do with a few miracles in our position. Oh, how I wished my dad was by my side. He'd sort them out.

At last we heard someone coming.

'Right, everybody in position,' Doug said softly. 'And remember — be careful,' he added.

The key rattled in the padlock and the chain was slipped through its hasps. My stomach tensed and my hands were sweaty as they gripped the stave of wood I had found as a weapon.

Sparky was behind the straw, ready to push it all on top of them, and I stood opposite him ready with my stick. The rest of the gang and Doug were trying to look as natural as possible, which was difficult, especially for Lump whose knees were knocking so much I swear I could hear them.

The door opened and the scruffy little man came in with the Hulk close behind. Right on time Sparky did his work and the bales came tumbling down. At the same time I leapt out and hit the Hulk on his back, knocking him to the ground. Everybody dived into the scrum, trying to keep the men so confused that they couldn't do anything. Looking up, I saw Doug making his way out of the door, then I dived back in with renewed enthusiasm.

Fists were flying in all directions. Sam was biting away at one man's arm, Chip was kicking away at a trousered leg for all he was worth, and Lump just sat on the heap of writhing bodies looking like a great Buddha. With all the punching and fighting from the rest of us, we were very effective for a while.

Eventually, however, all the noise and shouting roused the rest of the criminals back at the house. Suddenly we were all pulled apart and thrown aside. The fight stopped as quickly as it had begun. I looked up, and there was Booth!

'Right,' he ordered. 'Get up, everybody. You lot, back against the wall.' Then he turned to the Hulk and the other little weasel, 'Some guards you are, letting a bunch of kids nearly get away.'

'Sorry, boss,' grunted the Hulk, getting up from the ground and dusting himself off. 'Er, boss,' he continued.

'Shut up,' went on Booth. 'And get this lot sorted out.'

'But, boss. . .'

'What, you idiot?' shouted Booth, very red-faced and angry.

'The vicar's not here,' mumbled the Hulk apologetically.

'Oh no!' yelled Booth. 'Well, don't just stand there, get off and find him! Don't let him get away.'

We were left in the barn, locked up again.

'I hope Doug will be all right,' said Sam quietly.

'Yes, me too,' I added ruefully.

We were all quiet, then. Thinking about Doug, about our homes, our families. Nothing seemed to happen for ages, and we just sat around. Occasionally we heard shouts, but the criminals didn't seem to be having any luck. Later, we didn't hear anything. It was night now. In that long silence, in the dark, we all waited with a little hope and a little fear in our hearts.

Suddenly, the door burst open and a body was thrown in. Booth appeared in the doorway with a lamp held up to his face. He looked evil. 'Don't try it again!' he snarled and slammed the door.

'Can we have a light, for a little while at least?' Sam called out.

The door reopened and Booth put the lamp just inside, 'For a little while,' he said. 'And no tricks.'

We rushed to Doug's side. He had blood on his head and was unconscious. After a while his eyes opened and he groaned, raising his hand to the cut on his head.

'Are you all right?' I asked anxiously.

He gripped my hand. 'I'm OK,' he said weakly. 'Need to sleep.' Then he closed his eyes.

I felt terrible. It was all my fault. If it hadn't been for my 'bright idea', Doug wouldn't have been hurt.

What had I done now?

128

17

ESCAPE!

The night was a long one, the silence broken only by the occasional groan from Doug. Our lamp had been taken away and they had thrown us a bandage so that we could patch him up. It was very difficult in the dark. Just like with Aunty Edna's accident, Sparky's first aid work came in handy again, and even with only a faint glimmer of moonlight through a small hole in the roof, he managed to bandage Doug's head very effectively.

'Is he going to be all right?' I asked Sparky.

'I think so,' he replied.

'No thanks to you,' remarked Sam aggressively. 'You really sold us another useless idea.'

'Come on, Sam,' cut in Sparky. 'There's no point in all that. Leave him alone.'

I slunk off to the back of the barn in the dark. There I sat, reminding myself of all the awful things I had done to Doug and others in the past and thinking about my lousy temper and how impossibly bigheaded I was. I heard someone coming over and saw the dark outline of Sparky. Feeling how I did, really fed up, I turned away and hunched myself up, staring at the wall. I couldn't face being told what I already knew about my own stupidity. He sat down and didn't say anything. He didn't need to!

After a while I couldn't stand the silence. I felt

absolutely terrible about what had happened. I turned to face Sparky, thankful that it was too dark to see his face, and he mine.

'All right,' I said, 'I was wrong. I've been wrong all along, so there's no need to tell me what I know already.'

'I wasn't going to,' he replied quietly.

'Oh!' That surprised me. I was silent for a while, then, 'Where do we go from here?' I asked quietly.

'I think,' Sparky replied, 'that we do what Doug wanted in the first place. We must be patient for the right moment, and not rush into anything that will hurt anybody else.'

'Mmm,' I said. Well, what else could I say?

'As for now, we rest and wait until it's light,' he concluded.

Totally depressed, I settled down to sleep as best I could.

In the light of early morning I woke up with a start to find Sparky and Sam at work comforting Doug, who was conscious, but looked very pale. We had surrounded him with bales of hay and covered him with coats to keep him as warm as possible. I held back. Nobody seemed to want to talk to me.

'What do we do now?' asked Whizzer of nobody in particular.

I said nothing, but Sparky called everybody together. I was so low and numb with depression that I didn't protest. After all, I wasn't such a good leader. Sparky suggested that we all pray for Doug and also to ask God for a way of escape. For once, praying seemed to be a good idea.

I sat back and quietly joined in as Sparky began to pray. Was it really true, as Sparky said, that God was always with you, and listening, and helping?

'Oh God,' he began, 'thank you for being with us here. Thank you for promising that you will help us if we ask. We ask you to make Doug better quickly and please help us to find a way to escape. Thank you for the help you're going to give. In Jesus' name, Amen!'

Nobody talked much after that. I was feeling a bit low and the others were either helping Doug or talking together. They didn't seem to want to talk to me. Sparky was messing about in a quiet corner of the barn.

'Hey look!' he suddenly yelled.

'What is it?' asked Sam impatiently.

'Look at this!' went on Sparky. 'I've found a loose brick.'

'What?' asked Whizzer. 'Where?'

'Over here,' he said, pointing to the area I had hastily passed by when looking round soon after we were thrown into the barn.

'Yes, look, it's a loose brick,' Raj added, joining Sparky. 'Let's loosen the others round it. One good shove will make quite a hole.'

'Why didn't we see it before?' grumbled Sam, 'it would have saved a lot of fuss.' Everybody went silent, and some looked at me. I went red and looked at the ground wishing I was invisible.

There was a long pause, then Sparky began to spark. 'I've got a plan,' he said, looking round at us all. 'What we do is this. We make up a dummy using straw and some of our clothes, then when they come in, we sit in a circle close together with the dummy turned away from them. They never look closely, only quickly count heads. That will give someone a chance to get right away without being missed, especially if we put back the bricks.'

I looked around and could see everyone thinking about this. I personally thought it was a great idea and wished I had thought of it myself. If only *I* had noticed the loose bricks. I also wanted to make sure I was the one to take the risk and make the escape.

'It's a great idea,' I said, stepping forward. 'But I want to be the one to make the break.'

Sparky thought about this for a bit, then replied. 'OK,' he said. 'I guess it has to be you. And it'll make you feel better as well,' he added bluntly. I didn't say anything, but he was right!

'But first,' Sparky went on, 'we must try the dummy idea out to see if it works.'

So we set to work. Sam looked after Doug while the rest of us loosened some hay and then sorted out clothes. We finished things off with Lump's scarf and Whizzer's bobble hat. From the back, with Whizzer on one side and Lump on the other, it looked very effective.

When the next meal-time came we tried it out. Two of them came in and dropped the food on the floor. I hid in the corner. They glanced round at the huddled group sitting around Doug, shrugged their shoulders and walked out. Magic! It worked!

'OK,' said Sparky. 'Success.'

'Yea, great,' added Sam. 'Which one is the dummy?'

'That one,' replied Whizzer, pointing at Lump.

Sparky turned to me. 'It's up to you now,' he said.

'Let's get on with it,' I replied enthusiastically. Underneath I was frightened rigid but I had to go through with it.

Just as I started to move the bricks, Sam ran over to me. She held my arm and put her lips close to my ear. 'Good luck,' she whispered. I blushed. For one moment, I had thought she was going to kiss me!

Sparky broke in on our romantic farewell. 'Take care, don't do anything daft,' he said.

I looked at him. He smiled, and so did I — it hid my terror. We turned and gently pushed at the brick. It fell back easily onto the earth outside and we soon had three others clear as well. There was just enough space for me to crawl through. I poked my head out and could see there was nobody round the back so I scrambled out.

'Push the bricks back,' Sparky called through the hole.

I pushed them all back into place, then turned to look for some cover. Just a little way off was a tractor. I ran and hid behind the large back wheel. From there I could see some of the criminals packing a lorry with things. They were obviously getting ready to move out so it was as well I hadn't waited until night-time when it would have been too late.

I waited there until I saw them stop work and go into the farmhouse. Seeing my chance, I ran for the fence, jumped straight over it, then ran along in the shadow of a hedge, away from the farm and towards the road. I was about halfway when I heard a shout from the farmhouse. Looking round, I saw someone leaning out of an upstairs window, pointing. I had been rumbled!

I turned and ran as fast as I could towards the road. I turned back once more to see if I was being followed, and ran straight into a tree. I hit my head and gashed my arm on a branch. A huge lump was coming up on my forehead and my arm was bleeding but there was no time to stop, so I carried on. I leaped through a hedge on to the road and looked round frantically for help. There was no one in sight!

Turning right, I ran along as fast as I could. The sides of the lane were lined with trees which gave me good cover, but there was still no one to help. By now I was feeling exhausted and couldn't go much further, so I stopped and leaned against a tree and slumped down, gasping for air.

I longed for a friendly car to come along and rescue me but all was silent except for the distant shouts from Booth's mob. Then I heard a vehicle approaching very fast. Without thinking, I ran into the road, ready to stop it. But something made me dive back into cover, just in time! From the trees I saw the car rushing past with the Hulk and another man looking out. I breathed a sigh of relief! That was close!

Then I heard another vehicle, much slower. It was a risk, but my arm was hurting more and my head was reeling. I had to take a chance! I jumped out onto the road and waved the approaching vehicle down with my good arm. It stopped. My stomach churned as I looked in, trying to see whether it was friend or foe. A man got out. I quickly realized from his perplexed look that he wasn't one of the criminals. He was in fact a farmer, taking his van full of produce to the market.

'What's up, lad? You all right?' he asked, looking at my arm and my head.

I tried to tell him what had happened and he put me in his van and we drove off to find a telephone box. I'm sure he hardly understood a word I said! Rounding a bend, we saw the other car ahead at the crossroads and the two men looking around.

'Climb into the back, lad,' the farmer said, 'and

hide among the boxes.' At the crossroads the Hulk waved us down, and the farmer opened the window.

'Not seen a lad about, have you?' asked the Hulk.
'Er, it's my nephew and I think he's lost.'

'Sorry,' replied the farmer. 'Don't see much down this road and certainly nothing this morning.'

He wound up the window and drove off steadily, trying not to give any clues that I was in the back. I looked out of the back window and saw with relief that they didn't seem suspicious. At the next phone box the farmer rang the police. It wasn't long before a white car came speeding towards us, blue light flashing.

It was fantastic! In the car was my dad, and I quickly told him everything. He called up the station on his radio telephone and passed on everything I had said. Then he turned back to me. 'Let me have a look at that arm,' he said. It was quite painful now, and it felt very bruised and sore. Dad bandaged it up using his car's first-aid kit. He looked at the huge bruise on my forehead and shook his head. 'I think you ought to see a doctor with that,' he said. 'Are you feeling OK?'

'Yes, I'm fine,' I said impatiently. 'Can we go to the farm now?'

'OK,' he agreed. 'I'd like to see that everyone's all right as well. But we must get you to a doctor before long.'

'I'm coming too,' added the farmer. He had never had a day like this before.

So Dad and I went in the police car and the farmer followed in his van. By the time we got to the farm the place had been surrounded and the police officers were rounding up Booth's mob. It was really good to see Booth, handcuffed, being pushed into a police van.

We got out and went over to the barn. Dad broke the lock and out came the gang. They were all in one piece, to my great relief. An ambulance had been called and Doug was carried into it on a stretcher. They insisted I went too. My head was really aching by then, so I didn't protest.

Before I went into the ambulance I had a quiet word with Sparky. 'Thanks for everything,' I said. 'You're a good pal, and I think I am just beginning to understand what you're on about.'

Sparky smiled, but he didn't say anything.

18

NICK & CO.

'Give me the ball,' I yelled.

Raj looked up as he heard my shout and passed the ball over Sam's head, to me, hurtling down the other pavement. I hit the ball hard on the run, and it thudded against Booth's garage door. Our goal was the garage entrance at the back of Mr Blake's butcher's shop, and so far it hadn't received a shot. The goalie, Lump, dived for cover when he saw me getting lined up to shoot. It was a very satisfying goal, and was greeted with shouts of glee from Chip and Raj, the rest of my team.

'You great lump, Lump,' groaned Sam at the unhappy goalie.

'Well,' retorted Lump, 'I hate football, I hate being in goal, and I hate being hit by one of Nick's piledrivers.'

It was just like the old days. It was half-time so we sat with our backs against the fence and Lump passed around some chocolate biscuits from his vast supply of tuck. Oh, it was good to be back together again. What a great bunch of mates we all were.

As people passed us they smiled and said hello. It's funny how you can suddenly change from being public enemy number one to being the best thing since sliced bread, I reflected.

Boy, my Dad had felt really stupid when he pieced together what had happened. He had actually taken

Mr Booth's word for it, when he and the Hulk claimed they were with the Chief Constable at the time Aunty Edna was knocked down. It wasn't true, of course. They *had* been there in the morning, but not the afternoon. Mind you, the Chief Constable was very embarrassed to find out that he had bought his son a stolen car. Not only was the Hulk in trouble, but Mr Booth would get a stiff sentence at the court too.

With all the publicity we had got over the Booth case, my mum reckoned I soon wouldn't be able to get through the door because of the size of my head. There's no pleasing parents!

Of course, it wasn't all good news. Nothing anybody could do would bring us back our club hut, but all the fuss had caused a lot of people in the church to think again about the use of the church hall. In fact, they had all pulled together and promised to buy us some new equipment, which was really nice of them considering the damage I had caused. I still blushed to think of the piano incident.

It wasn't just that they had changed, I had as well. You couldn't go through all the things that had happened to me and not be changed. Some of the things that had made Sparky the way he was had now started to become a part of my life. By talking to Doug and Sparky, I realized that God was actually interested in *me*, and how I lived. And that Jesus wasn't someone to get embarrassed about, or a name just used for swearing. Things were starting to make sense to me. Being a Christian wasn't about *trying* to be good, but something to do with trusting in Jesus. Already my bad temper was more under control. And I was starting to realize how bigheaded I had been. Poor old Doug was still in hospital, but he was nearly better. He had promised us a really great new club in the church hall. . .

I was woken from my dreaming by a warm, wet tongue. Staring me in the face was 'Wally'. He was my pride and joy! Dad had relented, and said I could have a dog. We had been to the Dogs' Home to choose one and of course I had to pick the oddest dog in the place. It was his look. You know, the look that says, 'I only want to be a friend, and if you take me away from here, I will worship you for ever.' He is a cross between an Old English Sheepdog and something else much smaller, and looks like a walking floor mop. He had to be called Wally!

'Oh, Wally,' I spluttered through the damp licking. 'Stop it, stop it!'

I turned to Little Mo, who was struggling at the other end of the lead. 'Sorry,' she said. 'I tried to take him to the park, but he heard your shout and dragged me this way.'

'It's all right,' I replied.

'We don't mind you at all,' I said to Wally. You really get daft with pets — as if he could understand! We all kept Wally entertained by throwing sticks out into the street, which he returned, his tail wagging, eyes bright, and giving the occasional deep 'Ruff'. Then Whizzer reminded us that we were in the middle of a game, and shouldn't we get on with the second half.

'OK,' I said cheerfully. 'I'll just tie Wally up to the lamppost.' 'Now you just stay there,' I said to him, 'and behave yourself.'

'Ruff,' he replied.

We carried on, with Little Mo joining my team. The ball bobbed about up and down the street, and we all tried to keep it away from Wally, who was attempting to play for both sides whenever it came near the lamppost. I had been teaching him to play nose football, and he showed a natural talent, but didn't have much goal sense. He tended to keep going in whichever direction the ball was going.

I was on the run again, hurtling down the pavement, Sparky facing me in defence. I closed in on him, with the ball at my feet. With the outside of my foot I flicked the ball against the wall, and slid past him on the other side. I controlled the ball again and looked up. Raj was standing by the goal, waiting.

'To my head, to my head,' he yelled.

Lump stood quaking by his side. Sam was running back to help.

I kicked the ball over to Raj, who leaped to head it just as Sam arrived to defend. Lump just stood there.

With an incredible crunch they all met. Raj was wedged between Sam and Lump like a sardine sandwich. The ball hit Raj's head, popped up in the air and gently sailed over the locked gate of Booth's garage.

There was a stunned silence. Sam, Raj, and Lump picked themselves up.

'Here we go again,' groaned Lump.

'What do we do now?' asked Chip.

'Well, *I'm* not going to try and climb over,' I said.

'Nor me,' added Whizzer.

'And I'm not going to let anybody use me as a stepladder,' grunted Lump.

There was a pause.

I really had to laugh, and what started as a chuckle, turned into uncontrollable laughter. The others joined in till we were all rolling about the street laughing. Eventually, when the laughing

140

subsided, the inevitable question was asked.

'Well, what *are* we going to do to get the ball back?' Sam asked.

'You'll never guess where it's landed,' said Sparky as he looked through a gap between the fence post and the rest of the fence.

'Where?'

'It's lying by that heap of old tyres,' he said.

We all groaned. It brought back such memories.

'Ruff,' added Wally, who thought he had been forgotten. That gave me an idea. I untied him, and walked over to the gap.

'What are you up to?' asked Sparky.

'Wait and see,' I replied with a smirk.

'Now, Wally,' I said to the dog, 'go through the gap, fetch ball, fetch ball.'

'Ruff,' he responded.

I pushed him through the gap and, with wagging tail, he waddled over to the heap of tyres. 'Football, Wally, football,' I encouraged.

He nosed the ball, and began to push it away from the tyres. The only trouble was, he didn't have control or direction, so he just chased up and down the yard, wagging his tail. But eventually he came near enough for me to grab the ball through the fence and he followed it out, tail still wagging.

We patted and cheered him till he got thoroughly excited, which was a big mistake. He was leaping up and down for all he was worth. Whizzer kicked the ball away, and Wally was so excited he chased after it, and began his daft game of nose football all over again, this time down the street.

We all chased after him, yelling for him to stop. In the end we had him cornered and he stopped. However, as we closed in on him, he took it into his

141

head that this was another game.

As I reached out for the ball he grabbed it in his teeth.

'No, Wally, no!' I yelled.

Too late! He might be stupid but he has really sharp teeth. The sound of air escaping from the football was unmistakable.

There was nothing for it. With a sigh, we all sat down. With a wagging tail and winning eyes Wally dropped the ball at my feet, punctured and useless.

We all looked at each other and laughed. Another disaster for Nick and Co!

NICK & CO. on Holiday

NICK
& CO
ONHOLIDAY

Bob Croson

CONTENTS

1

A BIT OF BOTHER

Church Street wasn't the best cricket pitch in the world, but in my imagination it was smoother and flatter than any Test Match wicket I had seen on TV.

My best pal Sparky passed me the ball, and I paced back from the lamppost, striding into the distance trying to look mean and hard. I turned and looked round. The batsman was waiting impatiently.

'Oh come on, Nick, get on with it!' she said. It was Sparky's sister, Sam. She was really good at most sports, which was a bit maddening at times. Both Sam and Sparky played in school teams for all sorts of things and were very athletic and quick.

I looked at the rest of the gang to check if they were all in the right places. Sparky was standing ready for a catch, and Raj was looking very correct behind the wicket, made from an old cardboard box. He was ace at cricket and dead keen to play for England when he grew up.

But the rest!

Whizzer was leaning on a lamppost, clicking his fingers to the rhythm coming from his headphones. Chip — a computer-freak — was bent over his latest game. And as for Franco Granelli

151

— Lump to friend and enemy alike — he was, as usual, eating!

That only left my pesky little sister Mo, who was busy holding on to Wally, our dog, who didn't understand the rules of cricket!

I didn't bother shouting at them all. It wasn't worth the effort. Besides, I thought I could get Sam out easily and they wouldn't be needed.

'Botham races in, one ball to go, one wicket to take. Will he win it for England yet again?'

I raced in and bowled as hard as I could. The tennis ball sped in Sam's direction and, 'WHAM!' She socked the ball high in the air.

'Get it,' I yelled.

Now I didn't mean Wally, but the ever-obedient if slightly stupid dog didn't understand. Hearing his master's voice, he wrenched himself free of Mo and hurtled off after the ball.

Lump never moved, Chip didn't notice and Whizzer clicked his fingers in time to the music only he could hear, with a blank smile on his face.

'Mine,' I yelled as I sped off after the ball.

'Mine,' yelled Sparky as he did the same.

'Come back, Wally,' Mo shouted as she chased after our daft dog.

Now, it would have been a brilliant catch if it hadn't been for Mr Marchbank. He was a very correct, retired teacher. You could set your watch by him. He always bought sausages on a Tuesday at exactly the same time from Mr Blake's butcher's shop on the corner of Church Street, opposite our youth club. It was also right on the boundary of our pitch. Just at the moment he stepped out of the shop, Sparky and I arrived to catch the ball, closely followed by Wally.

There was a terrific 'CRUNCH!' as we all collided. Mr Marchbank fell to the ground, his sausages beside him. Sparky and I lay in a tangled heap at his feet.

The ball bounced off the bald top of Mr Marchbank's head, and with great skill Wally leaped in the air and caught it. He brought it to me in his mouth, his tail wagging wildly.

Then Wally saw the sausages. The prize for all his hard work! He dropped the ball and grabbed them.

'No!' yelled Mr Marchbank.

'Leave!' I screamed at Wally.

His tail drooped, he dropped the sausages and skulked off to Mo, wondering what he had done wrong.

I picked up the sausages, dusted them off and sort of pushed them back into shape, smoothing over the dog bites, wrapped them in what was left of the paper, and handed them back to Mr Marchbank. He did look a funny colour. Sort of purply-red!

'Are you all right, Mr Marchbank?' I asked politely.

It was like watching a kettle come to the boil. Suddenly the steam came out.

'You blithering, idiotic, wicked children,' he shouted angrily. He was obviously struggling for words.

We just stood there, feeling rather uncomfortable. And it was a relief to see Doug arriving on the scene. He is our youth club leader, and is brilliant at rescuing us from scrapes.

153

Doug raced over to pick Mr Marchbank up, helped by Mr Blake the butcher.

'They should have taken my advice and closed down that blessed youth club, it's nothing but a nuisance,' Mr Marchbank complained.

That made me see red. When I thought of all we'd done to keep our youth club! But I kept my mouth shut.

'Are you all right?' Doug asked, ignoring the outburst. 'I'm sure the boys didn't do it on purpose. It was a very unfortunate accident. When the new playing-field at the back of the club is finished this sort of thing won't happen.'

'And none too soon,' Mr Marchbank grumbled.

'Now,' Doug went on, 'those sausages are beyond repair. Mr Blake, will you give Mr Marchbank some more and add a couple of those lovely chops you have in the window? I'll pay now and the gang will pay me back later.'

We all looked at each other, horrified. I got little enough pocket-money as it was, without keeping 'Old Grumblechops' in breakfasts!

'Right you are,' Mr Blake said and went into the shop.

'Bang goes my new cricket bat,' I muttered grimly.

'Anyway,' Doug cut in sharply, giving me a sidelong glare, 'as I'm taking this lot off camping for a week, you'll have some peace, and by the time we're back, the playing-field should be ready.'

'Thank goodness for that,' Mr Marchbank grunted and disappeared back into the shop to collect his goodies.

'Right, you lot,' ordered Doug. 'Into the hut. Quick march!'

We all trooped into the club hut, with Wally following, wagging his tail. Dumb dog!

'At least I got you out,' I said to Sam, as we flopped down on the chairs.

'You never,' Sam complained. 'It was a six!'

'No way. Wally caught you, off Mr Marchbank's head.'

Wally wagged his tail in agreement.

'He doesn't count!' Sam said, angrily.

'Hang on, hang on,' Doug cut in. 'It's not important. And before you leave I want contributions for the sausages.'

'Wait a bit,' Lump complained. 'I wasn't playing.'

'Guilty by association,' Doug replied. 'And I haven't got time to argue.' As well as being our club leader, Doug was also the curate of our local church, a sort of trainee vicar. But if you think religious people are just softies, you should meet Doug. He can be tough, but he's always fair.

When I first got to know him, he really got on my nerves, going on about Jesus and God and things, but after a while I began to realize what he was on about. He actually did all the things he talked about. Actions speak louder than words, they say.

Through him and Sparky, most of us had become regulars at Doug's club meeting after Friday games nights. That was when Doug would tell us stories from the Bible and make them really come alive. I used to think they were dead boring. But with Doug they made a lot of sense. He really made me change my mind about God and Jesus,

155

and take being a Christian seriously.

'Before you lot all slope off,' Doug went on, 'I want some help in packing up things for the camp.'

'I'll do the food,' Lump chipped in, quick as a flash.

'No, you won't,' Sam said. 'We want some left.' Lump's parents owned the local chip shop and the whole family was, shall we say, keen on food.

After a bit of arguing about who did what, we helped Doug pack the camping gear which we had borrowed from the local scout troop, as well as the food. We were off to Tidesbourne the next day, Doug's home village, and his mum and dad would be getting some of the equipment to save us transporting it in the hired van.

It was the first time any of the gang had been camping, and I noticed Doug was looking rather nervous.

'Right, you lot,' he said, 'be back here, tomorrow morning, nine o'clock sharp. And don't be late.'

The next morning dawned bright and clear — just the day for a holiday. I said goodbye to Wally — and waved to Mum and Dad — and set off for the church hall. Little Mo had already gone to call for Sam.

The van was the oldest and most beaten up vehicle I have ever seen. In my humble opinion it should have been cut up into little pieces and used for making tin cans years ago, but Doug insisted it was perfectly all right. Anyway, it was all we could afford.

After we had packed our gear and sleeping-bags, Doug called us together for a final chat.

'Now look,' he started, 'this holiday has been paid for as a reward for all that you did last year to help the police catch those car thieves.'

We all glowed with pride as we thought back to the excitement of last year (though there were *some* incidents which I'd rather forget).

'Now, this time,' he went on, 'we are going on a holiday. Right?'

'Yes, Doug,' we replied.

'And we are not looking for any adventures.'

'No, Doug.'

'And we certainly don't want to get involved in anything dangerous, do we?'

'No, Doug.'

There was a long silence.

'I'm telling you this because there has been a bit of bother recently in the village,' Doug said. 'But we're not going to get involved. We're there to have a holiday. Right?'

'Yes, Doug,' replied Chip and Lump.

'Cowards!' I grunted at them. Then I asked Doug, 'What trouble?'

'Never you mind,' Doug replied. 'I'm just telling you to keep your nose out! We are on holiday and not getting involved. Right?'

'You know me, Doug!' I responded, with a twinkle in my eye, nudging Sparky.

There was a pause. I leaned back in my seat, looked up at the ceiling and spoke, to no one in particular:

'Nick and Co., righters of wrongs, modern-day Robin Hoods, England's answer to the A-Team . . .'

157

I was suddenly bombarded with cushions from all sides.

Doug just held his head in his hands and groaned.

I just couldn't wait to get there!

2

RUN FOR IT!

'Old Macdonald had a farm,
Ee-i-ee-i-o.
And on that farm he had a four-eyed, one-legged,
flat-nosed, green-eared,
duck-billed platypus, and his dog, Spot,
what a lot,
Ee-i-ee-i-o.'

The van trundled through the Derbyshire countryside, with us singing to relieve the boredom.

I was sitting between Sparky and Raj. Opposite us sat Whizzer, Lump and Chip, and piled all round our feet were all the bags and junk. Mo and Sam were sitting up front with Doug.

'Only a mile or two to go now,' said Doug cheerily, joining in with the chorus.

'BANG!'

Suddenly the organized tangle of bags jumped up and hit me in the face, Lump bounced podgily to the floor, and the rest of us lurched around all over the place.

'Hold on!' Doug called out.

'That's great,' I thought. 'He says hold on, when it's like being inside mum's washing-machine!'

Then I was thrown on top of Lump who groaned loudly as the wind was knocked out of him.

'Good job he's so fat,' I thought, grateful for the soft landing. We skidded to a stop and Doug turned round to see if we were all right.

'Everyone OK back there?' he asked.

There was a muffled and painful groan from underneath me and the pile of cases. My comfortable landing-mat had now become an erupting volcano as Lump surfaced from the bottom of the van growling, 'Gerroff!'

Doug came round and opened the back of the van and we all fell out, a pile of bags and bodies. We were in the country, by a wood.

'Wh-what happened?' asked Whizzer, pulling his earphones off. How he managed to keep listening to Reggae music through all the chaos I'll never know.

'Sorry, fellas,' Doug apologized. 'We had a puncture — a front tyre — and I nearly lost it.'

'I don't think you ever found it,' I grumbled.

For some reason Doug didn't seem to like this remark. I can never understand why adults get so touchy about their driving. My dad becomes a raving lunatic behind a wheel, especially when he sees a woman driver. But you tell him if he does anything wrong and he goes berserk!

'I don't think your driving is getting any better,' added Sam.

'No, it's always been terrible,' said Little Mo rubbing her bruised shoulder.

'Where are my sandwiches?' complained Lump, digging around for the 'snack' he'd been eating.

160

We all fell about laughing, because it was obvious to everybody else exactly where Lump's sandwiches were. He must have landed on them and now they were stuck very firmly to the back of his jeans!

He groaned and began the messy business of scraping them off, while we stood watching Doug trying to change the wheel of the van.

'You're not very good at it, are you?' put in Chip, knowingly.

Doug just turned and looked at him. 'Why don't you go away and have a wander round while I sort this out?' he asked through gritted teeth.

'Come on,' said Sparky, 'let's have a game of hide-and-seek.'

It was better than sitting around getting bored, so I agreed.

'Last one to the tree's on!' I shouted as I made a dash to the nearest one.

The others hurtled after me, all except Whizzer, who had been fiddling with his headphones. When he realized what was happening he was so far behind us he couldn't even beat Lump to the tree. So we left Whizzer to count to a hundred while we all dashed off in different directions, leaving Doug to deal with the wheel in peace.

I ran as fast as I could for a narrow lane which branched off the main road. The trees leaned over, making it like a dark tunnel, and I looked around for somewhere to hide. The undergrowth was thick with nettles. Suddenly I saw the back of an old lorry parked by the side of the lane ahead of me. It had a tarpaulin cover, and I jumped up

161

on to it, looking for a place to hide. It smelled horrible, piled up with dirty, smelly sacking. I jumped down quickly, holding my nose, and ran into the clearing behind it. In the gloom of the wood I could see an old caravan. It looked disused. The curtains were closed.

I could hear someone coming down the lane, so I hid round the back of the caravan. From my hiding-place I saw Lump approaching, red-faced and looking for somewhere to hide. He looked around and then ran over to a large tree and tried to hide behind it. No way! Sticking out one side I could see a mop of black hair and on the other a large backside, still carrying the remains of the squashed sandwiches.

I almost laughed out loud, but that would have given me away, so I just clamped my hand over my mouth and held on tight. I crouched behind the caravan for what seemed an age. In the distance I could hear faint sounds of laughing and shouting.

Eventually, along came Whizzer.

It was funny watching him creeping round the lorry and into the clearing, trying not to make a sound, crouching down and then standing on tiptoe, looking for us.

In the end, he resorted to cheating.

'One, two, three. Nick, I see you,' he shouted.

But I wasn't fooled — he was looking in the other direction.

Then Lump erupted from behind the tree. A wasp, attracted to the sandwich remains, had been buzzing around him. Suddenly it attacked Lump with a well-aimed sting!

'OWCH, OW, GERROFF!' screamed Lump, holding his backside, and leaping into the clearing.

At the same moment the door of the caravan burst open and a man came storming out. He was wearing a pair of greasy, stained trousers and a dirty shirt. His angry, stubbly face jutted out as he looked round to see where all the noise was coming from.

Whizzer was rooted to the spot in surprise. But Lump couldn't stay still because of the sharp pain in a certain tender part of his anatomy. The man grabbed Whizzer's arm, dragging him over to Lump, who was imitating a Red Indian war dance.

'What're you two doing here?' he bellowed angrily. 'This is private land. You're spying, aren't you! Sid, Sid, get out here and give me a hand,' he called in the direction of the caravan.

I watched in horror from behind the caravan. I had to do something to help. But what? I didn't think walking out and explaining that we were only playing hide-and-seek would really work.

'Who sent you here?' the man went on, looking very nasty.

There was nothing for it; I had to do something quick and drastic. I jumped out from behind the caravan, making as much noise as I possibly could. I pushed the man over, and Whizzer broke free.

'Whizzer, Lump, run for it!' I yelled. We all dashed round the side of the lorry and into the lane. It took the man by surprise and gave us a head start on him and Sid. But Lump was having difficulty in running and holding his wasp-sting at the same time and he tripped and fell over,

163

groaning and complaining. Whizzer and I hauled him up, totally ignoring his complaints, and dragged him on down the lane. I could hear the men shouting behind us.

'Get your fat frame going,' I shouted. 'Or we'll all be caught.'

'I'm trying, I'm trying,' he replied breathlessly. 'But I am in pain, you know,' he said.

'Come on, man, come on,' urged Whizzer. Together we dragged Lump along the lane. What a weight! But we did it, and before long we burst out onto the main road.

The van was all ready to go, and the rest of the gang were already inside, waiting for us.

'What on earth's the matter?' asked Doug, as he saw us arrive.

'Don't ask, I'll tell you later,' I replied breathlessly.

We heaved the complaining Lump into the back of the van and Doug started it up.

As we set off, I looked out of the back window to see the men running out onto the road, and shaking their fists at us . . .

'What on earth was that all about? You haven't been up to something you shouldn't, have you?' asked Doug.

'Oh, it was nothing,' I replied. 'A misunderstanding.'

I didn't think it would do any good to explain. Anyway, Doug might want to go back and talk to those men and I for one didn't think that was a good idea.

We weren't far from the village — and I just hoped we wouldn't come across those two again.

But I had a feeling in my bones that it wasn't the last we had seen of them!

3

IN AT THE DEEP END

It was very quiet in the van. Well, we were quiet, but the van sounded as if it was shaking itself to bits.

'Look, there it is!' Doug said, as we came over the crest of the hill. The village of Tidesbourne was below us, nestling in a wide green valley dotted with farms. Beneath the heather-topped hills, we could see the village, a higgledy-piggledy tumble of houses.

'Cor, isn't it pretty? Like an advert on the telly,' Sam said.

Even Whizzer had switched off his Walkman and was looking out of the windows with the rest of us, admiring the view. When we reached the village we drove past old stone cottages and gardens packed with flowers. In the middle of the village was some grass and a pond with ducks. A bit further on we turned into a gateway and drove down a tree-lined drive.

'Hey Doug, do you live here?' Chip asked.

'I used to,' Doug replied. 'You know where I live now — it's only just down the street from you.'

'Come down in the world, haven't you?' inquired Lump. 'What did you do wrong?'

'I didn't do anything wrong,' replied Doug. 'I

wanted to work in the city.'

'You must be stark raving mad,' Whizzer said.

Before the conversation could continue, we skidded to a halt on the gravel drive in front of a big house.

'Right, everybody out,' Doug called.

This time we climbed out very slowly. It was very grand and I had great difficulty stopping my mouth dropping open.

The door opened, and out stepped a grey-haired lady in a tweed skirt.

'Douglas, where have you been? We were quite worried about you,' she said, putting her arms round Doug. She gave him a hug and a kiss. It was funny seeing your youth club leader and church curate being treated like a little boy by his mum. I could tell Doug wasn't that keen and made a mental note to tease him later.

'Hello, Mum,' he replied sheepishly.

We all looked at each other and sniggered.

'I hope she's not going to try that game on me,' I thought, and edged behind the others.

She turned towards us and I could feel everyone leaning towards me, trying to get as far away as possible from the chance of a sloppy kiss.

'These must be our guests,' she went on with a smile.

We all smiled nervously back. I could feel that knotted tingly feeling you get in your stomach when you are not sure what's going to happen next.

She reminded me of an aunty of my mum's who visited once a year. I looked forward to it the same as I looked forward to a visit to the dentist.

167

Every year it was the same. When she arrived it was like being enveloped by a huge, lavender-smelling duvet, and when you surfaced from that there was a walloping, sloppy kiss. Ugh!

Doug introduced us one by one, and I decided on a distant 'Hello' from behind the protection of the rest of the gang. Thankfully she didn't try to kiss any of us.

'By the way,' she said to Doug after greeting us, 'it's our annual garden party in aid of the Old Folks Home today. I thought you wouldn't mind joining in.'

Doug turned and looked at us, then back at his mum. She didn't give him a chance to argue.

'Come on in, children,' she said brightly, ignoring Doug. 'Leave your bags in the van, I'll show you where the bathroom is, then you can join us. It's only a buffet.'

'What do we need a bath for?' Lump whispered in my ear. 'Does she think we smell?'

'No, you wally,' I whispered back through my teeth. 'She's telling us where the loos are.'

Mo looked confused. 'What's a buffet? What does it taste like?' she asked.

'It doesn't *taste* like anything,' Sam replied. 'It's what you have at a wedding.'

Mo looked puzzled. 'Are we going to a wedding?' she asked.

Doug butted in. 'Don't worry, Mo. You're not going to a wedding. What Sam means is that the food's on a table, so you can help yourself. It's like that at a lot of weddings.'

The talk of food spurred everyone to action. We followed Doug into the hall and waited while

168

Whizzer tried out the bathroom. Soon he came bounding down the stairs.

'Hey man,' he gasped, shaking his head, 'that bathroom's incredible, fantastic. It's like something in a film.'

After that we all had to try it! It was *huge* — with gold taps, and plants and a deep-pile carpet.

Eventually we were all ready and made our way into the garden through some large glass doors. In front of us was an enormous lawn with tables of food and groups of grown-ups standing around.

It all went quiet. The gang huddled behind me. We didn't like being looked at. I stuck my hands in my pockets and tried to look relaxed, but inside I just wished I was home.

A man came up.

'Hello, everyone,' he said. 'I'm Doug's father. Come and have something to eat.' He had a kind face — just like Doug's.

We followed him down to the tables. Some people smiled and said, 'Hello', and I began to feel a bit better.

As we reached the food our eyes lit up. There was a fantastic spread of sandwiches and cakes. Lump looked ready to eat the tables as well!

Nobody moved until I picked up a plate and carefully placed a sandwich on it. Suddenly, as if that was some sort of signal, the rest of the gang all lurched forward after the food. The sandwich was knocked from my plate and I was pinned against the table.

'Back,' I hissed through clenched teeth.

'Sorry,' muttered an apologetic Lump, trying to clean bits of bread off me with his hands. I pushed him off and stepped back. The gang descended on the food like at the school Christmas party. I could see people looking at us, so I grabbed Sparky's arm.

'Calm them down,' I muttered. 'Everybody's looking at us. We're making real fools of ourselves.'

But before long everyone had piled food onto their plates and sat down on the grass to eat. I wandered round the garden, smiling at a few people and saying hello, trying to look as if I went to this sort of thing every week. Then some of the gang followed me about, staring at things and pointing.

'Cor, look at that swing in the tree.'

'Ain't there a lot of flowers, it's like a park.'

'Hey, look at all those goldfish in that pond.'

Eventually the girls got up and wandered over to talk to somebody by the house and Lump set off towards the table in search of more food. The others joined me and we walked over to the swimming-pool.

Raj and Chip ran off to the deep end to inspect the diving-board. Sparky and I stood by the side trying to work out who had got the most swimming certificates. Whizzer, behind us, was listening to his Walkman; I guess he was nervous and didn't want to talk to anybody.

As Sparky and I talked — well, argued — I could see Lump wandering back with the biggest piece of cake you've ever seen. It was topped with two sorts of ice cream. Lump was obviously looking forward to it. His eyes were fixed on the cake and he walked straight into a rosebush. I nudged Sparky and pointed, laughing as Lump picked his way out of the roses. His concentration restored, he headed our way.

I suppose I should have thought quicker, and remembered that Lump loses all functioning brainpower when focusing on food. Too late I realized that Whizzer, with his back to Lump and the Walkman on full blast, couldn't see or hear Lump approaching.

'Watch out!' I yelled.

Almost in slow motion, Lump barged into the back of Whizzer, who fell towards me, knocking me backwards into the pool. I felt the warm water close over my head, then surfaced, just in time to see Lump's huge bulk landing in the water right on top of me. He had slipped on the ice cream spilt in the collision.

Once more I went under and started to thrash about. Eventually I remembered it was the shallow end and stood up!

Lump was still spluttering and yelling, 'I'm drowning, I'm drowning,' when I grabbed his collar and made him stand up too.

'Sorry, Nick,' he muttered, sheepishly.

I could feel the anger rising up inside me. What was worse, there was a crowd of grown-ups standing around laughing. I didn't think it was funny. I had half a mind to climb out of the pool and punch somebody on the nose.

Doug rushed over. He took one look at my face and, with Sparky's help, got us both out of the pool and into the house, away from everybody.

They tried to calm me down as I dried off. Somebody brought our bags from the van.

'Huh, what's up with everybody,' I grunted as I rubbed a towel through my hair, 'laughing at me like that.'

'Oh, come on,' said Doug. 'It was funny.'

'Lump won't think so when I get hold of him,' I cut in.

Lump cowered in a corner.

'That's not fair,' Sparky went on. 'It was an accident.'

'Yeh, like the accident of my fist-accidentally-catching his nose!' I said.

I was really mad — steaming!

Eventually, after I had been left alone for a bit, I calmed down and started thinking straight again.

It was a bad start to the holiday. Over the last few months I'd been trying what Doug calls 'self-control', and asking God to help me. Just when I thought I'd learned how to stop losing my temper so easily, there it went again!

Carefully keeping our distance, Lump and I joined the rest outside.

It was time for us to leave and set up camp. We said our goodbyes and made for the van.

'Right, dear,' Doug's mum said to him, 'the rest of the things you need have been put under a tarpaulin in the field you'll be camping in. We've put up a couple of large tents and a toilet and a kitchen tent. All you have to do is put up the tents for sleeping. Mr Staples, the farmer, said there should be no problems — just to keep away from the animals and machines. With all the trouble he's been having he is a bit edgy, but it shouldn't affect your camp!'

My ears pricked up at the mention of trouble. I wished someone would tell us what it was all about.

We soon reached the campsite and set about putting up our four tents — not something we did every day. We were hopeless. There were tents, pegs, ropes, and other assorted bits and bobs everywhere. It was hysterical! Sparky and I made a good team. I held up the tent by standing inside it while Sparky banged in the pegs. But I couldn't resist making ghost noises at Mo, and frightened her to death. Unfortunately, at this point I collapsed, laughing, with the tent all about me.

Doug was not amused. In the end he had to put it up by himself, with us 'helping' — in between attacks of hysterical laughter which left us in a heap on the ground.

Doug sent me and Sparky to collect water from the tap in the corner of the field while Whizzer and Chip fetched wood from Mr Staples' farm to make a campfire. Good old Doug! While we put down our sleeping-bags and sorted ourselves out, he made cocoa on the camping-stove and we had some of his mum's fruitcake. It's funny how everything tastes better out of doors.

While we were sitting around the campfire, I suddenly remembered something said earlier in the day.

'Doug?'

'Yes,' he replied suspiciously.

'What is it,' I went on, 'that's been happening, that you don't want us to get involved in?'

He sighed. 'You really don't need to know,' he

said. 'It's nothing to do with you.'

I wasn't letting him off that easily.

'But if we don't know what it is,' I continued, 'we might get involved with it before we know we shouldn't!' The others all murmured in agreement.

At this point, Doug gave in.

'OK,' he said, 'I'll obviously have no peace till I tell you. Mr Staples has been having terrible trouble with a gang of sheep thieves. The police don't seem to be able to catch them and there are all sorts of rumours about who is involved and why they are doing it.'

'Is that all?' Whizzer complained. 'I thought it was something serious.'

'It is,' Doug continued. 'To city folk it doesn't sound a big deal, but to people around here it is very serious. If these people aren't stopped or caught, Mr Staples could easily go out of business.'

'Hmmm,' I said, my mind going ten to the dozen. 'Where do we start?'

'By going to bed,' Doug said flatly.

Eventually, we settled down in our tents. I was with Sparky and Chip. Sparky's been my best friend since we started school. It was difficult getting to sleep, and Sparky and I kept on thinking up jokes — until Doug told us to shut up. It wasn't exactly comfortable, sleeping in a tent. But, after wrestling with my sleeping-bag for hours, I gradually drifted off to sleep.

Suddenly, there was a terrific CRASH!!

Waking in an instant, I was ready for action.

'The sheep thieves,' I yelled. 'Let's get 'em!'

4

SHEEP THIEVES!

Leaping out of my sleeping-bag and diving out of the tent, I yelled for everyone to wake up. Almost immediately, Whizzer, Sparky, Sam, Raj and Mo were by my side. Lump never stirred, and Chip was still trying to get out of his sleeping-bag.

Doug sleepily emerged from his tent.

'What's going on?' he groaned.

'We're under attack. Didn't you hear the noise?' I hissed at him. 'I reckon it's those sheep thieves!'

'Good grief!' he muttered.

'Look!' Sam shouted. 'Over there!'

It was a clear, moonlit night, and in the eerie glow we could see the canvas of the kitchen tent moving.

There was someone inside!

Doug looked alarmed.

He picked up a piece of wood by the campfire and told us all to stand quite still. Slowly he crept over to the tent and pulled back the flap.

'Come out, whoever you are,' he demanded.

The tent moved again, but no one came out. So Doug decided to go in. There was silence for a moment, suddenly broken by Doug's voice.

'What on earth?' he yelled. Then even louder, 'Get out of here!'

There was a tremendous racket from inside the

175

tent, with pans and boxes falling everywhere. Before we could make up our minds whether to run for it or jump in to help, two dark shapes leaped out of the tent, quickly followed by Doug.

With sudden relief, we all fell about laughing.

'Baaa,' the shapes complained as they scurried off into the night. It was two sheep, upset that their suppertime snack had been interrupted.

'Right, everyone, back to bed,' Doug said, sounding relieved. 'We'll sort the mess out in the morning.'

We woke up next morning feeling cold and stiff — and rather tired. But after our first breakfast, cooked by Doug, Chip, Raj and Mo, with only minor burning of the sausages and the merest sprinkling of grass on the bacon, we all felt better and set about tidying up.

Sam and I were on washing-up duty. She soon got me organized. My mum says I've got a 'soft spot' for Sam. She's not bad, I suppose, and, as she's Sparky's sister, I've known her for a very long time. I mean, I'm not keen on girls — but Sam's OK. Most of the time. I wasn't looking forward to doing the cooking. It was something that Mum always does in our house and is a complete mystery to me.

It was a good job that people in the village had invited us out for meals, and Mrs Staples, the farmer's wife, was making packed lunches for us every day.

In fact, the next thing we were going to do was visit the farm and say hello. Our field was by a stream some distance from the farm itself. We had to cross a couple of fields and go round the edge of a wood to get there. Perhaps it was just as well they couldn't see the field from the farm.

The farmyard was surrounded on all sides by buildings, and Mr and Mrs Staples were in the farmhouse kitchen. Doug had warned us that Mr Staples could be a bit stern and we were to mind our tongues. He was a big man, who didn't seem to smile much. His wife looked totally the opposite — small and jolly with twinkling eyes.

'Good morning, everyone,' Mr Staples said solemnly. 'Welcome to Staples Farm.' We all stood there quietly, rather frightened of him. I hardly heard what he was saying but I did hear him tell us he would let us have a good look round the farm that morning, but that he would appreciate it if we kept as much as possible to the field we were camping in.

'I haven't got time to show you round, so I'll send along one of the men,' he concluded, and marched off.

'Don't mind him,' Mrs Staples said, looking at our glum faces. 'His bark is worse than his bite. And he's got things on his mind. The sheep thieves, you know.'

'Is it that serious?' Doug asked.

'Why, yes m'dear,' she replied. 'If it goes on like this we could lose the farm before the winter.'

This really was something for Nick and Co., I thought to myself.

'But anyway,' she went on, 'you're here on holiday and nothing must spoil that. When you're ready, your lunches are on the kitchen table. Oh, and here comes Bill to show you round.'

A very brown and weathered, tough-looking man came over.

'Hello there,' he said. 'I'm Bill Groves, Bill to you lot. Shall we go?'

Leaving Mrs Staples, we followed Bill on a tour of the farm. After showing us the barns and machines, he took us to see the animals.

He showed us where the cows were milked, and a barn where some new calves were being kept with their mother. The calves were lovely — they sucked my fingers and nuzzled against me. It was the first time I'd ever really *touched* a farm animal. Next we looked at the hens that Mrs Staples kept. They were 'free-range' — just walking about the farmyard. Then Bill pointed to a large building a little way off.

'Let's go to the pig unit,' he said, and we trooped after him.

In one part of the unit were narrow stalls with lights hanging over them. In two of these pens were enormous pigs and rows of little piglets fighting for their mother's milk.

'Lots of lovely bacon,' Lump commented, smacking his lips.

It quite put me off breakfasts. While everybody was 'ooing and aahing' at the piglets, I wandered out to have a look round.

Round the other side of the building were larger pens with little houses at the back. Some were filled with pigs, but one or two were empty. I wandered into one of these empty pens to have a look round. But meanwhile Bill, still inside the building, had moved everyone on and was just about to open the inside door of the pen, not knowing I was there. Before I knew what was happening, what seemed like hundreds of pigs came screeching out at me.

I leaped into the air and as I landed the pigs started nipping at my ankles. An immediate strategic withdrawal was called for. Heading for the nearest wall, I vaulted it with a skill that could probably have taken me into the next Olympics.

In the Olympics, the high jump has a comfortable landing area; unfortunately my choice of landing was a rather large pile of muck. I landed well and truly in it. It smelt terrible — and so did I!

By now, the others had appeared. When they saw me, they just collapsed with laughter. I stood up, and with all the dignity I could muster, stormed off. Inside I was screaming with anger and embarrassment.

I made off along a farm track down one edge of a field. Running as hard as I could helped me to calm down a bit. When I was totally out of breath I had to stop. By then I had reached the wood that we'd passed on our way to the farmhouse. Bending down to wipe some of the muck from my trousers, I suddenly noticed something moving in the wood.

It didn't look like an animal. Could it be someone up to no good? A sheep thief? I walked on slowly and then turned quickly to face the trees. This time I definitely saw a pair of eyes looking back at me before they disappeared. Was this a chance for Nick Baker, single-handed, to catch the sheep thieves? Forgetting Doug's advice, and without thinking about what might happen, I decided attack was the best form of defence.

179

I suddenly turned and leaped into the wood. A dark shadow flitted away through the trees and I hurtled into the undergrowth in pursuit. Suddenly I burst out into a clearing and grabbed my quarry round the ankles. He fell, and I sat on him.

'Ouch,' he shouted. 'Gerroff.'

I was pushed off and a boy about my age ran across the clearing to where two other people were standing, looking at me in disbelief.

'Good grief,' I thought. 'What have I got myself into now?'

They stood there — a boy and a girl, both with bright ginger hair, and an old man.

'He's mad,' the boy said to the others, pointing in my direction.

The old man, who had a kind, reassuring face, looked across at me.

'Are you all right?' he asked.

'Yes,' I replied cautiously. Then I turned to the boy. 'Why were you watching me?' I asked.

'Why were you running like a lunatic?' he replied. 'And why do you stink so much?'

'Why don't you mind your own business?' I barked back.

'Who are you anyway?' he said.

'Hold on, hold on,' cut in the old man. 'This isn't getting us anywhere.'

'Ginger,' he said to the boy, 'that's not the way to talk to people.'

Then he turned to me. 'Don't mind Ginger,' he said quickly. 'He thought you might be up to no good.'

'A sheep thief, you mean?' I replied, looking quizzically at them.

He didn't answer. Instead, he told me who he was. His name was Tom Marsh, and he lived in the smallholding next to Staples farm, the boundary of which went right through the middle of the wood. The two kids, Ginger and Mave, were his grandchildren. Tom also told me that Mr Staples wanted the wood cleared, but that he was against it because it contained so much wild life.

'Lots of people think it's me taking the sheep,' he went on. 'But it isn't.'

Before I could ask him about it we were interrupted.

'What's going on here then?' came a loud and very stern voice.

5

MORE MYSTERIES

The voice startled both of us. I turned to see Mr Staples standing there, looking very angry.

'Marsh,' he said, 'I thought I told you to keep off my land.'

'We were in "our" part of the wood,' replied Tom, 'when Ginger here heard something suspicious.'

'Huh,' Mr Staples grunted, then he turned to me. 'I thought I told you not to go wandering. Get back to the others,' he said angrily.

I was just about to object when he said, 'Now!' in a voice that I didn't dare disobey. Tom and his grandchildren went off in the other direction.

'Keep away from them, boy,' Mr Staples said as we set off back to the farm. 'They're a bad lot, always involved in bother. I'm sure it's them taking the sheep, but he's so fly the law haven't managed to get him yet. But I will!'

I was going to argue, but decided not to. Mr Staples didn't look in the mood to discuss anything.

When I got back to the farm nobody wanted to come near me. They all held their noses and Doug said, 'Nick Baker. How *do* you do it?'

Mrs Staples was kind and helped me get cleaned up. When I went outside again I was introduced to Frank, who also worked on the farm. He was much younger than Bill, and a very friendly sort of guy.

While I was in the farmhouse, I had overheard Frank telling Mr Staples that some more sheep had been rustled sometime during the night. Mr Staples had said he was going to set the law on old Tom Marsh, as it must have been him.

We were standing outside, wondering what was going to happen next. Looking at Mr Staples, Doug decided to cut short our farm tour, and we gathered up our sandwiches and trooped back to the campsite.

On the way back, Sparky had a go at me.

'What are you playing at?' he complained. 'You're already in bother and it's only day one.'

I told him all about Tom and about what I had overheard, but he was unimpressed. Sometimes Sparky really gets on my nerves, especially when he's right! I knew that as usual I was beginning to go over the top and get carried away.

We had a really good afternoon playing cricket. Then it was my turn to help cook. Trust me to get the grotty jobs! First I had to peel the spuds, millions of them, and then help Doug cook a strange mixture that he called hot-pot. While we were stirring it like two old witches, he had a word with me.

'About earlier,' he began.

'I know, I know . . .' I interrupted. 'There's no need to go on.'

I could do without being told where I was going wrong on the very first day of the holiday.

Seeing he was going to get nowhere, Doug left

me to stir the horrible brew, making a comment as he left about me being good at stirring. I didn't like that.

My mind drifted away during this boring occupation, and I was dreaming about how, one day, I would have a house like Doug's parents, with a swimming-pool. I would sit in the garden, stirring my drink, and listening to the sounds of birds calling.

'Nick!'

It wasn't a bird calling, it was Sam yelling at me.

Coming out of my daydream, I realized that the delicious cool drink I was stirring was a horrible hot-pot, and the revolting brew was bubbling over the side of the pot and spilling on to the cooker.

Sam turned off the gas, and then turned on me.

'What are you playing at, and where's Doug?' she demanded.

'I don't know, and I don't know,' I replied grumpily. 'And anyway, this is a woman's job!'

I shouldn't have said that. You should have seen Sam's face!

'How dare you!' she blasted back. 'I suppose you think that all a woman should do is shut up, wash the clothes, cook the food, and do anything else that her lord and master commands her.'

'Well I . . .' I began to reply.

Fortunately, Doug came back and rescued me.

'Come on, you two,' he said. 'Save your arguments, there are more important problems to deal with!' He pointed to the burnt mess in the pan. Sam flatly refused to help, so Doug and I had to open some more cans of beans!

After the meal we had what Doug called a

'camp time'. We had a sing-song, a few games, and finished with a talk from Doug before bedtime. He talked about Jesus and how he forgave people — even the ones who condemned him to death, when he had done nothing wrong. We talked about how God could help *us* to forgive other people.

That started me thinking. It's a whole lot easier to be thankful when God forgives, than to forgive other people when they say sorry for the things they've done to me!

I thought about how I felt about Lump at the pool, and Mr Staples. Forgiving people was easier said than done!!

Just then Sam came up to me and apologized for losing her temper with me. That really hurt, because I knew I was the one who should have done the apologizing. I mumbled something back but I felt terrible inside.

'Time for bed,' shouted Doug. 'And don't forget to clean your teeth.'

'Grown-ups!' I muttered, beneath my breath. But I managed to get into my sleeping-bag without Doug noticing I hadn't been near a toothbrush.

The following day, Sunday, we went to church. It was OK. In the afternoon it poured, and a 'kind' lady asked us to go to a concert in the village hall. It was an old wooden building, a bit like our old club hut. I hoped the concert would be good fun, but it was boring — very, very boring! Most of it was a choir of old ladies singing old-fashioned songs. I suppose they were doing their best, but before long, my mind began to wander. At least we weren't out in the pouring rain.

Looking round at the others, I could see they were bored as well. Whizzer was listening to his music with an earphone under one hand. Sparky, Sam and the others just sat there — bored out of their skulls.

Then it was time for a poetry reading by the village postmistress, a very — shall I say, large? — lady.

I glanced across at Lump.

Disaster!

He was gently nodding off, having eaten too much lunch. I just knew what would happen next!

Sure enough, after a little while, a noise like sawing wood came from his direction — the dreaded Granelli snore. You couldn't take him anywhere! He had gently fallen over onto Chip's shoulder, who gave him a fierce jab in the ribs. This woke him up with a start — not a good idea with Lump.

'Whoa . . .' Lump groaned loudly, at the same time as lashing out with his arm, knocking Chip to the floor.

The resulting commotion stopped the show. The local District Nurse, sitting only a couple of rows away, was convinced that Lump had had a heart attack. Poor Lump came very close to being given the kiss of life by this formidable lady. Yeeuuch! Just in time, he managed to convince her he was all right.

After that little incident the show carried on — worse luck! I gave Lump one of my withering 'Don't you dare do that again' looks, but all he did was smile stupidly back.

At last, it was the end! We clapped wearily. What a relief! It had also stopped raining and the sun was shining. We all rushed out to the village green.

I sat with Sam and Sparky on a bench, tossing stones into the pond.

Suddenly I noticed Old Tom, Ginger, and Mave cycling along towards us. I waved to them, and they stopped.

'Hi,' I said, but before I could get talking to them Ginger interrupted.

'Let's go, Granddad,' he said.

'I think it's better that we go,' Tom said. 'There'll be another time.' And with that they were off down the road.

'What was all that about? Who were they?' Sam asked.

I told Sam and Sparky the little I knew about Old Tom and his grandchildren. I didn't know *why* they'd been in such a hurry, though.

Then I saw the reason. As I looked back to the hall I saw the local policeman wandering round the side of the church, pushing his bike. He just smiled at us and set off up the road — in the opposite direction to Old Tom, Ginger, and Mave.

We got up and went to find out where Doug and the others were. I heard the noise of something coming along the road behind us. Looking over my shoulder I saw an old lorry stop by the village green. Turning round, I could see two people in the cab, but couldn't make out what they looked like.

There was something about the lorry that made

me curious, and I started to walk back towards it. However, before I could get anywhere near, it roared off at speed down the road. I turned back, deep in thought.

Just at that moment there was a screech of brakes. We all ran towards the noise. Tom was lying in the road with Ginger and Mave kneeling over him. Their bikes were scattered round, and the lorry was nowhere to be seen.

'What happened?' I asked breathlessly as we arrived on the scene. Tom was just coming round.

'That stupid lorry came hurtling down here at a stupid speed, and we had to throw ourselves out of the stupid way!' Ginger shouted.

Tom began to struggle to his feet.

'Are you all right?' Mave asked, helping him.

'Yes,' he replied. 'Just winded.'

'I'll go and get the policeman, he can't have gone far on that bike of his,' Sparky said in his usual efficient way.

'No, it's all right, no harm done, no need to get the police, they only make a fuss,' Tom insisted.

Tom, Ginger, and Mave picked up their bikes, and without another word, set off.

Why didn't they call the police? And why were they in such a hurry to get away? Strange!

I looked down the road in the direction the lorry had gone, to see the three cyclists disappearing into the distance.

'There's something fishy going on here!' I said out loud.

'Oh no,' groaned Chip. 'No more adventures, please. Let's just have a quiet holiday.'

6

THE CHURCH STREET CHASERS

'By the way,' Chip continued, taking my mind off the mystery of the crashed bikes, 'what about the races tomorrow. You haven't forgotten, have you?'

I had! The next day was the Tidesbourne annual village sports and we had persuaded Doug to let us enter as a team. We'd show 'em! We'd take on the kids from local villages. After all, we'd been practising for weeks. Doug had said I was taking the whole thing too seriously, but I wasn't having anybody laughing at us and calling us weak townies. We'd spent ages choosing our team's name. I suggested 'Nick's Army' — it had a sort of ring to it, I thought, but I was out-voted! We eventually agreed on 'Church Street Chasers' — Sam's idea — not bad, I suppose. It looked good on our banner. Sam flatly refused to wear a short skirt and prance around as our cheer-leader — I thought she would have looked rather good — but we did think up a great chant:

'Church Street Chasers are the best,
Church Street Chasers'll beat the rest.
Run and race as hard as you might.
We'll still beat you out of sight.'

'You *have* forgotten,' said Chip accusingly.

189

Thankfully Whizzer joined in. 'Yeah,' he interrupted, 'I've been looking forward to it, man. All the practice has made us into finely-tuned machines ready for anything!' He flexed his muscles, then turned and pointed up the road. 'I mean, look at Lump!' he said.

I looked in the direction Whizzer was pointing.

'Grief,' I groaned to everyone. 'What chance do we stand with him? It's not that Lump's fat particularly, he's so dumb with it.'

'That's a bit mean,' cut in Sparky. 'You shouldn't talk about him like that, and he's not so dumb.'

I just looked at Sparky and raised my eyebrows.

'OK,' Sparky went on, 'he may make the odd mistake, but don't we all?'

I hadn't got time to argue, I had to fix my mind on the competition ahead, so we decided to get together the next morning for a final practice.

The practice was absolutely hopeless. This time I was determined not to lose my cool, but only just succeeded. The field where we were camping wasn't exactly right for running, what with long grass and hidden humps and hollows. Added to that, nobody was taking it seriously, and the more I went on, the more daft they became. I thought we should just practise running, catching and jumping but even that seemed too much for them.

Raj and Whizzer kept hiding in the long grass and popping up suddenly making daft noises. Sam and Sparky got a giggling fit and couldn't even stand up! Chip wouldn't concentrate at all, and kept drifting off to play with an electronic game he had brought. Little Mo tried hard, but her legs were so short that she couldn't keep up with the rest of them. And as for Lump — well, what can you say! It wasn't that he was so big, but you would think that a bigger person had more brain cells. Not in this case!

I dreaded to think how we'd do!

It was a lovely day and there was lots to do and watch at the sports. There were sideshows and stalls, and everyone was enjoying themselves so much that I threatened our team with terrible tortures if they didn't turn up on time for the races. I killed time by trying out various side-shows, and won a couple of coconuts, which I passed on to Doug for that night's tea.

As it got close to the start time we made our way to the sports-field. There were six teams in the competition — ours, one from Tidesbourne village, and four from neighbouring villages.

The first event was the egg and spoon race. We had put Chip into it because he was the technical sort. What a mistake! He might be good at pressing buttons and connecting circuits, but asking him simply to balance an egg on a spoon was something else.

He set off all right, but twenty metres down the track he tripped over his own feet and the wooden egg went rolling off in another direction.

'Pick it up, you dimbo, and keep going!' I screamed at him from the side of the track.

Obediently he ferreted around until he found it, replaced it on his spoon, and chased after the rest. Fortunately some of the others had similar difficulties and he managed to finish third. He was pleased. I wasn't.

'A blind bat with a wooden leg could have done better,' I grunted.

'Oh Nick, you're not starting again,' groaned Sparky beside me. Sparky didn't have time to hang about for my response because he was in the next race. He is the niftiest and quickest sack-racer I know, so I was quite confident there would be nobody to beat him. There was a lad from the village who was also in the race, and I heard him telling anyone who would listen about how he would easily win this race.

'Not this time, sunshine,' I said quietly under my breath.

The starter lined them up and I could see the village lad slyly looking across at Sparky. The gun went off and first they had to get into their sacks. It was here that the lad pulled his stunt. While he was getting in he leaned over, pretending to slip, and knocked Sparky over.

'Eh, ref, come on,' I yelled to the starter, but he took no notice.

I began to get worked up, but thankfully Sparky was more cool-headed. He leapt back to his feet and dived into the sack. The others were off down the track, and it was a while before he caught up with them, leaping along like a kangaroo with its tail on fire. There was no way that he could catch the leader, but then pride got the better of Tidesbourne's sack specialist.

What he did was very understandable, but all the same it was very foolish. He made the big mistake of looking round, admiring the cheers of the crowd and seeing just how far he was ahead.

'Arrgghh!' he yelled as his foot caught in the sack and he fell full length, just two metres from the winning tape. Quick as a flash, Sparky was past him, and had won.

Pride really did come before a fall! The lad was so miffed that he threw his sack down and stormed off without even crossing the line to get a point. I would never do a thing like that!

Next came Little Mo in the obstacle race. She couldn't run very fast, but was so nippy through all the hoops and nets that she came in a very honourable third. I was very pleased with my little sister, and didn't even rise to Sam's comments about girls being able to do just as well as boys.

I was dreading the next event. One of the rules was that everybody in a team had to do something. Now it was Lump's turn. We had chosen the potato race, because it was the shortest distance to run. He had to throw three potatoes into a bucket. Surely he couldn't muck that up?

The gun went off and Lump, under pain of death, put everything he'd got into it. He set off down the track like an Olympic sprinter — well, sort of! He lurched to a stop at the first potato, picked it up, and carried on to throw it in the bucket. Then he turned, ran for the second potato, grabbed it, and set off back to the bucket again.

Unfortunately, success went to his head and he turned to wave at the rest of us watching him. This spoilt his concentration and, as he passed the third potato, he trod on it, reducing it to a squidgy pulp. Only he didn't notice.

Triumphantly he threw the second potato in the bucket, then turned to look for the last one. His face dropped as he realized what he had done, saw the 'mashed' potato, and heard the laughter of the spectators. Even I felt a bit sorry for him. He looked confused, then decided to carry on. Much to everyone's amusement he set about picking up the bits of potato. Unfortunately, in doing it, his ample bulk strayed into the next lane, where another lad was coming along.

The effect was like a snooker shot. The lad bounced off Lump and into another racer, who lurched across the path of the guy in the end lane. Lump meanwhile cannoned off, and into the path of the remaining two competitors, who tried to take avoiding action and ran into each other. There were potatoes, buckets, and bodies everywhere.

It was so funny.

I laughed so much I was nearly sick.

The race had to be declared a draw, which was a better result than I had expected, so I was quite pleased.

The last event in the team competition was the relay, and we had to win it to claim the team trophy. We had saved our strongest team: Sam, Whizzer, Raj, and myself. We would win it easily, of that I was sure. In fact, I felt supremely confident. The village teams looked easily beatable and in Raj we had a county standard runner.

It was a complicated race. The first two runners did a hundred metres each, the next runner did two hundred, and the last four hundred.

Sam and Whizzer would take the first two legs,

Raj the third, and me the fourth, which wasn't run in lanes.

At the gun, Sam set off and kept a reasonable position; Whizzer then took over and pulled us into the lead with a fantastic run. Then Raj built up an even bigger lead — until the last twenty metres, when he pulled a muscle. In spite of the pain he struggled on to pass the baton to me. One of the village lads had already warned me to be careful of one of the boys I was racing against. He was called 'Grabber', and was determined to win, however he did it.

As I waited for Raj to reach me with the baton, Grabber pushed me out of the way to get the inside track. After taking the baton I set off in pursuit of the leaders, having fallen back into fourth place. I quickly made up the gap and slotted into second place, behind Grabber. He looked over his shoulder at me and sneered. Along the back straight, away from the crowd, he began to slow down till we were all bunched up tight, but when I tried to get past he speeded up again. What was he playing at?

Suddenly he slowed down again, this time catching me off guard. His foot hit my leg and knocked me off balance, and I fell to the ground. The lad who was third fell in a heap on top of me and we were left to sort ourselves out while Grabber raced away to victory.

I complained loud and long about what happened, but no one would listen. And, to make matters worse, Grabber's team won the cup.

'There ain't no justice,' I growled, and stormed off.

7

LUMP GOES MISSING

I got away from the crowds and sat down grumpily. I started pulling up tufts of grass and thinking of all the nasty things I could do to that swine Grabber.

'Come on, Nick,' said a voice. It was Sparky.

'Shut up,' I replied quickly. 'Don't start lecturing me, and don't give me a sermon.' And I added as an afterthought, 'If you do, I'll punch you on the nose.'

He sat down beside me and never said a word.

Slowly the boiling mood inside me calmed down, and I began to think straighter.

'All right now?' Sparky asked.

I grunted.

'You've done it again, haven't you?' Sparky said.

'What?' I growled.

'Completely lost your head. You always do it, and it never works!'

'Hmm,' I responded. He was right as usual.

Sometimes I could cheerfully strangle him, but I couldn't do without him. Like all real friends, he was always there to help when he was needed, however badly I treated him. And he often had the right thing to say. Not that I always listened straight away!

'Remember what Jesus said about forgiving,' Sparky went on. 'Even people who treat you rotten, like that lad on the track.'

I grudgingly admitted he was right.

It wasn't easy, but I began to feel better. I would try to forgive Grabber, but I still wished he hadn't won the last race.

'Worse thing is, there's no one to stop Grabber in the sprint now Raj is injured,' I grumbled.

We had no answers.

I looked across at the sports field and noticed three familiar figures watching events from outside the fence.

One of the village lads who was walking past noticed them as well.

'It's a pity . . .' he said. 'But he wouldn't.'

'Who are you talking about?' asked Sparky.

'Ginger over there,' he replied, pointing. 'He's the fastest runner I know, but he won't race.'

'Why?' I grunted.

The lad just shrugged his shoulders and walked on.

We just had to win the sprint! Not being able to think of any other idea apart from hitting Grabber, I decided to try persuading Ginger to join us.

'Wait here,' I said to Sparky.

I wandered over to where they were standing, trying to think of what to say.

'Hello,' I greeted them.

Ginger and Mave said nothing.

'Hello,' Old Tom replied. I noticed he was sporting a black eye.

'How'd you get that eye?' I asked.

'Oh, it just happened, must have walked into

the door,' replied Tom.

But at the same time Ginger added, 'Got it when he fell off his bike!'

I looked at them and wondered what on earth they were trying to hide.

'What do you want?' Ginger asked aggressively.

'Oh, someone says you're a very fast runner,' I replied. 'And I wondered if you would like to enter the last race.'

'No,' was all he said in reply.

I guess that would have been the end of it if Grabber himself hadn't come along.

'Nasty eye you got there,' he said to Old Tom, with a wicked grin on his face.

'Why you . . .' Ginger said as he lunged out at Grabber.

Tom pulled him away, but Grabber just laughed and walked off.

Then I had an idea.

Turning to Ginger I said, 'You don't like him, do you?' Not waiting for a reply I carried on, 'Bet you'd like to find some way of beating him! Now, my pal who was to race against him is hurt, but if you entered the last race you could take his place and beat Grabber out of sight.'

'No!' put in Old Tom quickly.

'Yes,' contradicted Ginger, still obviously fuming from Grabber's comments. Before he could be stopped he jumped the fence and followed me over to the others. We fixed it up with the race organizers and then made our way to the start.

Grabber was looking evil.

The gun went off on this last, special 200 metre

sprint for the individual prize. Ginger was off like a rabbit from a trap, and was miles ahead before the rest even got going. He didn't need any protection from me! There was no way anyone could get near him, and he had already finished before the others were halfway down the final straight. He stood with his hands on his hips watching the rest struggle to the finish.

'I'll . . . get . . . you . . . for . . . this . . .' gasped Grabber.

Ginger just turned and walked back to Tom and Mave. He didn't even wait for his prize.

I leaned on the fence, watching them go, and tried to work out what on earth was going on in this village. I hadn't cracked it yet, but supersleuth Nick had never been beaten — yet!

The day after the sports, Doug organized a hike. Before we came away he had made a hike sound great fun, a spectacular adventure.

I should have known better! Grown-ups are brilliant at making things sound fantastic. You know the sort of thing. 'Oh, by the way, Nick, tomorrow we are going to see Uncle Arthur. You won't be bored, he's great fun.' Uncle Arthur is ninety, and can't stand children. Last time we went I took my remote control car to liven things up and he nearly had a heart attack when I drove it between his feet.

Right from the start, things went wrong. The lovely weather of the weekend had changed to a cloudy, misty and very grey day. I had geared myself up in an old, thick sweater, school anorak, old jeans, football socks and trainers. The rest of the gang looked equally bizarre in a strange selection of gear.

Chip looked really miserable. 'I don't want to go,' he moaned. 'I'm cold. If God wanted us to climb mountains, why has he made it so difficult?' All he wanted to do was to play with his computer games.

We hadn't named him Chip because he liked a certain food that goes with salt and vinegar. It was because of his crazy passion for computers. His family came from the West Indies and his dad was a teacher at our school. They encouraged him. As far as I was concerned, computers were only useful for playing occasional games on. The rest left me cold, especially when we did it at school. But for Chip computers were his life — much more exciting than going up one hill and down the other.

'I'm not The Grand Old Duke of York, and don't want to be,' he went on. 'All we'll do when we get to the top is come down again. Waste of time!'

As for Lump — he was whining louder than my dog Wally when he got a thorn in his foot. He wasn't keen at all.

'What are we doing this for anyway?' moaned Lump. 'It's cold. Wouldn't it be better if we left it for another day? Or year?'

'Oh, do stop moaning,' Doug said as he hustled us along through the village. 'You'll enjoy it.'

I goose-stepped behind him and said in a German accent, 'Ve haf vays of making you valk!'

Doug didn't like that.

The others did!

Sam laughed so much she nearly fell in the pond.

'Come on, you lot,' Doug bustled, 'or we'll be late.'

Doug led us to an old house just outside the village. There was a sign outside saying, 'Outdoor Pursuit Centre'. It was run by two men who looked about nine feet high. I decided straight away not to be cheeky to them! I think the others felt the same. They were called Joe and Dougal. Looking across at Sam, I could see her going weak at the knees. Pathetic!

'Gather round,' Joe ordered us, and we dutifully stood and listened. 'Inside,' he went on, 'we have kit for anyone who needs it. We will check out what you have and supply anything extra. I think we should be able to kit all of you up.'

I could see him looking a bit dubiously at Lump.

We were taken inside and shown racks of clothing and boots, and set about getting ready. Sparky pulled on a pair of boots and did an impression of Charlie Chaplin. Then he put on an enormous cagoule and a woollen balaclava hat and did his Donald Duck voice. What a hoot!

Meanwhile Lump was struggling to find suitable gear. If the trousers and cagoules were big enough round the waist, they were far too long. If they were the right length, then everything was too tight. Whizzer suggested a shoehorn or a pot of vaseline. But eventually Lump found something to fit.

We all gathered together at the entrance again. Sam was already there, swooning around the two instructors. Honestly! A few muscles, a stubbly chin, and she breaks into the 'You Tarzan, Me Jane' routine. You know, all fluttering eyelashes and the old, 'Aren't you wonderful' looks.

Sparky looked at my face as we went out. 'Careful, Nick,' he said, with a twinkle in his eye. 'Someone might think you're jealous.'

I trod on his foot hard, and he yelped with pain.

We had only gone a mile or so when it started to drizzle. After another mile the drizzle turned to rain, and then we climbed into the damp and soggy mist.

Lump dragged along at the back, looking totally miserable. I could hear Dougal encouraging then bullying him, trying to keep him up with the rest of us. Poor old Lump, it really wasn't his day.

At last, we reached the top of the peak — to find it wasn't a peak at all. What a con! It was an enormous, smelly peat bog. The mist was very grey, and the ground very black. It looked more like something from a horror movie than the top of a hill in the Peak District.

We stopped for a break and Sparky and I dropped into a gully to share a bar of chocolate.

'You enjoying your holiday?' I asked Sparky.

'If you mean right this minute, not a lot,' replied Sparky. 'If you mean all together, yea, it's cool. What about you?'

''S'alright,' I responded. 'Mind you, some of the things that happen are a bit odd, like disappearing sheep, and people behaving mysteriously.'

'Don't you think you're exaggerating a bit?' he asked.

I ignored this and went on, 'Look at the way

Old Tom is treated. It's not right, it's odd.'

'Mr Staples was saying that Tom and his family had been in trouble with the police before,' Sparky added.

'Your trouble is . . .' I started to reply, getting a bit cross. But I was interrupted.

'Gather round, everybody,' Doug called urgently.

When we looked out from the gully we got a shock. The mist had come down and you could hardly see your hand in front of your face. We clustered together, a grey and bedraggled group of figures.

'Here's another fine mess you got me into,' I muttered at Doug.

'Don't worry,' Doug said with a worried look on his face.

'Right,' Joe said. 'Rather than go on with the weather closing in, we're going to turn back and go straight down the way we came.'

Chip started to sing 'The Grand Old Duke of York' sarcastically, but stopped when he saw Doug's face.

'Listen carefully,' Joe went on. 'I want you to walk in line, staying within sight of the one in front. If you do lose sight, I want you to shout out loud and clear and we will all stop. Don't talk to anybody and lose concentration. If you do as you're told there will be no problems at all. I will go in front and Dougal will be at the back.'

I thought he was going a bit over the top, but he was bigger than me, much bigger, so I didn't argue.

It was wet and misty, really grotty, and nobody

203

looked happy. What a lovely way to spend a holiday! Tired, wet, and fed up, we made our way back to the village.

It was horrible, not knowing where we were going. None of us would admit to being scared, and when we got back we all made a great show of how clever we had been. I guess by the time school started in the autumn the story would sound like the first ascent of Everest, but all we wanted to do at that moment was get out of our wet clothes.

'Er, Doug,' Chip said suddenly. 'Have you noticed anything?'

'What do you mean?'

'Where's Lump?'

Lump was nowhere to be seen. We called and called but there was no response.

Where had that stupid idiot got to now?

8

NICK BLOWS HIS TOP

There are days when Lump drives me right up the wall.

There are days when he just irritates me.

There *are* times — a few — when he is actually useful.

But if ever there was a prize for being a pain in the neck, Lump gets the gold medal!

Joe and Dougal decided to call out the mountain rescue team and, as we stood at the entrance to the Centre waiting for them to arrive, I could only think badly of Lump. I wasn't so much worried about him being lost, just angry at all the inconvenience he was causing.

'I do hope he is all right,' Sparky said.

That made me even more angry, because I knew I ought to feel like that, too.

'He's just a stupid pain,' I replied sharply, angry at both him and myself. Just then a land-rover screeched to a halt and several people got out. It was the mountain rescue team who had been on a training exercise nearby.

Joe turned to us.

'Who was behind him on the way down?' he asked. Timidly, Chip stepped forward.

'I was,' he admitted. 'And Nick was in front of him. But I swear that I never lost sight of Lump in front of me, unless I . . . I . . . er . . . mistook Lump for Nick.'

'You what!' I exploded. 'There's no way I could be mistaken for that fat freak, especially from behind!'

I turned away in disgust.

Doug then turned his attention to Chip.

'Are you *sure* of what you are saying?' he demanded. 'If you had paid more attention, we might not have been in this mess. Honestly, you lot are about as reliable as . . . as . . . my old van!'

If he hadn't been so angry, I would have laughed.

Chip looked crestfallen. 'I can't understand it,' he muttered.

Joe turned to Chip. 'Don't worry,' he said. 'It could happen to anyone. We'll find him all right.' And with that the rescuers, including Joe and Dougal, got into the vehicle and set off in the direction of the hills.

Doug turned again to Chip. 'I'm sorry,' he said. 'I guess I got carried away and didn't think. I shouldn't have gone on at you like that.'

Then to us all he said, 'I think it would be good if we all prayed that Lump will be found safely.'

Every time we get in a pickle, Doug suggests we pray. It's not that I don't believe in God, because I do. It's not even that I don't believe that praying, talking to God, works, because I do — I've seen it work. It's just that it's very embarrassing standing around in public and talking to someone you can't see. People might think you're mad!

However, at Doug's insistence, we asked God

206

to look after Lump and bring him back safely. Then we all set off back to the camp to wait. On the way Sparky walked with me as I grumbled along, kicking a stone.

As we got to the centre of the village, I noticed Ginger and Mave sitting by the village pond looking at the ducks. I wandered over, forgetting Lump for a bit, once more intrigued to find out what was going on.

'Hello again,' I said.

'Huh,' Ginger replied.

Mave looked at me and forced a half-smile.

I had been thinking a lot about how they fitted into the mystery, and why they didn't seem to have any parents, just Old Tom.

'Er, Ginger,' I asked. 'I was wondering. Why haven't we seen your parents about?'

Both Ginger and Mave looked sharply at me.

'What's it got to do with you?' Ginger grunted aggressively. Then, changing the subject, 'What are you doing here anyway? You're supposed to be up there walking or something, aren't you?'

He gestured with his thumb in the direction of the hills, invisible in the thick mist.

'What's the matter?' he added sarcastically. 'Was it too wet for you towny softies?'

I was too cheesed off to rise to the bait, so I told him about the events of the day, and the loss of Lump. Instead of looking concerned, he just burst out laughing.

'What are you laughing at?' I complained angrily.

Ginger and Mave just laughed all the more. I had never seen them happy before. A funny thing to be happy about, I thought.

All Ginger could manage to say was, 'I think you should go to the chip shop.'

Then he and Mave walked off, holding each other up!

I looked at Sparky, who looked back at me, equally confused.

'What do we do now?' I asked.

'Well, what about taking a look at the chip shop?' he replied. 'What have we got to lose?'

It wasn't just curiosity that led me to agree. By now my stomach was ready for food.

The chip shop was at the other end of the village, and, turning the bend in the road, I could see the sign ahead.

Outside was a huddled figure, enjoying what he had bought. It made my mouth water to think of hot chips with lashings of vinegar. My pace speeded up at the thought. As we got nearer, I thought I recognized the eater. It was Lump!

We broke into a run. When we reached him, I grabbed his arm, spinning him round and spraying chips all over the floor.

'What are you doing?' I screamed at him.

He looked startled. 'What's the matter with you?' he protested. 'Look what you've done to my chips!'

I flipped! What with all the trouble he'd caused, and the miserable end to a miserable day, I was ready to carve him into tiny little pieces using the wooden fork he was still clutching. What made matters worse, was that he just stood there, wondering what all the fuss was about.

'Have you seen all those mountain rescue

people rushing about the village?' Lump asked innocently. 'Somebody must have got lost.'

I shot him a look that made him go pale.

'When we got back to the village,' Lump continued, 'everybody spread out and I sort of drifted to the back. I was hungry, so I decided to get some chips before returning to the Centre. Doug's not angry, is he? What's the problem, anyway?'

That was too much!

'What's the problem, what's the problem?' I shrieked. 'There's half the climbers in the north of England out on the hills looking for you, the mountain rescue team have been called out and the police, and probably the army by now, for all we know. And you ask what the problem is?'

Lump backed off nervously, looking shocked.

'Oh dear,' he said, in a pathetic voice.

As I grabbed him by the collar, he cringed.

'Er, don't you think you're going a bit over the top?' Sparky asked from a safe distance.

I grabbed Lump's collar even tighter, and then eased off as I began to calm down a bit.

'I think we all ought to go back to the Centre and sort this out,' Sparky said.

He turned away and began to set off in that direction.

'Well, are you coming or not?' he called over his shoulder.

We followed with different degrees of reluctance, Lump giving me a particularly wide berth.

As we approached the Centre, Doug saw us coming and ran towards us.

'What? . . . Where? . . . How? . . .' was all he

could gasp.

'Never mind that now,' Sparky interrupted. 'Don't you think we ought to get the rescue team back?'

Without answering Doug turned on his heels to go and get everyone recalled and sorted out.

By the time everybody had returned and the whole story had been told, they all agreed it was 'just one of those things' and were simply relieved that no one was hurt.

But not me!

I was still furious.

I was mad with Lump for being so stupid.

I was mad with Doug for getting us into the mess in the first place.

I was mad with Sparky for stopping me thumping Lump.

I was mad with everybody for not being mad.

And I was mad with myself for being mad!

As we walked away from the Centre I could feel myself boiling up inside like a coke bottle which has been shaken up. I blew my top.

'Why have you brought us here, Doug? Is this a prize or a punishment?' I complained. 'Because I've had enough. I'm fed up and want to go home.'

The others all went quiet. Doug grabbed my arm, stopped me, and looked me straight in the eye. 'Everybody else is having a reasonable time, except for the occasional problem,' he said. 'You, as usual, are going right over the top about anything that doesn't go exactly how you like it. Then you start complaining that being a Christian doesn't work. It works for Sparky, doesn't it?'

I didn't say anything but I had to agree.

'It works for me,' Doug went on. 'The trouble is that you want it, like everything else, on your terms. Being a Christian is more than just saying you are one — it has to be worked at like anything else. If you want to be good at football, you have to practise. It's just the same.'

I was flabbergasted. He was right.

He was right, and I didn't like it.

I couldn't think of anything to say, so I ran off towards the camp, feeling like a real wally.

9

GORGEOUS GEORGINA

The next day I got the feeling that everybody was avoiding me so I just lay in my tent feeling sorry for myself.

Suddenly there was a call from outside.

'Go away,' I grumped.

The tent-flap flew open.

'I didn't hear that,' Sam said as she climbed in, followed by Little Mo.

'Hi, big brother,' Mo greeted me cheerfully.

'Get lost,' I replied.

They just kept on talking and ignoring my grumpiness.

'All that business over Lump was really stupid, wasn't it?' Little Mo went on.

I sat up, looked coldly at her, then fell back. 'Why don't they go away?' I thought. But they wouldn't give in.

'We thought you might like to come for a walk,' Sam said.

'No thanks,' I grunted.

'Oh, come on,' Little Mo went on. 'Dad'll be really mad if he thinks you haven't been looking after me, especially when I tell him you wouldn't even take me out for a walk.'

'You rat,' I replied sharply, sitting up. She was using blackmail. I knew there was no way I could get out of it. Grudgingly I gave in.

'All right,' I said, getting up. 'Let's get on with it.'

It was a nice day and as we walked I gradually relaxed, letting my bad feelings go to the back of my mind. There was no one to shout at or push around and it was hard to keep angry.

We were walking along a narrow lane with high walls, which skirted round the edge of Staples farm. We leant on a gate at a gap in the wall and looked across the fields. It was great! Then, about two fields away, I noticed a lorry.

'That's odd. I didn't know Mr Staples had a lorry like that,' I said to Sam. Then we saw some men with big sticks cornering a sheep. It was the sheep thieves!

Before I could work out what to do, one of the men saw us watching them. He pointed in our direction and they quickly left the sheep and ran for the lorry.

I leaped the gate and made off after them, followed by Sam and Mo. Suddenly there was a 'BANG!' and we dived to the ground. I heard the lorry making off, then turned to see Mr Staples standing at the side of the field, a smoking gun in his hands. He didn't look very pleased.

'What on earth are you playing at?' he shouted angrily. 'I nearly caught the blighters. Why did you have to get in the way?'

'Charming,' I replied angrily. 'We didn't know you were there. All we could think about was saving your blinking sheep, and this is all the thanks we get!'

He wasn't in a mood to discuss the point, and Sam, seeing my face and knowing what I was like, interrupted.

'We're ever so sorry, Mr Staples, but honestly we were only trying to help,' she said, and, together with Mo, pushed me towards the gate and back to the road.

I wasn't in the mood to carry on with the walk, so we went back to the camp. It wasn't just that I was angry. I had seen something else that I hadn't told Mr Staples about, and I needed to think.

That moment when I had looked up and seen Mr Staples, I had also seen, further down the road and obscured from him by a hedge, Tom, Ginger and Mave. They had disappeared immediately but I had seen them.

What were they up to?

Were they involved after all?

The next day was an important one on Staples farm. It was the day for sheep-dipping, and we had been invited to go and watch. We were even getting breakfast cooked by Mrs Staples.

In the huge farmhouse kitchen we had as much bacon and eggs as we could handle, sitting round an enormous table. Mr Staples sat at one end behind a newspaper.

'Morning, Mr Staples,' Mo chirped.

'Hmmm,' he grunted in reply from behind the paper. And then to no one in particular, 'I hope everybody's on time.'

Why is it that grown-ups like to communicate in a morning from behind a newspaper? Is it that they can't stand the sight of anybody at that time? Or is it a way of hiding their faces because they look so awful in the morning, before a shave or

214

putting on their make-up? My dad always picks his nose behind his newspaper. Disgusting!

First the sheep were gathered in from the large field they had been put in the day before and put into large pens.

'Where's Frank?' Mr Staples complained. 'He's never around when you want him.'

Before long we saw him coming along the lane, looking very bedraggled. For all his friendliness, there was something about him that I didn't like. But my eyes wandered quickly to somebody else following him down the drive. It was the most beautiful girl I had ever seen, with long blonde hair, and dressed in riding gear.

'Who's that?' I said to nobody in particular.

'Why, bless you, love, it's my niece, Georgina,' Mrs Staples said from behind me. She walked up to the girl to say hello.

After a while, Mrs Staples went in and Georgina wandered over to us.

'Hello,' she said, 'I'm Georgina. Who are you?'

I smiled weakly at her and opened my mouth, but nothing came out.

'He's called Wally,' Mo said, looking hard at me.

'Hello, Wally,' she gushed.

Sam and Mo fell about laughing. I could feel a blush gradually rising up my face, as I turned the colour of a cooked tomato. I couldn't do anything about it.

'No, Georgina,' Sam eventually said. 'That's Mo's joke. He's her brother, Nick.'

'Oh,' replied Georgina blankly.

'Are you here to help with the sheep?' Sam

215

went on.

'No fear,' she responded quickly. 'Dirty smelly things. I much prefer horses. I've just come to pick up some eggs.'

It was a mouth-before-brain situation, and before I knew it my mouth had put me in a situation I was going to regret.

'I prefer horses, too,' I chipped in.

'Can you ride?' Georgina asked innocently.

'Yes,' I continued, as if it was the only word I knew.

'Liar,' muttered Mo under her breath, but loud enough for me to hear.

I wasn't strictly lying. I *had* ridden a horse — once. When it was the police open day I had been given a lesson on a police horse. Well, actually, it was twenty minutes riding round a field with someone leading.

Georgina perked up at my reply.

'Oh lovely,' she said. 'Would you like to come for a ride with me tomorrow?'

'Great,' I replied. Caught!

Then she tripped off to collect the eggs.

'Oh no,' groaned Mo. Sam just looked hostile.

We watched the sheep being guided down a narrow concrete channel filled with liquid. As soon as Georgina reappeared at the door I hoped I looked like a macho farm-worker.

'See you tomorrow then,' she called. 'I live at Valley Farm. You can't miss it. It's about a mile down the lane from here.'

I waved. Whizzer groaned. Sam looked like thunder!

I was so busy looking at Georgina and des-

216

perately trying to think of something to say, that I stepped forward, not noticing the sheep-dip in front of me. I suddenly lost sight of Georgina as I cartwheeled into the dip.

I surfaced among the sheep to see a crowd of laughing faces looking down at me. Did I feel embarrassed! They helped me out and I made a run for it.

After a short while Sam appeared round the corner of the barn. I couldn't look at her.

'I've no sympathy,' she said. 'You've made a complete wally of yourself and I should leave you to rot, but Mr Staples says you should be cleaned up as soon as possible, so just stand still.' Wondering what was going to happen next, I stood dripping against the wall. With a glint in her eye as cold as steel, Sam reappeared round the corner holding a hose in her hands!

Before I could take evasive action someone turned it on, and I was getting my second soaking of the day. This one was even wetter than the first, and Sam was none too gentle about it.

The next day dawned bright and clear. After all the things that had gone wrong, I had real hopes that the day would be a good one! After all, I was going out riding with 'gorgeous Georgina'.

At the back of my mind there was the slight niggle that I really didn't know how to ride a horse — but I could ride a bike, and it didn't look much different. Anyway, the old 'Baker magic' should see me through!

I wasn't getting on too well with the rest of the gang. Everybody seemed to be in a funny mood except me! The rest of the lads had gone wandering off downstream from the camp to play near a bridge that was a great spot for paddling. I didn't know where the girls had gone. I think Doug was asleep in his tent.

I combed my hair and put on some clean jeans and set off down the lane towards Georgina's farm, dreaming of riding along with the wind rushing through my hair, Georgina trying to keep up on her smaller pony, just like an advert on TV.

'PAARRP!!'

The noise shook me awake, and I leaped for the wall by the side of the road as a lorry whooshed past. It wasn't until it had gone that I realized it was the lorry I had seen in the field when Mr Staples fired his gun. And by the time I struggled to my feet, I also realized it was the same lorry that had run down Tom.

'If I was Sherlock Holmes, it would be easy,' I muttered as I dusted myself off and carried on walking.

Suddenly the silence was broken by another unexpected noise.

10

ANOTHER FINE MESS!

'Whiiii, wheeeeew!'

It was Sparky, I'd know that wolf-whistle any-where.

I had reached a bridge over the same stream that ran past our campsite. Looking down I could see Sparky, Whizzer, Raj, Chip, and Lump paddling in the stream.

'Who's a pretty boy, then?' Sparky yelled.

'Going somewhere special?' added Whizzer, sarcastically.

I bent down, picked up the biggest boulder I could find, and lobbed it into the stream beside them. It landed with a terrific 'SPLASH!' and they had no time to get out of the way.

'Ugh!' 'Yuk!' 'Oh no,' they yelped in chorus.

I leaned on the bridge, looked down, and smiled at them.

'You look a bit wet,' I said. 'Has it been raining?'

They started to splash water in my direction, and I ducked for cover.

'Peace!' I yelled from behind the bridge wall, and the barrage of water stopped. I carefully and slowly raised my head to look down, holding a boulder in my hand in case of a double cross.

'OK. Peace,' Sparky replied, looking apprehensively at the boulder in my hand. I put it down and started to climb down to them. Then I noticed Old Tom walking along the path by the stream towards us all.

'Hello, lads,' he said. 'Doing a bit of fishing, are we?'

'Going for a swim more like,' I laughed, pointing out the others' wet clothes.

Whizzer kicked some water in my direction.

'Watch it,' I warned him, jokingly.

'Did you see that lorry go by?' I asked, changing the subject.

'We saw *a* lorry,' Sparky replied.

'That's just it,' I said excitedly. 'I'm sure it belongs to the sheep thieves. But I still couldn't get the number or see who was in the cab.'

'Have *you* seen that lorry before?' I asked Tom.

There was a strange look on Tom's face.

'Look,' he replied, 'I think you should keep away from what's going on.'

'What do you mean?' I responded.

'Never mind,' he continued mysteriously. 'Just enjoy your holiday, go home, and let somebody else sort it out.'

Then, abruptly, he changed the subject.

'Have you caught any fish?' he asked.

'We weren't really trying,' Sparky replied. 'Anyway, we're not quite in your league.'

'What do you mean?' Tom said quickly. 'I gave that game up a long time ago.' He turned to me. 'When I was younger, much younger,' he went on, 'I was a bit of a poacher, but that was a long time ago.'

'How did you catch the fish?' Sparky asked.

'I tickled them,' was Tom's strange reply.

'You're kidding,' Whizzer said, shaking his head.

'No,' Tom said. 'But it wasn't really tickling. One way to do it is to stand in the water with your legs apart and your hands down under the water until the fish swim between. You have to keep very still. Then, when the fish swim over your hands, you lift them quickly, and fling the fish on to the bank.'

The rest of the lads bent down and tried it in the stream.

'Very strange,' muttered Raj.

'It's a funny way of catching tiddlers,' added Sparky.

'I think I'd rather get my fish from the super-market,' Whizzer concluded. 'Sort of tickle it out of the frozen food department!'

'Hey, Grandad,' we suddenly heard.

Up on the bridge Ginger and Mave had arrived.

'Gotta be going,' Tom said. And with that, he climbed up to his grandchildren and was away without so much as a wave.

'Some folk are very strange,' I said, shaking my head. Then, without thinking of the con-sequences, added, 'Gotta be going myself. Got a date.'

'Whe-hey,' they all chorused.

I tried to give them one of my best withering looks.

Walking on, I continued down the lane. It took me round Tom's smallholding — a few fields, a cottage, some outbuildings, and part of the wood. Rounding a bend I almost walked straight into the back of an estate car. The tailgate was open, but nobody was about. A very flashy sports car was parked in front of it.

Then I heard voices coming over the wall from one of Tom's fields. Something stopped me from looking over and I hid behind a bush.

I saw two men appear, hopping over the wall and back into the lane. One man had a kind of tripod that I had seen surveyors carry and he put it in the estate car, slamming the tailgate shut.

The other bloke was a real 'medallion man' type, all flashy clothes and jewellery.

'What do you think?' Medallion Man said.

'Perfect,' the other bloke replied. 'When do we start?'

'I need to do a bit of . . . er . . . negotiating first!' Medallion Man replied.

The other bloke laughed and they got into their separate cars and drove off.

When they had gone I came out from behind the bush. 'What on earth was all that about?' I said to myself, shook my head, and once more set off for my 'date'.

I soon arrived at Georgina's house and I made my way along the drive and round the side of the house to the stables. As I walked along I quickly ran my hands through my hair. Yes, I was still the same handsome hunk I had always been!

By the stables 'gorgeous Georgina' was waiting!

'Sorry I'm a bit late,' I apologized.

'That's all right,' she replied. 'I've really been looking forward to our ride together.'

I blushed. I tried not to, but could feel the colour rising up in my face. It was as if somebody had opened up the top of my head and poured

red dye in.

'I've put you a hard hat out,' she went on. 'I hope it fits.'

I tried it on and wondered why it was necessary. It did nothing for my carefully prepared hairstyle.

'By the way,' she said, 'your sister and her friend are already here. They said you wouldn't mind!'

I groaned! Why couldn't they leave me alone?

'The horses are out in the field already,' Georgina added. 'Shall we go?'

'Lead the way,' I said, trying to sound like John Wayne.

I followed her out, like a lamb to the slaughter.

When we got to the field, Sam and Little Mo were leaning on the gate, waiting.

'Here comes Clint Eastwood,' chirped Little Mo.

I gave her one of my looks. I felt a right wally in that helmet, though.

But when I looked at the horse I was going to ride, I suddenly felt very grateful for that hat. The saddle was a long way off the ground!

Georgina was already on her pony and sat waiting.

The moment of truth had arrived. It was at this point that I began to realize that horse-riding wasn't as easy as it looked on TV. But there was no turning back now.

Having watched my fair share of cowboy films I knew what I had to do, vaguely. I got hold of the reins with my left hand, put my left foot in the stirrup, grabbed the saddle, and hopped up. Now, that horse had seemed to be a very well-behaved, friendly sort. He hadn't moved a muscle so far. Until that moment! Just as I hopped, the brute took a careful, measured step forward, knocking me off balance and landing me with perfect aim in the only patch of mud for yards. I swear it looked round and smirked at me. It was just then that I decided I didn't like horses. There I lay, in my best gear, covered in mud, right in front of Little Mo, Sam and, worst of all, Georgina.

Sam and Mo buried their mouths in their sleeves, but I could see their eyes watering.

'I think you missed,' Sam's muffled voice spoke from behind her sleeve.

'Sorry,' Georgina said very apologetically, 'I should have warned you. Dad's horse can be a bit awkward sometimes, but you assured me you were a very experienced rider, so I didn't bother.'

I struggled to my feet and tried to repair my somewhat battered image.

No way was this horse going to beat me. I grabbed the reins and hopped up very quickly this time, before it had time to think of another devious way to land me in the dirt. Gingerly I sat up straight, then smirked down at Sam and my sister.

'Great,' Georgina said. 'Shall we try once round the field to get used to things?'

'OK,' I replied. 'Lead the way.'

She set off at a gentle trot.

'Right,' I said to myself, 'now to get this thing started.'

In the movies I had seen cowboys get their horses going by a sharp dig in the ribs with the heels. Seemed as good a way as any!

I smiled down at Sam, stuck my tongue out at

Mo, and dug hard with my heels.

The effect was electric! The horse bucked furiously, then galloped away.

I passed Georgina at speed, who looked on in amazement, her wave frozen in mid-air. The horse was snorting and bucking. All I could do was hang on tight to the reins. At that point I lost sight of the others.

We were coming to the end of the field. Now, although you see a lot of horses stopping and starting in films, you very rarely see them turning corners. At this point I couldn't remember ever seeing *anybody* turn a corner on a horse.

It was a split-second decision. I decided to let the horse choose which way to go. He chose to leave the field, which meant jumping the fence! I decided to hang on as tight as I could and firmly shut my eyes. I shall never know how we both managed to clear that fence.

When I opened my eyes again I had lost all sense of direction. All I knew was that I was still on top of this mad beast and trees were rushing past me at an alarming speed.

I desperately tried to think how to stop. How did you put on the brakes? It seemed logical to try pulling on the reins, but how hard? In the movies they pulled very hard. I was getting really fed up with this stupid horse, so it was time for decisive action. I grabbed hard on the reins and pulled!

Well, the horse stopped. Boy, was it fitted with good brakes! Only trouble was, the horse stopped quicker than I did. Suddenly I was sailing gracefully through the air.

Another fine mess I'd got myself in to!

11

NICK DOES IT AGAIN!

Flying is best done in an aeroplane. After leaving the horse behind, I was hoping for a soft landing. I got it!

That horse was a brilliant shot. He catapulted me with great precision, right into an enormous pile of cow-muck. I sat up and looked around to see Georgina approaching. She passed me without a glance and went to gather up the reins of her father's horse. She seemed more worried about him than me! After a short time she came back with it in tow.

'Are you all right?' she asked coldly.

I nodded.

'You were lying,' she continued. 'That'll teach me to trust boys! You could have really hurt yourself — and what's more, you could have seriously damaged the horse!'

I smiled weakly at her, but she just turned and walked away back to her own horse.

Up ran Sam and Mo.

'Are you OK?' Sam asked.

'I think so,' I replied, trying to sound fragile.

Little Mo just stood looking scornful as I removed the helmet and shook my head.

'I think — er — you'd better take this back. I don't think I'm exactly flavour of the month with

Georgina.'

'Liars get found out in the end, don't they?' Mo said, rather unkindly, I thought, as she took the helmet.

'Anyway,' Sam went on, 'with the smell you're giving off, you're nobody's flavour of the month.' Then, turning to Mo, she said, 'Come on, let's go.'

They turned and left. I just sat there.

I staggered to my feet and began to clean myself up using a handkerchief and some big dock leaves. But, although I managed to get most of the gunge off, I couldn't get rid of that persistent, long-remembered, stomach-churning smell.

Grimly I looked around for some recognizable landmark to show me the way home. In the end, I just wandered down the path in the direction the girls had taken, hoping that I would find a way that didn't take me past Valley Farm!

I soon heard the sound of a car and saw a road the other side of the next field. There didn't seem much point in worrying about my gear now, so I climbed over a wall, across the next field and over the next wall, to find myself back on the road to the campsite.

I set off gloomily towards the camp. It wasn't long before I was back at the bend before the bridge where Sparky and the rest were playing. I stopped to think.

My — er — unfortunate disagreement with the horse was bound to get out eventually, but just at that moment I couldn't face the teasing. How was I going to get past the stream without being seen?

I could hear the lads making a lot of noise

227

as they mucked around, so I crept forward cautiously. I could see the low wall of the bridge. Now, if I crouched down and crawled along on my hands and knees, they just might not see me. First I looked through the trees to see where they were. I could see some figures happily messing about throwing stones in the water. Now was my chance!

Crawling along, I was just thinking to myself that I would make a great recruit for a spy film, 003½ perhaps, when . . .

'Hey, Nick, why are you crawling along on your hands and knees? Have you lost something?' It was a voice I instantly recognized. Lump!

My heart sank!

I turned my head, and there he was, sitting up against a tree, stuffing himself with crisps. I put my finger to my lips to tell him to be quiet, but, as usual, he misunderstood — the wally!

'You want one?' Lump said. He struggled to his feet and came over, holding out the packet.

Suddenly he stopped. With a noise that could have been heard the other side of Glasgow he cried, 'PHEW!' and gripped his nose as if it were about to fall off.

'What a pong!' he spluttered through his hand.

Before I had time to move, the others joined us.

'Hey, Nick,' Sparky said, surprised, 'what are you doing?'

'Oh er . . .' I replied lamely. 'I'm er . . . I er . . . dropped something.'

Quick as a flash, Sparky and the others were by my side, keen to help.

'What have you lost, man?' Whizzer asked.

Then suddenly, 'PHEW!' Chip said, stepping back, as did the others, holding their noses.

'What have you done?' Sparky said, then they all burst out laughing.

'All right, all right,' I said. 'Look, I slipped in some muck, OK?'

I wasn't going to tell them exactly what happened. They'd find that out soon enough from Sam and Little Mo, my big-mouth sister.

'What happened to the horse ride?' Whizzer asked innocently.

'Look,' I went on, ignoring the awkward question, 'I've got to get myself cleaned up. I haven't got time to stand here talking to you lot!'

'But what about whatever it was that you lost?' Sparky asked, with a curious look on his face.

I groaned inside. Like all lies, you have to keep on lying to make the story work, and gradually get into deeper and deeper water.

'Yes,' I replied, trying to look worried and desperately trying to think quickly. 'It was my watch. I must have lost it when I came past before and threw that rock at you.'

It was a bit weak, but the best I could do in an emergency. With great energy, like true friends, they immediately began searching all around. I thought I had escaped.

I was just about to say that I must have lost it somewhere else when Sparky sat bolt upright.

'Just a minute,' he suddenly said. 'I went with you to town a few days before we came on holiday to take your watch to be repaired. You never brought it with you!'

Quick as a flash, before anybody had time to

229

add two and two together and make even more than four, I replied, 'Oh, so did I, how silly of me. Still, that's all solved, so I can go off and clean up now.'

I didn't dare to look at Sparky's face as I turned and made off in the direction of the camp, but I could easily imagine his expression. I could feel his eyes piercing the back of my head as he tried to work out why I had lied, and what it was all about.

My ears burned so much you could have used them to light a fire. As I walked I began to grumble to myself about everything and anything, talking myself in to a mood. I thought about all sorts of horrible things that ought to happen to various people, friends and enemies alike. I also told the trees about how horrible the holiday was and what a vile place Tidesbourne was. What made me feel worse was the fact that everybody else was having a great time. It just wasn't fair!

That old Baker temper was surfacing again!

My mum always said I took after my dad in that. My dad always reckoned I took after my mum. I knew it came from plain old selfish me, but at the moment I didn't want to think about that.

In a grim mood, sunk in gloom, I wandered back till I reached Staples farm.

But my mood soon left me when I saw there was a car outside the farmhouse — a police car. What was up? I ran over, curiosity making me forget everything else.

By the car stood Mr Staples, very angry, with arms waving. Frank and Bill stood alongside and a very patient policeman, his notebook open, was taking notes and nodding his head. He did remind me of my dad, who was a policeman as well.

Nobody noticed me, until I got near. The smell got to them before I did. I could see their noses twitching as they turned to stare at me. Bill came over to me while the others carried on talking.

'Phew, Nick,' he complained, holding his nose. This was getting monotonous. 'You don't half pong,' he continued. 'What have you been doing?'

I had neither the time, nor did I want to tell him what had really happened.

'Never mind,' I said sharply. 'What's going on here?'

'Some sheep gone again,' he replied.

I turned to the others and listened.

'I'm really fed up with all this,' Mr Staples said angrily. 'When are you going to do something about it, that's what I want to know?'

'Look, Mr Staples,' the constable replied, 'I'll make a report and we'll keep a careful look-out. Sooner or later we're bound to catch them.'

'Later is what I'm worried about,' Mr Staples snapped back. 'I'll have no sheep left by then!'

The policeman ignored Mr Staples' anger and carried on writing.

'Now, did anyone see anything suspicious?' he asked generally.

'Well, I saw Old Tom hanging about,' Frank said.

I really didn't like that guy, he was too sly, and I wasn't going to let him get Tom into trouble.

'Just a minute,' I said, stepping forward and

butting in.

Everyone took a step back as I came towards them.

'I saw Old Tom earlier, by the stream, nowhere near here,' I added.

Frank looked hard at me, then asked, 'Which direction was he coming from?'

I knew what he was getting at and didn't want to answer. He was a bit too keen to get Tom into trouble for my liking. The stream passes through Staples farm before it flows by the bridge where the gang were playing, then it goes by Tom's smallholding, then round Valley farm.

Eventually, after a long silence, I admitted, 'Downstream,' trying to make it sound unimportant.

'That proves it,' jumped in Mr Staples. 'I knew that old rogue was involved.'

He turned to the constable. 'What are you going to do about it? Go and arrest the man.'

'All it proves,' replied the policeman patiently, 'is that Tom was near the farm around the time that the sheep went missing. If I arrested everybody who was near here at the time, my little lock-up would be full ten times over. You leave it to me, Mr Staples. I'll have a word with Tom in the next few days. In the meantime, don't worry, we're bound to catch them soon.'

'Bah!' grunted Mr Staples, and stormed into the house. The policeman got into his car and drove off.

'Cor, you really do niff,' Bill said at my side. 'Why don't you go and have a bath or something?'

'Later,' I replied sharply, gave a hard look at

232

Frank, and turned on my heels. I was determined to find Old Tom and tell him about the policeman.

I ran all the way back to Tom's cottage, not even stopping to talk to the gang who were still at the bridge. The cottage was off the main road, down a long, dark, overgrown lane, all on its own.

I knocked on the door.

No answer.

I knocked again.

Still no answer, but I heard a scuffle from inside.

Something was wrong. What had I walked into?

Suddenly the door opened — just a crack!

12

THE SLIPPERY SNAKE

A voice spoke sharply from behind the door.

'What do you want?' it grunted.

It was Ginger.

'Can I talk to your grandad?' I asked.

'Why?' he replied. 'We don't like nosy parkers.'

'I've got something important to tell him,' I went on.

There was silence. After a while the door opened and Tom put his head round.

'Hello, Nick,' he said. 'What do you want?'

'I came to warn you that some more sheep have been taken from Staples farm. The police were called, and everybody's blaming you.'

'Tell me something new,' Tom laughed. 'But thanks for coming round to tell me.'

There was a long silence as we stood looking at each other.

Then Tom opened the door some more.

'Come on in,' he said.

I was about to step in when I suddenly thought and stopped.

'I pong a bit,' I said. Then, before they got the wrong idea, added, 'I fell in a pile of muck.'

'That won't bother us,' Tom said kindly. 'A bit of muck won't make any difference.'

What I saw when I got inside took my breath

away.

It looked as if a bomb had gone off. There were books, pots, and furniture thrown about all over the place. Ginger and Mave were trying to put things straight.

'What on earth happened here?' I asked, looking around.

'Let's just say we had some visitors who wanted to tell me something!' Tom said mysteriously. Then he put a hand on each of my shoulders and looked me in the eye.

'Now, Nick, I want you to listen very carefully,' he went on. 'I don't want you to ask any more questions about what has happened.'

'But why?' I interrupted.

'Never mind. No more questions, and I don't want you to tell anybody — *anybody* — about what you have seen. Is that clear?' he added.

'OK,' I said doubtfully. I didn't think it was right, but, at that moment I couldn't think of anything else to say. He was a friend, and if that was what he wanted . . .

I set to work helping them to tidy up, trying to put the mystery together in my mind. There were lots of interesting things in the cottage, and every so often Tom would stop to tell me about a particular photograph I had found, or the history of a piece of furniture.

I was desperate to ask questions, but Tom just kept changing the subject. When I left I was no wiser. I was even more puzzled about what was going on. What was Old Tom trying to hide?

One of the highlights of our holiday had been

planned for the next day, and I'd been looking forward to it ever since Doug said he would take us. About twenty miles from the village was the biggest theme park in the country, called 'Beacon Manor', and we were going there for the day. It was one day none of the gang was going to miss. I woke up that morning feeling really excited.

But even as we stood around waiting for Doug to bring the van along, I had a feeling it wasn't going to be my day. Instead of being her usual chatty self, Sam turned her back on me. Over the years we had often fallen out, but we had always made it up before. This time I had really blown it! Nobody seemed that keen on me, but the way Sam was treating me was the worst. She was madder than I had ever seen her.

The journey to the park was as uneventful as any ride could be in that awful boneshaker of a van, but we made it — just! Even though we had set off early, there was still an enormous queue to get in, and then it took ages to find a place in the enormous car park. Through the trees we could see the bright colours of the rides, and the excitement began to fizz up in my stomach. This would be something to boast about next term at school!

We got out of the van and stretched our legs.

'Wow, man. Fantastic,' Whizzer said as he switched off his Walkman. 'What a place, what a place!'

Raj, who rarely said anything, just looked around with his mouth open.

Everybody was looking round, pointing things out to each other. Back home we had talked about how many times we would go on the famous loop-the-loop roller-coaster we had seen on TV, called the 'Slippery Snake'. Seeing it through the trees and hearing the screams and rattling of the cars, some doubts began to creep into our minds. Now we would see who was just talk!

Me — I was ready for anything. It would be a good time to show everybody how tough I was and win back a bit of respect!

I turned to Sam, putting on my best 'macho' manner.

'Come on, Sam, let me take you on the "Pirate Ship". I'll look after you,' I said.

If looks could kill, I would have died on the spot.

'Why don't you go and ride the horses on the merry-go-round, or are you afraid you might fall off?' she replied. Then she turned to Mo. 'Come on, Mo, let's go on the "Pirate Ship", I don't like creeps.'

The rest of the gang fell about laughing.

My heart turned to stone. My jaw dropped so far open it must have nearly reached the ground!

Still laughing, Raj and Whizzer headed off for their first go on the 'Slippery Snake'. Lump waddled off in the direction of a hot dog stall, and Chip made for the electronic games.

I just stood there.

'What about a go on the log flume?' Sparky asked me.

I exploded. 'I can do without your goody-goody sympathy,' I snarled at him. 'Push off and leave me alone.'

Without waiting for a response I turned on my heels and stormed off. Unfortunately, the way I had chosen to go was past the 'Pirate Ship', which was swinging high into the air with its load of screaming passengers. I could clearly see — and hear — Sam and Mo screaming with pleasure.

'I'm not interested in girlfriends, but she shouldn't treat me like that,' I said to myself. I must have said it rather loudly because I got some strange looks from people walking past. That made me feel embarrassed as well as angry. I strode off quickly, seeing a lake ahead with some boats. Fortunately there was no queue, so I paid, stepped into one and rowed furiously out into the lake.

There I could drift into my dreamworld where *I* was in charge, everybody agreed with me, and did exactly as I said.

Reaching the middle of the lake, I pulled in the oars and lay back in the boat, staring up at the sky. Around me all was peaceful, except for the distant squeals coming from the rides, and all I could see was the white clouds drifting across. Boy, was I fed up!

Suddenly, the boat lurched as something hit the side, and there, looking down at me, was Doug.

'What do you want?' I growled. 'I don't want to hear any sermons.'

'Are you all right?' he asked, ignoring my nastiness. 'I was — er — just rowing past and — er — thought I might stop for a chat.'

I glared up at him with a 'Who are you kidding?' look, but I was quite happy to see him really.

I was famous for my 'I want to be alone' trick. 'King of the sulks', my mum said, but I never quite knew what to do with myself after I had stamped off!

'You are a bit of a wally, aren't you?' Doug said.

I just looked at him. What could I say? He was right!

He and Sparky were the best friends I had, and they stuck with me whatever I was like. I suppose that's what being a real friend is. If I were Doug, I would have walked away from me and left me to rot — if you see what I mean! But Doug never did.

'Any mess you get in is usually your own doing, you know,' he went on. 'Then you expect your friends to forgive and forget — when you don't even do it yourself.'

He didn't have to remind me about that again, I knew all too well. I knew that I had to do something about it, too. I just didn't want to!

But I still didn't answer.

'A suggestion,' he continued. 'To begin with, how about swallowing your pride and saying sorry to Sam for the way you treated her? You might then try and think about letting your friends be the kind of pals *they* want to be, instead of how *you* want them to be.'

He didn't say anything else, but rowed off, leaving me to think about what he'd said. The battle was on — would I be able to swallow my pride and apologize?

I wasn't very good at it, but not many people are. It's dead easy when you're at fault to think of all the things wrong with everybody else and forget your own mistakes.

I sat up, flicking the water with my fingers,

remembering my pals, and all the things we had done together. I remembered a lot of the scrapes I had got into and all the times Sparky and the rest had been on hand to rescue me. For some daft reason I remembered the time when we were little and I got my head stuck in the park railings. Sparky and Sam between them kept me calm, just, while the fire engines came. I laughed to myself.

And then I thought back to last year. When Sparky said he was a Christian, I thought that would be the finish between us. But it wasn't. He became an even better friend, in spite of me!

What should I do? I wasn't going to enjoy it, but I had to make things up with Sam for a start.

I pulled myself together and rowed slowly back to the boathouse area, trying to think of the best way to apologize. Whatever I thought of, it sounded really stupid. I guess any apology sounds stupid to the one doing the apologizing.

First, I had to find her.

There she was, queuing for the 'Parachute Jump' with Mo. I didn't know whether to wait, or get on with it. But, figuring I might chicken out if I waited, I decided now was the time.

Marching up to them in the queue I could see that they hadn't noticed me. Sam didn't seem very happy, sort of bored and cross!

I tapped Sam on the shoulder, and she turned and looked at me blankly.

Words failed me. My mouth opened and shut but nothing came out.

'Yes?' she said coldly. 'What do you want?'

'Er — I — er,' I stuttered. 'Can we talk?'

'Go ahead,' she responded. 'I'm all ears.'

'Not here,' I said defensively.

'If you think I'm going to lose my place in the queue for you,' she went on, 'you've got another think coming.'

A large man behind them suddenly grabbed my shoulder.

''Ere,' he said, 'we'll 'ave no queue jumpin'. You get to the back.'

He was too big to argue with. I had to get on with it.

This was awful!

13

NICK & CO. ON THE TRAIL

I turned to Sam.

'Look,' I blurted out. 'I want to say, I'm sorry for the way I treated you.'

Sam looked at me.

'I treated you badly, sorry,' I went on.

'Are you going to move?' the man behind me said. 'Or will I have to move you?'

I grabbed Sam's hand and pulled her out of the queue.

'I think I'll go and find Doug,' Mo said, smiling. What a great sister!

Sam and I stood looking at each other. Eventually she spoke.

'You ever do that again, and I'll kill you,' she said.

'What about a go on the "Slippery Snake"?' I asked. She nodded. We sat off in that direction.

It wasn't until I heard loud whistles and shouts from above that I realized I was still holding Sam's hand. It was Sparky, Whizzer and Raj up in the cable car above us, pointing and making a lot of noise.

I quickly drew away my hand and shoved it in my pocket. Sam looked at me and burst out laughing.

'You are daft,' she said. 'Come on, let's get in

the queue.'

We spent the rest of the day very happily on the white-knuckle rides. We all had a great time, and even got Doug to go on them. I wasn't sure if it was the sort of thing vicars ought to do, but he said it was quite all right.

In the middle of the afternoon we had a big meal in a café, where Lump in particular packed away a huge lunch. I didn't do too badly, either!

Then after lunch it was back on the rides — the gentler ones to start off with. I didn't fancy seeing my lunch return. At the end of the day we had to have one last go on the 'Slippery Snake'. We even got Lump to go on it. He had been avoiding it all day. It was a great machine, with twists and turns, and a loop-the-loop that sent your stomach up to your throat and down to your boots in turn.

We had thought that was the perfect end to the day. Then Doug, who was pleased to see us all happy, bought us all waffles, piled high with everything sweet and sickly you could think of. Lump had looked a bit green when he came off the 'Snake', but he could never resist food . . . which would have been fine, except Sparky suggested one quick last go on the 'Pirate Ship'.

We all thought it was a great idea and dragged Lump along as well. He was *very* reluctant, but before he had time to argue we were all on, and the swaying had begun. Higher and higher we climbed, and as the screams got louder, Lump's face got greener. That lovely feeling at the top of the swing when you leave your stomach behind must have been agony. I took a look at him. I didn't think he would get off without 'unloading the dumptruck', so to speak.

He might have been reluctant to get on, but he was *very* quick to get off, rushing for some nearby bushes. When he had recovered we set off home in the van, although nobody wanted to sit next to our green-faced friend. We actually got nearly home before Lump yelled for us to stop, and dashed into some trees to be sick. I recognized the place — it was near where we stopped on the way to Tidesbourne with the puncture.

We all got out and were standing around waiting, when Sparky caught my arm and pointed down the road. In the distance we could see that lorry again — I was sure it was the same one! We hadn't told Doug about all the things we had seen, and he couldn't understand when we tried to get everybody back in the van and go in pursuit.

By the time Lump had sorted himself out and we had set off, there was no sign of the lorry. It must have disappeared into thin air.

Suddenly there was a 'PAARRP', and Doug gripped the wheel tightly in surprise.

We dived to the back window and looked out. Trying to get past us was a great, flashy, open car with two people in it. It wasn't just the driver that I recognized, but the passenger as well. It was Grabber! Medallion Man was driving, in the car that I had seen on the way to Georgina's!

We waved our fists at them and the driver blew on the horn and squeezed up against the van with his car. The road was very narrow, but that didn't stop him, and Doug had to take avoiding action. We lurched along with two wheels on the verge and Doug slewed the van to a halt.

Poor Lump had to leap out to be sick again with all the jolting about we had taken.

The car didn't stop, but drove on at speed, its horn blaring.

'What a stupid driver!' Doug said.

Sparky and I just looked at each other!

It was a lovely day for our last Sunday in Tidesbourne. We were taking part in the morning service at the church, by doing some drama. Doug's fancy clothes, which vicars wear for such occasions, looked whiter than white. You could have used him for a washing powder advert.

We were going to act out two scenes from the Bible about the life of one of Jesus' close friends, called Peter. And I was playing the part of Peter.

Before we started rehearsing Doug said that he couldn't think of anybody better to play the part. I *think* it was because I am good at acting, but Sparky's laugh made me wonder! *And* Doug's answering smile.

The first scene was the one where Jesus was in the garden of Gethsemane and the men came to arrest him. Sparky was playing Jesus and Whizzer played the soldier who got his ear cut off when Peter tried to stop them. That was good — except that I nearly *did* take Whizzer's ear off with the wooden sword. It was a good job I didn't manage it because, good as Sparky was, I don't think he'd have been able to put it back on for real, like Jesus did!

The second scene was when Peter denied he knew Jesus three times, after Jesus had been arrested — and then the cock crowed, just as

Jesus had told Peter it would. That went well, except for Raj getting too carried away. He was doing the crowing of the cockerel from the back of the church, and nearly gave the old ladies heart attacks, he was so loud and unexpected!

I really liked Peter. When he first knew Jesus he was always opening his mouth and putting his foot in it. But Jesus stuck with him, kept forgiving him and helping him, and eventually Peter became the leader of all the Christians at the time.

Doug talked for a bit at the end of the drama, about how Peter started off being a bit of a loud-mouthed aggressive sort of a guy, and then learned through Jesus about how that wasn't the best way of going about things. I felt as if Doug was looking straight at me all the time he was saying this. But I didn't care! I reckoned that if Peter could survive all that and finish up the way he did, so could I. And I knew that Jesus wouldn't give up on me.

After the service we stood outside and shook people's hands, which was all right, except for the sweaty ones! Some of the old people looked at me a bit strangely and said things like, 'Very nice!' and 'How interesting!'

I wandered off on my own to go back to the camp. As I walked down the lane, I thought about what Doug had been saying, and tried to sort out in my mind all the things that had happened since arriving in Tidesbourne.

It's dead easy to lose your cool and crash about like Peter did. But in the end, Peter had to stop behaving like that. It was a bit like me really. I guess in the end I had to do what Doug was always going on about — to calm down and not be ashamed to ask for God's help. Talking to God wasn't that hard really. It was only embarrassing if you didn't really believe it worked. So, quietly, on my own, I asked God to forgive me for being so stupid — and to help me change.

Before I knew it I had arrived at the bridge where the gang liked to mess around, but there was no fun going on there this time. As I got nearer I could hear voices. Now, it's not that I'm nosy but, just like most people would, I found myself walking very quietly, trying to pick up some of the conversation.

What's more, I noticed, further on, that sports car that had nearly made us have an accident in the van. Now I was really curious!

Quietly, I raised my head over the parapet of the bridge and looked down. Below me, and leaning against the stonework of the bridge, was Ginger. Facing him, and stopping him from getting away, was that grotty pig, Grabber and the man from the car — Medallion Man.

They were both having a real go at Ginger. I couldn't pick up exactly what they were going on about but I saw enough to know that Ginger was in trouble.

'Just tell that grandfather of yours to do as he's told and keep his mouth shut, or it won't just be your dad that gets dealt with,' I heard Medallion Man say.

There was a lot of prodding and pushing going on. I had to do something to help, but what? I didn't want to get caught myself. Looking round,

I saw a large stone lying by the road, and remembering the effect it had on my pals the other day, I picked it up, aimed carefully and threw it down alongside Grabber.

It had the desired effect.

'Run for it,' I yelled at Ginger, and he didn't need telling twice. He was off down the path like a scalded rabbit. Medallion Man was too worried about his gear to think about chasing, but Grabber clambered up the bank after me.

I made off down the lane as fast as I could, hoping to get far enough ahead not to be caught. Grabber chased me for a bit, but eventually gave up. I stopped running and turned round. We looked at each other from some distance apart on the road.

He pointed his finger at me. 'You stay out of this,' he threatened. 'Or you'll regret it.'

I put my hand to my nose and waved a very rude goodbye before running off in the direction of Staples farm.

At the farm I was in for another surprise. In the yard was the estate car that I had seen with the surveying gear in it. The man who had been nosing about Tom's fields was talking to Mr Staples. I waited for the man to leave then went over to Mr Staples.

'What do you want?' he asked suspiciously.

'I was wondering what that man was doing,' I replied.

He sighed heavily. 'Don't you ever mind your own business?' he grumbled.

There wasn't a lot I could say to that, so I just stood there twiddling a bit of straw, figuring he would either tell me eventually or tell me to push off.

'I called him in to work out how to pull up my part of the wood and what to do with the land. He's an estate agent,' he said eventually.

Then, before I could start arguing with him about the wood, he carried on. 'While he was here he also offered to buy the whole farm,' he continued. 'A very generous offer.'

'But you can't sell,' I replied.

'Why not?' asked Mr Staples. 'If I wait much longer I'll be out of business anyway!'

I wanted to talk to him, to tell him about the things I had found out, but he just walked away sadly. I don't think he would have believed me anyway. But I had to do something.

In the evening we all went for a walk into the village. We stopped and sat down by the pond. Doug was going off to see his mum and dad, and had threatened us with various tortures like extra washing-up, if we got into any bother. As usual Lump got into bother chasing food. He had some sandwiches in his pocket and Whizzer did the unforgivable. He sneaked the sandwiches out of Lump's pocket and launched them out into the middle of the village pond on a piece of wood. You should have seen Lump's face when he saw his precious food sailing into the distance. He went berserk! He ran up and down the edge of the pond like a wild man, screaming abuse at Whizzer.

'You pig, Whizzer, you swine,' he shouted.

He was uncontrollable, getting redder and redder in the face. There was no way he would give up the idea of getting his snack back, but he had some competitors who also had their eyes on the goodies. The ducks on the pond had taken note of the free lunch sailing out into the middle of their own particular dining area and, never ones to refuse a hand-out, were making a beeline for Lump's sandwiches.

Lump now diverted his anger away from Whizzer and towards the ducks.

'Go away, you stupid ducks,' he screamed. 'They are *my* sandwiches.'

At the same time he jumped up and down in anger. I kept wondering what the odds were on him starting an earthquake!

The ducks took no notice, so Lump took drastic action. Without thinking of the consequences he leapt out into the pond, fully clothed!

He beat the ducks to the sandwiches by a short head. They obviously thought he was some sort of large duck trespassing on their territory and his return from the centre of the pond was even quicker than the outward journey, the ducks in hot pursuit!

Lump had the sandwiches, very wet trousers, and filthy shoes!

When I had stopped laughing, I felt really sorry for him, and, much to the amazement of the rest of the gang, lent him my sweater because he was looking a bit cold.

We had decided that while Doug wasn't about we would have a look around to see if we could find out some more about what was going on. Mr and Mrs Staples were out as well so it seemed an ideal time. Sparky wasn't that keen, but I convinced him that we wouldn't do anything illegal.

Also, Sam threatened to throw her brother in the pond if he didn't shut up!

We split up into small groups to cover the area around Staples farm, where most of the sheep had been stolen from.

Chip, as the technical expert, had thought up a system of communication using different numbers and types of yells. It all sounded good when he explained it, but I had my doubts. Still, we could only try!

'OK, gang, split up and let's see what we can find,' I told them. Then added, 'And if all else fails, just yell anything as loud as you can!'

I hoped that this general nosing around would lead to something.

As usual, we got more than we bargained for!

14

EVIDENCE

We split up in pairs and went off in different directions. Before long, I was sure, Nick and Co. would be hot on the trail. Someone was bound to come up with a good clue, or see something suspicious.

I set off with Sparky. We were heading towards the back of the wood where I first met Old Tom. It was a lovely evening and there were birds singing in the trees.

'Great, isn't it?' I said to Sparky.

'Yes, smashing,' he replied. 'But you've changed your tune,' he added. I was about to start telling him about why I felt different when something happened.

The trouble with the countryside is that the animals, in this case cows, have a nasty habit of leaving what my little sister Mo calls 'country pancakes' all over the place. Once again I found myself magnetically drawn to things that didn't smell nice! Before I knew what was happening I slipped in some muck and landed flat on my back, looking up into Sparky's laughing face.

'I'd better not say anything, had I?' he said, smirking down at me.

'You'd better not!' I replied.

I got back on my feet and cleaned up the

damage. I was getting good at this!

Suddenly I heard a shout and Sam came rushing towards me, closely followed by Mo. She was pointing towards a hilltop at the other end of the farm, in the direction that Lump and Chip had gone.

We all hurtled off in that direction, clearing gates and stiles like Olympic athletes, and diving through hedges with no thought for the scratches. On the way we picked up Raj and Whizzer who had also heard the shout.

I reached the hilltop first, completely breathless, to be met by Lump and Chip, looking confused and upset. Yes, they'd done it again!

Lump had been startled by a sheep and barged into Chip, who had bounced off into a patch of nettles. The effect of a sudden stinging sensation in the rear caused Chip to scream. He wasn't amused when we asked him why he hadn't used the correct coded shout for a nettle sting in the backside!

We all spread out again and carried on searching. Sparky and I walked back across the farm, this time a bit more slowly.

We started to look around in the wood. Then Sparky grabbed my arm.

'Not Lump again,' I groaned.

'No,' Sparky replied. 'Didn't you hear it?'

I listened. He was right. From the area where Whizzer and Raj had gone there was a clear shout. Two steady shouts, which meant, 'Come quick, we've found something.' Once again we rushed towards the shout.

Whizzer was waiting for us by a wall.

'Over here,' he yelled.

We followed him round the back of the wall to where Raj was standing in a field of sheep looking at something.

'I heard the noise of a big truck,' Raj said. 'But it had gone before we got here.'

'Look,' Whizzer went on, 'there's some wheel tracks.' He pointed to some marks in the mud at the gate to the field. But that wasn't much help. As Sparky pointed out, it could have been one of the farm vehicles.

We also found some scraps of sheep's wool and signs of some sort of struggle, but nothing that could really prove anything There was nothing else to see, apart from a scrap of blue cloth that Sam noticed caught on some barbed wire.

'I think we'd better go and tell Bill,' Sparky said. I couldn't argue with that. Bill was looking after things while Mr and Mrs Staples were out.

We all trooped back to the farmhouse and told Bill the story. When they returned, Mr Staples wasn't pleased, which I thought was a bit unfair because we had *nearly* caught whoever was taking the sheep. He just went on about us taking the law into our own hands, and what would our parents say if we got into bother, and stuff like that. Although the police had promised to keep a close watch over the farm, they weren't interested in our 'evidence'.

I'll never understand grown-ups!

Before bedtime Sparky, Sam, Mo, Whizzer, Raj and I met up in the village for a quick knock at cricket. Raj and Whizzer in particular were dead keen. Whizzer fancied himself as the next demon West Indian fast bowler, and Raj was an ace batsman.

Using a tree for wickets we played with everybody batting and bowling in turn, and no sides. It was my turn to bowl:

'And now, from the Trent Bridge end, coming in to bowl is the latest successor to Ian Botham, the new find for England, Nick Baker.'

'Get on with it,' Sparky complained from the other end, leaning on his bat, waiting for me to come out of fantasy-land.

I ran in to bowl and he played the ball away for Whizzer to chase and throw back. Eventually I got him out, yelling at a non-existent umpire!

Whizzer was an incredibly fast bowler, and he got us all out, one after the other. It may only have been a tennis ball, but he could make it come at you so fast you could hardly see it.

We had been playing for about twenty minutes when that flashy sports car whistled past us and stopped at the village chip shop. We all watched as Grabber and Medallion Man bought some chips.

'Come on,' complained Raj. 'Never mind them, let's get on with the game.'

It was my turn to bat again and I took up my position at the crease, not noticing that Grabber had wandered over. It was Sam's turn to bowl and she was very good, getting me out the next ball, and I didn't play soft because she was a girl!

'What a Noddy!' Grabber called out from the side. 'Getting out to a girl. Is that the best you can do?' He didn't stop there. Leaning on a wall he continued to take the mickey out of me.

'I thought you were a bit soft when you fell over in the race,' he went on. 'Now I'm sure of it. Come on, give me the ball and I'll show you how to play.'

'Right, Dad,' he called to the man by the car. 'Watch this!'

So that was who Medallion Man was!

Grabber snatched the ball from Sam and went over to the bowler's mark. From the area of the chip shop we heard Grabber's dad cheering, and Grabber waved back in salute. They were obviously trying to wind us up.

'Come on,' he demanded. 'Somebody bat. It won't be for long!'

I handed the bat over to Sparky who was next man in. Grabber came rushing in and sent the ball down very fast, hit Sparky hard on the leg, and really hurt him. To add insult to injury he also claimed that Sparky was out leg before wicket. I was just starting to argue when Raj stopped me, winked, and said loudly, 'I'm next.'

Grabber leered nastily at him and said, 'Great, I always like to sort you "foreigners" out.'

What a stupid thing to say! For a start, Raj wasn't a foreigner, he was born in the same hospital as me! And anyway, it really gets on my nerves how some people think that the colour of a person's skin makes him different from anybody else.

Grabber came in again to bowl and Raj stood waiting with the bat. The ball flew down the pitch and *Wham!*, Raj walloped it into the distance.

'A four, I think,' Raj said politely as Mo went off

to retrieve the ball. The next three balls went just as far and Grabber was getting angry! He sent down the next ball at head height and not even Raj could reach it. It just missed his face and he fell as he dodged it.

I was in a mood to go over and get Grabber, but Whizzer stopped me.

'Leave this one to me,' he said.

We helped Raj out of the way and sat him down to recover.

'Why don't you have a bat?' Whizzer suggested to Grabber.

'OK,' Grabber replied sarcastically. 'Do you think you can get me out, then?'

'I'll have a go,' Whizzer said. 'If you don't mind a "foreigner" bowling at you, that is.'

Grabber just sneered at him.

Boy, if I had been Whizzer I would have gone for his throat!

Grabber got himself ready to bat and Whizzer ran up to bowl with his steady run, then whirled his arm over fast and, before Grabber knew it, the ball had hit the tree.

'Howzat!' we all yelled.

'I wasn't ready,' Grabber lied.

'Boy, what a cheat,' I thought.

Whizzer looked at him, took the ball, and set off to bowl again.

The next ball bounced up wickedly and hit Grabber right in his stomach. He yelped in pain and doubled up.

'This pitch isn't safe to play on,' he whined.

I was really ready to take the mickey out of him now, but my attention was suddenly taken by his blue shirt. It had a huge rip in it. What's more, it was exactly the same colour material as that piece on the barbed wire at the farm!

Grabber noticed my stare. He looked guiltily at me, then without saying another word went over to his dad and they drove off.

'Why did he have to go so soon? I was just beginning to enjoy myself,' Whizzer joked.

I told them about the tear in Grabber's shirt and reminded them of the piece of cloth on the barbed wire.

'I think things are beginning to fall into place nicely,' I said.

The others just raised their eyebrows and groaned. 'Elementary, my dear Watson,' I said, puffing on an imaginary pipe.

15

OLD TOM VANISHES

The next morning Mr Staples came over to our campsite to see us.

'Oh no!' I groaned under my breath, expecting another ticking off for something or other.

He must have read my mind.

'Don't worry!' he called. 'You haven't done anything wrong. I just wanted a word.'

This was adult-speak for a lot of words!

'I wanted to finish off what I was saying yesterday,' he went on. 'I didn't want you to think I wasn't grateful for what you tried to do. But I was worried for you. You must remember that while you are staying here you are my responsibility. What would your father have said if you had got hurt?'

I dreaded to think! Dad always seemed to 'flip his lid' at the way I attracted trouble like a magnet. To my way of thinking, there was nothing I could do about it, but my dad and now Mr Staples obviously didn't agree with me.

'I still don't think Old Tom had anything to do with it,' I said, changing the subject.

Mr Staples sighed and raised his eyebrows.

'Maybe you're right, Nick,' he replied. 'But you must admit, he always seems to be around when something happens.'

That was true, but I was sure that there was a reason for that, something I hadn't figured out yet.

I looked across at Doug, who didn't know much about what had been happening. He had a funny look on his face.

When Mr Staples left, Doug turned on me. 'Right,' he demanded. 'What's been going on, then?'

'Sparky will tell you,' I replied quickly. 'Got to go and . . . er . . . post a card.'

Before I could be stopped I hurried off, avoiding Sparky's eyes. I'd landed him in it, as usual! I was really keen to see Tom and find out a bit more about what was going on, so I decided to go to his house. By the time I reached it, I had a list of questions in my head to ask him. But I never got the chance!

I should have realized that something was wrong the moment I reached the gate. The front door was open, and I knew that wasn't right.

'Hello,' I called round the door. 'Is anybody ho-ome?'

There was no response and I began to get nervous but, being Nick Baker, I had to go on. I pushed the door open and made my way inside. There was no one about. I looked into every room but there was no sign of life. But there were signs of some kind of a fight. The lounge looked like my bedroom after a pillow-fight with my sister Mo.

Straight away I was convinced they were in trouble and I had to do something. I turned on my heels and ran to the village to find help.

I went to find the village bobby, who was sitting in a deckchair admiring his garden. He seemed a nice guy, but very slow, the original P.C. Plod. I told him about what I had seen, but he obviously didn't want to move.

'Tom does that sometimes,' he said from the comfort of his chair. 'He'll be back, don't you worry. He's probably heard about some hurt animal or something, and rushed off to help. That's what the mess will be about and why the door was open. I've been up there a few times myself and found it like that, and he's always returned.'

I was only half convinced, but there was no way that this guy was going to move. I don't think he would have moved if half the robbers in England had walked past his front lawn.

A bit grumpily I wandered off to find my pals. They were having a picnic lunch at our favourite spot, the bridge. When I found them and told them what I had seen, Sparky suggested we go back and have another look at Tom's cottage to see if he had returned. 'Or to pick up some clues,' I added eagerly.

Back at Tom's place there was still no sign of him or his grandchildren. We looked all over the cottage, and were just about to give up when Lump of all people found something.

'Hey, look at this!' he yelled from the kitchen.

'He must have found some food,' Sam laughed.

We went to see what Lump had discovered. Triumphantly he was holding up a piece of crumpled paper.

'Wow!!' Whizzer said sarcastically. 'What a find!'

'Look,' Lump said excitedly, ignoring Whizzer

and waving it in my direction. 'Read it!'

I flattened it out on the table to make it easier to read. It was just a letter to some shop in town, written by Tom, then crossed out.

'Good grief, Lump,' I complained. 'What's special about that?'

'On the back, on the back,' he protested.

I turned it over. On the back, in the same hand-writing, was a list of dates and times, and at the bottom the words *caravan, surveyor, sheep, Staples*.

I couldn't make head nor tail of it!

'Don't you see?' Lump went on. 'Either Tom is involved in what's going on and this is a list of what he's been up to, or he is trying to find out what's going on, and these are "doodles" of the things that he's been thinking about.'

I was impressed. I was always underestimating Lump.

But it still didn't really help us. I just hoped Tom wasn't involved. I couldn't really believe it of him.

Then Lump had another idea.

'Caravan,' he said. 'I wonder . . .'

'Go on, go on,' I said.

'The men from that old caravan off the main road must have something to do with it,' he said. 'You know — where we stopped on the first day.'

Lump had more cause to remember the caravan and the men than anybody. I thought it was a bit of a long shot, but anything was worth a try! We had no other leads.

We sat down to think about what to do.

'Do you think Tom's in with these men?' Sam asked.

'No,' I replied firmly. 'But if we went to the police they would think so, on the evidence so far!'

'What do we do then?' Sparky asked. 'And shouldn't we tell Doug?'

Telling Doug didn't seem a good idea at this stage, but I promised Sparky that I would when we had something better to go on. We agreed to do a bit of quiet spying on the old caravan, keeping well out of trouble, if we possibly could!

By now we had begun to find our way round the area without getting lost. The main road back to the caravan led out of the village, up the hill, but in fact this road wound round the back of Staples farm, and so the caravan was only a few fields further on in a thick wood. We just had to cross the farm, and climb through the fields by a steep path to get to the wood.

As we walked along, carefully avoiding the farmhouse and Mr Staples, we spread out. I walked with Sparky.

'Lump does have some uses, doesn't he?' I joked.

Sparky was in one of his 'I've got to have a word with you' moods. Boy, friends can be really trying sometimes, especially when they are right.

'Look, Nick,' he said. 'You go on at other people because they say something about Whizzer, Raj and Chip to do with the colour of their skins, but you're as bad with Lump, just because he's, well, a little overweight.'

'A little overweight?' I choked. 'You mean fat.'

'You know what I mean,' Sparky went on. 'You treat people really badly. You were rotten to Sam

— and then there's Lump, and a whole list of other people. I heard Doug talk in one of his sermons about not being a hypocrite. You know, he was talking about what Jesus said about taking the plank out of your own eye before complaining about the splinter in somebody else's.'

'Yes,' I replied. 'Never did understand what he was talking about.'

'Oh, Nick,' Sparky went on. 'He *did* explain. The splinter is somebody else's little fault; the plank is your own big one!'

'Oh!' I replied. The light dawned!

'You can be a real hypocrite,' Sparky went on painfully. 'You're great at criticizing other people for the little things they do wrong, but lousy at noticing your own whopping great blunders.'

He was right again. I was just grateful that Sparky was a lot more patient with me than I was with anyone else, or with him. I don't know where I'd be without Doug and Sparky, but the message was getting through at last.

Why was I so dim?

We had nearly reached the wood where the caravan was.

'OK, everybody,' I said. 'We're nearly there, gather round.'

We had come round the back of the woods, so I told everyone to follow me and to be very quiet. It was a matter of crawling through the undergrowth and Lump had to be restrained from calling out loud as branches, thorns, and thistles grabbed at him.

Soon we reached the caravan and crouched in the bushes a little way away. The two men were outside the caravan talking. The lorry was now missing.

Suddenly from behind me came a noise.

'TISHOO!!'

I had forgotten Chip's hay fever!

'What was that?' one of the men said sharply. They turned in our direction and began to walk towards us.

Now we were for it!

Then there was another noise, and the men just as suddenly turned back.

We all breathed a sigh of relief — very quietly!

Coming along the lane towards the caravan was the car belonging to Grabber's dad, and he was in it!

The men greeted him and must have told him about the noise they had heard.

'You're too jumpy,' he told them. 'Get in the car. We've got to pick up the lorry. Is everything secure here?'

They nodded their heads, climbed in the car and were off.

You could feel the relief among the gang as the car went away.

'What do we do now?' Chip asked nervously.

'We go and see what's in the caravan, of course,' I replied. 'Sam, Sparky, you come with me. The rest wait here, and if we get into trouble, run for help.'

When the three of us got to the caravan we carefully looked around to see if there was anybody about. Suddenly we heard a muffled noise from inside and jumped back.

I looked at the others and made a decision.

Reaching forward, I turned the handle and
opened the door . . .

16

THE MYSTERY DEEPENS . . .

From inside the caravan I heard a noise.

'Mmmmm.'

I leaped back from the door and fell on top of Sam and Sparky who were close behind. We scrambled up and rushed back to cover.

'What on earth was that?' Sam asked.

'Dunno!' I replied.

We sat in the undergrowth in silence for a while. I could feel myself shaking inside with fright. I was so frightened I decided I just had to talk to God about all this. It's what Doug does a lot of — praying. It's funny, but the only time I find talking to God easy is when I'm in a mess!

In my mind I said to him, 'Look God, I've not exactly been getting things right, and I'm sorry for all the ways I let you down, but I could sure do with some help now to get this one sorted out.' I suddenly remembered the drama we had done in church. How Peter had denied Jesus three times, and Jesus still forgave him. That helped. If Jesus could forgive Peter, he could forgive me.

Sparky was all set to give up and go back to the village to tell Doug. I could see all sorts of problems if we did that, so before anyone could agree with him, I summoned up all the courage I had and marched straight back to the caravan. I looked back to see a number of worried faces staring out from the undergrowth.

I gulped.

The door opened easily and again I heard the loud 'Mmm. Mmmm. Mmmmm!'

I stepped into the caravan and looked round. It was a grotty, dirty tip. Stepping over a pile of old clothes I went over to another door, to what I thought must be the bedroom. The noises were getting louder, coming from behind the door. By now the whole gang had plucked up courage and had come to the entrance of the caravan.

I opened the door and nearly died of shock when Ginger fell out onto the floor of the caravan. He was bound and gagged, and behind him I could see Mave and Tom in a similar state.

'What are you doing here?' I demanded.

'Mmmmm,' was Ginger's reply.

I undid his bindings and took the gag from his mouth. He fell back, taking in great breaths of air.

By now the others had come in to the caravan and were staring at Ginger in amazement.

'Get him outside while I see to the others,' I said to Sparky. Sam helped me to untie Tom and Mave, and then help them outside.

We started to fire questions at them, but all Tom could do was hold his hands up and say, 'In a bit,' between taking in gasps of fresh air. From somewhere Sam found some water and they drank it gratefully. I got very impatient waiting for them to get their breath and getting the feeling back into their legs and arms.

'Will you calm down,' Sam complained. 'And give them a chance? Just think what you would feel like after you had been trussed up like that!'

She was right, but when I get into something like this I hate having to wait. Patience is not one of my strong points, or as my mother often says to the point of ultimate boredom:

> 'Patience is a virtue,
> Possess it if you can,
> Seldom found in woman,
> But never in Nicholas Baker!'

Eventually, after what seemed like an age, Old Tom said, 'I suppose I had better explain what's going on.'

'Are you sure, Grandad?' Ginger put in. 'They look like a load of blabbers to me!'

I didn't like that. Nobody had ever called my gang 'blabbers' and got away with it!

'Look,' I responded fiercely. 'Nick and Co. never blab. If they did, they would be dealt with. Right?' I looked round at everyone and they nodded their heads in agreement.

Ginger didn't look convinced, but Tom went on anyway.

'Now come on, Ginger,' he said. 'They have tried to help, and they did come and rescue us.' Without waiting for any more comments from Ginger he told us what was happening.

Old Tom's story was long and complicated. We listened in amazement as he told us everything. Ginger and Mave's dad, Tom's son, was awaiting trial for a post office robbery which he didn't do. He had been framed by a gang led by Grabber's dad. Tom and his grandchildren had been trying to find some way of getting to the truth when they had stumbled into the sheep-stealing racket. But Tom didn't want to tell the police about what he had seen until he had got some evidence to clear his son of the robbery.

What's more, Tom's and Grabber's families had been involved together for many years in a little local poaching. When Tom was young he used to go poaching with Grabber's grandad and they were always trying to get him to join them again, but Tom had gone around breaking their traps. Now the two families hated each other.

'Ginger had been out looking at a badger sett,' Tom went on, 'when he saw the lorry. He fetched us from my cottage. I rooted round and found my old camera to get some pictures to add to our other evidence. Trouble was, we got too near and they grabbed us, brought us here, and tied us up. I don't know what they're planning to do with us.'

The scene at Tom's house, together with all the other things we had seen since arriving in Tidesbourne began to make sense. 'It's all got very complicated,' Tom said sadly, shaking his head in despair.

'What was that surveyor, or estate agent, snooping round for?' I asked.

'Oh him!' Old Tom replied. 'Well, you see the sheep-stealing isn't the end of the story. Just recently I found out what they are really trying to do. They are trying to put Mr Staples out of business, as well as me. There are plans to build a huge housing estate on this land for people from the city. That would make our village what they call a dormitory town. If they get the land there would be no stopping the development and they would make tens of thousands of pounds.'

'Was that why your things were all thrown about when I first came to your house?' I asked.

'Yes,' Tom replied. 'They were trying to frighten me off my land.'

'Who's involved then?' I asked.

'Most of Grabber's family,' Ginger replied. 'The two men you have seen here are his uncles. Oh, and of course there's that bloke who works at Staples farm.'

'Frank!' I said. 'I knew it!'

'Yes, Frank!' Ginger continued. 'Another of Grabber's uncles!'

'What are we going to do now?' I asked of nobody in particular.

'I think we should tell the police,' Sparky put in.

'No!' Tom said fiercely. 'Not yet. I still want to try and clear my son's name. And I don't want you kids involved. It will be dangerous!'

'How can you stop us?' I responded quickly. 'We *are* involved!'

There was a long silence.

'All right,' he said eventually. 'But you must do exactly what I say, and not do anything on your own.'

Well I'd try. Actually, for once I agreed totally with Sparky. We should go to the police. But I could see Tom's point of view as well.

'To begin with, we have to find somewhere to hide,' Tom went on. 'They've gone off on another job, but it won't take that long.'

Then I had one of my ideas!

'I know just the place,' I said. 'Your wood! You know it so well that no one would be able to find you, and there's enough shelter.'

'Yes,' Ginger said. 'That's a good idea, Grandad. We could use the old gamekeeper's hut. Nobody ever goes there.'

We set off for Old Tom's wood with Ginger leading the way. When we got near the village we decided it would be best if the gang split up. So Sam, Sparky and I went with Old Tom, Ginger and Mave, and the others went back to the campsite.

We made it to the wood without being seen, and they took us to the gamekeeper's hut which was hidden deep within Old Tom's part of the wood. When we left them, I promised to come back with some food. We went out of the back of the wood and returned down the drive to the farm so that we didn't give the game away.

Back at the camp Sam, Sparky and I went to the kitchen tent to make some sandwiches. Things were running a bit low because it was nearly the end of our camp, but we managed to get together enough to feed them.

I had thought Doug was up at the farm talking to Mrs Staples and we would get away with it nicely. But suddenly and unexpectedly he stepped through the tent-flap.

'What's this then?' he asked. 'Off on a sneaky picnic?'

'Er, yes,' I replied, thankful for the ready-made excuse.

'No,' Sparky cut in. Then, turning to me, 'I'm not lying, not even for you!'

After that we had to tell Doug everything. As he listened his mouth dropped open.

'Are you *sure* about all this?' he asked disbelievingly.

'Come and talk to Tom if you don't believe us,' I countered.

He accepted my invitation and followed us into the wood and along to the gamekeeper's hut.

By this time the light was fading and it was getting dark. I was glad that Doug had brought his torch.

'Tom,' I called softly. There was no reply. I pushed the door open.

Tom, Ginger, and Mave weren't there.

They'd disappeared again.

17

ACTION!

Where had they gone? They couldn't just have vanished!

I looked anxiously at Doug. I couldn't quite make out what he was thinking.

We began to search around for signs of what might have happened to them. Suddenly I noticed Mave waving from behind some trees and putting her finger to her lips. She looked anxious and excited.

I told everyone to be quiet — then clapped my hands fiercely over Whizzer's mouth. As usual he had his Walkman on and didn't know how loud he was really speaking.

Signalling everybody to stand still, I went over to Mave. She said nothing but beckoned us to follow, and then put her finger to her lips again to make sure we kept quiet. I repeated her signals to the others and we followed in line through the trees.

After a short time, Mave turned and again signalled with her hands, this time to crouch down and stay still and quiet.

We were at the back of the wood. I noticed that Sam was taking the precaution of making Chip hold his nose, so that his explosive hay fever sneezes wouldn't give us away.

Mave parted some bushes very carefully and I looked through.

Straight ahead was the lorry — the one we had seen around the village and that had knocked Tom down, the same one we had seen by the caravan on that very first day.

Looking past the lorry, Mave pointed out Tom and Ginger hiding in some bushes. They waved to us and pointed further on.

In the field, and coming towards us, were five people, dragging along two very reluctant sheep. Even in the twilight I recognized them straight away — and I don't mean the sheep! It was the two men who had been in the caravan, Frank, Grabber and Grabber's dad!

Something had to be done!

We couldn't leave these men to get away.

I had my own ideas, and Doug and I had a whispered argument trying to sort out what to do. He could see that we couldn't just back off and leave, but Doug was also concerned that we didn't do anything stupid and dangerous.

We began to get everyone organized. Raj was sent off to get Mr Staples and the police, while the gang spread out to hide all round the lorry.

Chip had his own idea to do something and went round towards the front of the lorry.

'Trust me,' was the last thing he said over his shoulder as he crawled away. I hadn't a clue what he was up to.

By now the men and the sheep had almost reached the lorry. I had to time the next bit dead right! I let them get to within a few metres of the lorry and then yelled as loud as I could.

'NOW!!' I screamed.

From all round the area, hidden in the under-growth, everyone began to scream, shout, and make as much noise as possible.

You should have seen the look on the faces of the sheep thieves. They nearly died of shock!

I suppose if I had thought about it for any length of time I might have realized how risky it all was, but things were happening so quickly there was no time to think. Fortunately for us, the thieves were so frightened that they didn't think it might be just a load of kids making a noise. They just panicked.

The sheep added to the confusion as they jumped about trying to escape, and it finished up like something from an old movie with everyone trying to go in different directions and finishing up falling over each other.

We just kept up the noise, with Tom and Ginger joining in.

'Get in the lorry,' Grabber's dad shouted. I had thought this might happen, but there wasn't a lot we could do. I hoped Raj had managed to get back to the farm and phone the police by now. But where were they? We needed them — *now*!

The thieves leaped into the lorry. Frank, who was driving, turned the key.

Nothing happened!

He kept trying to start the lorry, but it just wouldn't go! When I turned round, I saw Chip, a cheeky grin on his face, with his hands full of wires and things that he had removed from the engine.

Then came trouble. The men in the lorry saw

276

us. Angry because they had lost their sheep and furious because they couldn't get the lorry going, they got out and began to come towards me. One of the men from the caravan had picked up a spanner and was looking very menacing. I looked round and desperately tried to think of a way out. They were no more than five metres away when I heard the sound of a police siren.

Just at that moment Raj arrived with Mr Staples and Bill. The men and Grabber looked around and one of them shouted, 'Scatter!'

They all made off in different directions.

'Let's get 'em!' I yelled, and everybody got up and started leaping about.

The two men from the caravan were cornered by Mr Staples and Bill. Mr Staples had brought his shotgun and they didn't argue with him.

'Don't shoot, Guv,' one of them begged. 'We'll come quietly.'

I don't think Mr Staples would have fired it, but they didn't know that, and he sure looked mad enough to do it!

Frank was making a run for it towards the road. Sam saw him and was after him like lightning. She dived and floored him with a tackle that the Welsh Rugby Team would have been proud of.

Closely following her came Sparky and Chip, who dived onto him. Next came Mo and the final crushing blow for Frank was when Lump arrived. With a joyful whoop he jumped in the air and landed heavily on him. Luckily he didn't land on Chip and Sparky too.

'Get them off, get them off,' Frank pleaded, with what little breath he had left. It was obvious he was giving up the struggle.

Tom and Mave, together with Whizzer and Raj, had cornered Grabber's dad. He had looked threatening, but when the police arrived he gave up trying to get away.

That just left Grabber!

He had set off for the wood, with Ginger in pursuit. I thought Ginger might need a bit of help, and went off after them. It was a wild chase, as it was really dark in the wood. Grabber ran like someone possessed, not caring about the branches that snatched at him. I knew it must be hurting him, because it was painful for me too.

I managed to catch up with Ginger, who pointed for me to circle round and corner Grabber.

We eventually trapped him at the old game-keeper's hut. He stood there, his back to the wall of the hut, with one of us on either side of him. With a snarl on his face, Grabber raised his fists.

'Get out of the way, or I'll thump you both,' he snarled.

'Leave him to me,' Ginger said. 'I've waited a long time for this.'

Before I could do or say anything they were at it hammer and tongs. Now, I am the last person in the world to back away from a fight, but watching those two going at it I realized how stupid it all looked. I had to do something before Ginger knocked nine bells out of Grabber. He was like a lunatic. I guess there was a lot of anger pent up inside him, for everything that Grabber's family had done to Ginger's.

By the time I managed to separate them, Grabber was in no state to argue, and it wasn't too difficult to drag him back to the others, apart from stopping Ginger from setting about him again.

Back at the lorry, the police had started to push the criminals into the police cars. Then they took possession of a somewhat bedraggled Grabber. The car headlights cutting through the darkness made it look like something on TV.

Mr Staples took us all back to the farm, and his wife fed us and made us drinks. The police took statements from everybody until they were satisfied we had told them everything. This took ages and was very boring, but I knew from my dad how important it was to get everything on paper, and also not to tell lies or exaggerate. He had seen many criminals get off because a witness had exaggerated a story which made the evidence useless.

All the same, I was glad when the police eventually left.

The most pleasing thing was to see Mr Staples being so kind and apologetic to Old Tom, who for his part didn't seem to bear any grudges at all.

But the next best thing of all was falling into our sleeping-bags and getting a good, long sleep.

What a day!

18

THE WASP STRIKES BACK

The next day was our last full one in Tidesbourne.
Now it was nearly time to go home, I wanted to
stay. Funny, that! A few days before I had been
desperate to leave.

It was the day of the annual village fête — and
everybody from Tidesbourne would be there.
Honestly, all they seemed to do in this village was
have garden parties, sports, fêtes and all that sort
of thing — with lots of arguments in between!

In the morning I took the chance to have a last
walk round the farm. I left the others at the
campsite and set off on my own. After wandering
around the yard and talking to Bill, I strolled
around all the places that had become so familiar.

Together with the rest of the gang we also had a
last walk round the village. I hoped that all the
business over the housing estate could be stopped
now. It would be horrible to have such a lovely
place all built over. We all agreed that if they
wanted to build houses they should come to where
we live, knock down some of the old buildings in
the city that look such a mess, and build their nice
new houses there!

Back at the camp we started to pack up to make
the job easier the next morning. Lump helped me
take down the kitchen tent. He was a bit clumsy,

as it wasn't his sort of thing, but between us we got it packed into its huge canvas bag.

Only a week ago I would have been moaning at Lump at this stage, but I remembered what Doug had said to me in the boat. And Sparky's comments were fresh in my mind. It's very hard not to be a hypocrite, and very easy to notice other people's faults while at the same time quietly forgetting your own. Lump was a great pal really — he was just different from me.

The afternoon was great! There was even more food than at the garden party when we arrived, and the weather was absolutely boiling. The stalls and tables were all set out on the village green. We descended on the food like a plague of locusts, with Lump at the front.

Everybody was there. Even Georgina turned up and gave me a smile!

Before I could head off towards the food with the rest, Mr Staples caught my arm and pulled me to one side.

'I'm not very good with words,' he began. 'But I did want to tell you how grateful I am for all that you did. If I seemed a bit pig-headed it was because I was so worried.'

I shrugged my shoulders in embarrassment, blushed, and muttered, 'S'alright.' Well, what else could I say?

Fortunately, at that moment I noticed Tom, Ginger, and Mave appearing in the distance. They looked a bit nervous.

'I'll just go over to Tom and his grandchildren,' I said to Mr Staples. 'They look like they need some company.'

I hurried away, grateful for the opportunity to avoid what was becoming an embarrassing conversation. I think Mr Staples was quite pleased too!

'Come on over and have some food,' I said to the nervous threesome, but before we could get there Doug's dad, Mr Jones, started to make a speech. He was the chairman of the village council. He stood on a little platform with a microphone.

'Could you please be quiet,' he announced. 'And gather round.'

Everyone stopped what they were doing and walked over, except Lump, who kept eating.

'I'm not a one for long speeches,' he said — someone laughed, and Mrs Jones raised her eyebrows — 'but we as a village have a few thank-yous to make, and one or two things to put right. When my son first suggested bringing his young people to the village for a holiday, one or two people weren't very keen. I think that we have all learned something from having them here, but most important of all, we have to thank them for saving our village from being ruined for ever by some very wicked people.'

Everybody clapped furiously, and we all blushed uncomfortably.

Mr Jones continued, 'I also have some tremendous news. Mr Staples has generously donated the use of his woodland area to the village council. We are going to make it into a conservation area, to be used for groups of people who perhaps wouldn't normally get the chance to come and observe the wildlife of the countryside.'

Everyone clapped enthusiastically!

'And also,' Mr Jones continued, 'Tom here has been offered, and has accepted, the position of unpaid warden to the reserve.'

The clapping was even louder.

Tom looked embarrassed, but happy.

Mr Jones' speech was over, so I joined the rest of the gang who were getting their food.

We were sitting around on the green eating, when I heard a car draw up. I looked round to see a police car, and out got the village bobby. Another man got out from the passenger side. He looked a bit scruffy and tired, and rather nervous.

'It's Dad, it's Dad,' yelled Mave and Ginger. They leapt to their feet and hurtled over to him. The tears were streaming down Mave's face. They nearly knocked him flat as they rushed over to him and hugged him. Tom followed on behind, trying to choke back the tears. He wasn't the only one, I can tell you! I even saw Mr Staples begin to blow his nose.

The policeman came over to Mr and Mrs Jones who were standing near us.

'Er, special session of the court this morning, charges dropped, that lot we captured confessed everything. Er, thought it might be nice to, er, get him home as quick as possible,' he said, shifting from foot to foot.

'That was a very kind thought,' Mrs Jones said, wiping her eyes. 'Come on over and have something to eat.'

'Don't mind if I do,' he said, and stomped over to the food.

We left Tom and his family alone for a bit, but eventually they came over and joined us. They were so happy. The change in Ginger and Mave was incredible — you couldn't shut them up!

It was a bit embarrassing really, because they kept saying how we had done all this and they didn't know how to stop thanking us.

Just then, I felt a hand on my shoulder. It was Doug.

'I want a word with you,' he said.

We walked away from the others and sat on the grass.

'I thought I told you to keep out of trouble and just enjoy a quiet holiday,' he went on. 'Sometimes I wish I had never met you — you're a walking advert for trouble! But I don't think that often!' He gave me a friendly punch.

I liked Doug. Even though he was a grown-up, he seemed to understand.

'You know, Doug,' I said, 'I've learnt a lot this holiday. When I get it right, life is a whole lot happier. The trouble is I keep forgetting and wanting to do things the Nick Baker way, getting in a mess, then remembering. Thanks for sticking with me.'

Doug just smiled and winked, and then walked away to talk to Old Tom.

I got up and went to join the lads at the village pond. They were sailing their paper plates across the water. We got really involved in seeing who could make the fastest boat, leaning out to give an extra push.

None of us noticed the drama developing just behind us. Now, you know how Lump feels about bees and wasps. Well, a wasp was in dispute with Lump over who should have the piece of cake on his plate. Eventually it decided to take action, and go for Lump — in the usual place!

That was how Lump came to be heading towards the pond — and us — at a speed which he couldn't control. He raced along, knocking us in like a row of skittles, then dived in himself to avoid a sting!

We all surfaced, spluttering and laughing. As we crawled out, starting to pick off the green slimy weed that covered a lot of the pond, Sam, Mo and Georgina came along.

'Men,' Georgina said, looking down at us, 'are such fools!'

That was too much for Sam, a loyal gang member. She may think we are idiots, and often tells us so. But she wasn't going to let Georgina get away with it, so she reached round Mo and pushed Georgina into the pond.

When Georgina surfaced, spluttering for air, all Sam said, with a smile on her face was, 'Sorry Georgina, I must have slipped!'

We all roared with laughter. Georgina did too, eventually. After we pulled her out.

The next morning we said our final goodbyes as quickly as possible and loaded ourselves into the old van. The journey back was quiet — no wasps, and definitely no caravans hidden in woods! It had been a really smashing holiday!

It was good to see Mum and Dad, and especially my dog, Wally. He licked me so hard he nearly took the skin off my face! Mum and Dad asked loads of questions.

'Did you have a good time?'

'Great.'

'What did you do?'

'Lots.'

'Did you behave yourself?'

'Yes.'

'Did anything exciting happen?'

'Not much, really.'

After all, it was all in a day's work for Nick and Co.!

Also from Lion publishing

NICK & CO. TO THE RESCUE

Bob Croson

The gang is back! Despite their good intentions anything involving Nick & Co. seems to lead to trouble.

In this latest adventure the start of term sees them trying to save their school and on the trail of a con man. Then there's some dirty work in a local cycle race...

'Life is going to be busy...' reflects Nick in one of his rare quiet moments. How right he is.

ISBN 0 7459 1832 8

All Lion paperbacks are available from
your local bookshop, or can be ordered
direct from Lion Publishing. For a free
catalogue, showing the complete list of
titles available, please contact:

Customer Services Department
Lion Publishing plc
Peter's Way
Sandy Lane West
Oxford OX4 5HG

Tel: (01865) 747550
Fax: (01865) 715152